TREACHERY!

"Sir, we're under attack!"

The morning mist gave way to thick columns of smoke rising from the northeast. Through the smoke came the first wave of crab carriers, their metallic carapaces flashing, their big claw-like landing gear already flexing into position. Our rooftop cannon emplacements unleashed salvo after salvo, but those carrier pilots were running defense skins at maximum power. Our cannons would run out of ammunition long before they could gnaw away at those shields.

I contacted Diablo once more, and his answer to my request for atmoattack jets was anything but promising. "All of our forces are already deployed," he said.

"Very well then, sir. I've ordered a full evacuation."

He shut his eyes, rubbed his temples. "All right. Hold them off as well as you can, then get out."

"We will, sir. Have you made contact with our carriers?"

His eyes snapped open and his voice came through a shudder. "Major, our carriers are gone. It appears, Mr. St. Andrew, that we've been betrayed and ambushed. Now, if you'll excuse me, I've a battle to lose."

Also by
Ben Weaver

BROTHERS IN ARMS
REBELS IN ARMS

BEN WEAVER

PATRIOTS IN ARMS

An Imprint of HarperCollinsPublishers

This is a work of fiction. Names, characters, places, and incidents are products of the author's imagination or are used fictitiously and are not to be construed as real. Any resemblance to actual events, locales, organizations, or persons, living or dead, is entirely coincidental.

EOS
An Imprint of HarperCollins*Publishers*
10 East 53rd Street
New York, New York 10022-5299

Copyright © 2003 by Ben Weaver
ISBN: 0-06-000626-9
www.eosbooks.com

First Eos paperback printing: September 2003

Eos Trademark Reg. U.S. Pat. Off. And in Other Countries, Marca Registrada, Hecho en U.S.A.
HarperCollins® is a trademark of HarperCollins Publishers Inc.

Printed in the U.S.A.

10 9 8 7 6 5 4 3 2 1

*For all those who have ever been
Brothers, Rebels, and Patriots . . .*

Acknowledgments

Once again, I must thank Jennifer Brehl and Diana Gill at Eos for their encouragement and editorial expertise. With their help, this series has become far better than I could have imagined.

Thanks once more to my agent, John Talbot, whose enthusiasm can turn a lonely writing day into one with laughs and excitement.

I'm very much indebted to Nancy, Lauren, and Kendall, who understand the demands of a writing career and fully support me while I'm figuratively "blowing stuff up." I thank them for keeping the peace at home.

Finally, as I mentioned in the previous volume, both Robert Drake and Caitlin Blasdell helped me create this series. Their ideas, criticism, and strong belief in my writing are what made this happen.

Colonial Wardens
Articles of the Code of Conduct
Second Revision 2301
(adopted from 17 System Guard Corps Operations Manual)

ARTICLE I

I will always remember that I am a Colonial citizen, fighting in the forces that preserve my world and our way of life. I have resigned to give my life in their defense.

ARTICLE II

I will never surrender of my own volition. If in command, I will never surrender the members of my command while they still have the will and/or means to resist.

ARTICLE III

If I am captured, I will continue to resist by any and all means available. I will make every effort to escape and to aid others to escape. I will accept neither parole nor special favors from the enemy.

ARTICLE IV

If I become a prisoner of war, I will keep faith with my fellow prisoners. I will give no information nor take part in any action which might be harmful to fellow Colonial citizens.

If I am senior, I will take command. If not, I will obey the lawful orders of those appointed over me and will uphold them in every way.

ARTICLE V
Should I become a prisoner of war, I am required to give name, rank, and willingly submit to retinal and DNA analysis. I will evade answering further questions to the utmost of my ability and will not consciously submit to cerebral scans of any kind. I will make no oral, written, or electronic statements disloyal to the colonies or harmful to their cause.

ARTICLE VI
I will never forget that I am fighting for freedom, that I am responsible for my actions, and that I am dedicated to the principles that make my world free. I will trust in my god or gods and in the Colonial Alliance forever.

PATRIOTS IN ARMS

PART I

◄ ►

Heavy Losses

❯ The news reports all that morning had focused on the treaty violations and on the possibility that negotiations between the Colonial Alliance and Terran Alliances were about to break off. Nearly every correspondent on Rexi-Calhoon wanted to scoop the story, and even as I boarded my skipshuttle, bound for Rexicity and the capitol building, at least a dozen of them stood at the tarmac fence, hollering questions. Bren Dublin, senior officer of my personal security team, warded them off in his usual baritone, with about as much diplomacy as a man waving a particle rifle. "Colonel St. Andrew will issue a statement to the media at his convenience—not yours!"

"What's the matter, Bren?" I asked as he slammed the hatch and dropped his mammoth frame into the jumpseat beside me.

"I don't like these people," he groaned, then scratched his graying beard. His tone turned deadly serious. "You can't trust them."

Tat, Ysarm, and Jiggs, my other bodyguards, sat behind us, wriggling in their designer suits and probably wishing I hadn't asked them to look their very best. The three officers, all in their thirties, all South Point graduates, had over forty years' military experience between them, yet they, like Bren, had never seen real combat. I hoped they never would.

"I'll tell you why Bren doesn't trust reporters," said

3

Tat, the tallest of the group, a dark-skinned bird of a man with eyes nearly as small and definitely as keen. "He's never told you about his ex."

Bren gave Tat a fiery look that silenced the junior officer.

"I don't know," I began. "I'm not sure if you can trust them, but years ago a reporter saved my life."

"Six-seven-niner, copy. Cleared for departure," interrupted our pilot, who glanced back from the cockpit, his head draped in the translucent energy bands of his communications skin. "Colonel St. Andrew? ETA to the capitol building will be approximately nine minutes. Your tablet's up and running, so if there's any news you care to look at, it's there."

"Thank you, Lieutenant, but today I don't plan on watching the news—I plan on making it."

"Yes, sir."

With a hum and an appreciable rumble, the skipshuttle lifted off. As the G force drove me deeper into my seat, I glanced through a window at the reporters, some of who were delivering remarks and observations to their floatcams. I suspected that as they spoke, images of me boarding the shuttle were beaming out to all nine hundred million people on Rexi-Calhoon and were also being tawted out to the billions of others watching on all seventeen worlds and in the Sol system. That kind of media exposure scared the hell out of me, but it came with the territory these days. I shivered and turned back to Bren, thought of querying further about his ex, but his head hung low, his expression dark.

Ahead of us lay Rexicity, one of Rexi-Calhoon's six primary colonies. It was situated fourteen hundred kilometers south of Columbia Colony, and its skyscrapers rose up from an expansive valley to pierce a mantle of brown haze. The downtown district reeked of something oily and burned, a stench that often had me reaching for my breather.

"Aw, shit, look at that," said Bren, cocking a thumb at his window. Just off our starboard wing streaked two news shuttles, their logos flashing on their fuselages. "They want to capture every moment—even our routine flight. They call this news?"

"As long as they stay out of our zone, they have a right to be out there," I said. "And Bren, are you all right?"

"Fine, sir."

"I don't believe you." My tablet beeped. I withdrew the small computer from my seat pocket, keyed it on.

My executive assistant, Davyd Marke, gaped breathlessly at me from his desk in the capitol building. "Sir, I'm, uh, I'm afraid I have some bad news."

Bren and the others leaned in, trying to catch a glimpse of my screen. I gave Bren a look, then activated my communications tac to take the call privately. Once my head was enveloped in the skin's energy and the image of Davyd appeared in the Heads Up, I asked, "What's going on?"

"It's just . . . I can't believe it . . . it's insane . . ."

Davyd, fifty-two, a man who had spent his entire adult life working in colonial politics, had been with me for two years, and during all of that time I had never seen him as agitated.

"Report!" I boomed.

"Sir, less than a minute ago, thirty-nine capital cruisers from Earth tawted into orbit. They're setting up a blockade."

I sat there a moment, playing out every reason I could conjure why the alliances would do such a thing. I was

en route to Rexicity to put an end to the their treaty violations by suggesting four strategic compromises. For
nearly six months, Terran corporations like Inte-Micro
and Exxo-Tally had been holding the colonial tech market hostage by jacking up prices on tawt drive systems
and navigational equipment vital to space travel. Many
of the Sol colonies like Mars and those on the moons of
Jupiter refused to charge the higher prices, and the Alliances had threatened their own people with military
action, the same way they had threatened the extrasolar
colonies when we had expressed our desire to break
away to form our own alliance. Because it was in our
best interest to do business with Mars and Jupiter, we
saw their fight as our own, and had even offered them
membership in the Colonial Alliance.

"Sir, did you hear what I said?" Davyd asked.

I blinked hard. "Yes, I did. I assume the president has
been contacted?"

"She's on the line."

"Put her through."

Although my primary duty as security chief was to
serve as liaison between the joint chiefs of the Colonial
Alliance, the president, and the colonial congress, President Armalda Vinnery had asked me to deal directly
with the Eastern and Western alliance security chiefs. In
years past, President Vinnery would have met personally with them and with the presidents of both alliances, but given the many recent attempts on her
life—three in just the past year—she chose to negotiate
via satnet from her mobile command center aboard the
capital cruiser *Falls Morrow*. Presently, she was working
on matters involving human rights violations, the sharing of recently discovered Racinian ruins on Drummer

Fire, and on the release of forty-seven Aire-Wuian missionaries being held prisoner on Earth by leftist guerrillas.

Vinnery sighed at me from the tablet's screen. Her steely gaze, well-kempt blonde hair, and perfectly smooth black business attire allayed my fears, if only a little. She looked powerful, monarchal. But that image shattered the moment she spoke. "Colonel, what the fuck is going on there?"

"I'm not sure, Madam President. I haven't even reached the capitol building yet."

"Well, we're just outside Sol, and I've put in calls to President Holtzman and President Wong. We'll see if those idiots have the balls to call me back."

Admittedly, I had seen the president upset, but I had never heard her speak as coarsely. "Ma'am," I began tentatively. "I'm sure the other chiefs are either in the conference room or en route. I'll contact them immediately and demand an explanation."

"You do that. And network me in."

I nodded and tapped for a contact list. A sidebar appeared on the screen with the tablet numbers of Eastern Alliance Security Chief Paraven Nasir and Western Alliance Security Chief Leanne Kashnow. I dialed Nasir first, not because his name came first in the list but because Kashnow was as curt as she was egotistical, and, given the circumstances, there was no way in hell I would tiptoe around her like I usually did.

Nasir answered, and I could see he was on the move, heading down one of the capitol building's long hallways toward our conference room. "Hello, Paraven. Standby please," I said, then brought President Vinnery online. The screen divided to show both parties.

Nasir frowned, and while he was in his forties like me, the political arena's heat had not been kind to his dark skin. "Good morning, Colonel. And to you, too, Madam President. Is something wrong? Has our meeting been rescheduled?"

"Why are thirty-nine of your cruisers blockading my capitol world?" Vinnery demanded.

"What are you talking about? I know nothing of any cruisers."

"Don't fuck with me, Nasir!"

Oh my god, I thought. *I can't believe she's talking to him like this.*

"I repeat, I know nothing of any cruisers! Hold please. I have another call."

"He's lying," Vinnery told me. "He's lying through his fucking teeth."

"Ma'am, if there's anything I can do to help you *calm down*," I began.

"Colonel, I have every reason to be upset, more so because I've just ordered the entire Eighth Fleet to Earth."

Something deep in my gut gave way. "Ma'am, if you set up a counter blockade without congressional approval—"

"When our ships reach Earth, the first thing our captains are going to do is contact the defnet authorities and notify them that we're not setting up a *blockade* but are merely participating in a *parade*. So if congress wants to impeach me for ordering an unauthorized *parade*, let them try . . ."

"Of course our parade will block any ships trying to make Earth orbit," I said. "And this will escalate into a shooting war." I shook my head, my jaw falling slack.

"We can still salvage this," she said. "They pull out. We pull out."

"All right, I'm back," said Nasir. "I have President Wong. Linking him now."

My screen divided once more to include Vinnery, Nasir, and then Wong, whose face lacked color, emotion, pretty much everything that indicated he was actually human. But then, amazingly, his lips moved and his voice came in a reedy near-whisper. "President Vinnery, I share in your dismay regarding the blockade of your capital world. Unfortunately, we have just received requests for secession from all Mars and Jupiter colonies and provinces. Unfortunately, we must conclude that your alliance has been conspiring with these colonies to undermine our control of them. A treaty violation of this magnitude cannot go unpunished. We will keep our blockade of Rexi-Calhoon in place until the Colonial alliance officially rejects the requests from Mars and Jupiter. They are original colonies. They are properties of Terra. I assure you, that will never change."

"And President Holtzman concurs with this blockade?" Vinnery asked.

"I do," said Holtzman, appearing at Wong's shoulder, his stocky outdoorsman's physique and woodsy charm contrasting sharply with Wong's cool intellect. "I don't know what y'all were thinking, trying to get Mars and Jupiter to secede, but that was some dirty pool. And if you don't shut this down, we'll be putting you out of business."

Vinnery spoke to me across a private channel. "You believe these people?" she asked.

I knew what it felt like to be a naïve soldier, but at that moment, I received my first taste of being a naïve statesman. I had no idea until that moment that when push came to shove, politicians would rely on the tactics and behavior of the playground.

"Listen to me, Holtzman, and listen to me carefully," barked Vinnery. "If Mars and Jupiter wish to become members of the Colonial Alliance, there's nothing you can do to stop them."

"That's where you're wrong," said Holtzman, who suddenly turned to an aide, a scrawny man who whispered something in the president's ear. Holtzman's expression grew long.

"I see our fleet has arrived," said Vinnery.

"A very unwise decision," warned Wong, a hand to his ear as he listened to report. "We're not in the mood for any *parades* this morning."

I called up Vinnery on the private channel. "Madam President. They mean business."

"So do we."

"Let me talk to them."

She frowned. "You?"

"I don't believe they understand what's at stake here."

"They're big boys, Colonel."

"But they haven't seen what I've seen."

"Negative. Gut-wrenching war stories won't change their minds. We'll issue the ultimatum. In the meantime, we'll get the ambassadors from Mars and Jupiter up to speed and get a verbal commitment from them."

"Ma'am, please. Just let me try. You owe it to all those families who will never be the same because of the first war. *We all* owe it to them."

She studied me a moment, then closed her eyes.

Within the hour, my security team and I were on board a heavily armed Colonial Warden gunship, a hunchbacked hawk of machinery that we could fly directly into Manhattan and land outside the Western Alliance capitol. Wong and Holtzman had reluctantly agreed to meet with me, though they insisted that as a security measure we tawt into Mars orbit, then travel the rest of the way via conventional drive so their fighters could provide escort.

Once we reached Mars, we met up with those fighters and lumbered off. The trip to Earth would take about nineteen hours, so I settled back in my jumpseat, hoping to sleep away at least some of that time.

Before I could close my eyes, Bren, who was seated across from me, took in a long breath, then sighed. "Have you figured out what you're going to say to them? If I were you, I'd be thinking about three words: comply or die."

I was too aggravated to roll my eyes. "Last time I looked there was a balance of power between the three alliances."

"Yeah, but all their money is tied up with us. They need us more than we need them."

"Let's get some rest. I'm betting the days ahead will be very long. Very, very long."

"All right. But you still haven't answered me. What are you going to say to them?"

I closed my eyes and considered the question. If I was going to present a convincing argument to Wong and Holtzman, I had to turn statistics into blood, sweat, tears, and death. I would offer my experiences as a soldier. Perhaps war stories wouldn't be enough, but they would be a start. I thought of my early days in the corps, of the massacre at Columbia Colony, and of the friend who broke my heart.

*   *   *

I held the rank of major when Lieutenant Colonel Diablo gave me Fifth Battalion and sent my troops and I to the facilities of LockMar Randall, a Columbia Colony defense contractor who designed navigation and targeting systems for extrasolar craft. Our mission was to secure and defend the facility at all costs.

We had set up our headquarters inside the primary air traffic control tower, a glistening silver pyramid some three hundred stories tall. Just beyond my bank of displays and past the tower's viewport lay a grid of hangars, test facilities, and tarmacs that dematerialized into the morning mist. As I sat at my station, I imagined thousands of engineers out there and working warily around my troops. It wasn't every day that an entire battalion of Colonial Wardens showed up at your doorstep and told you that your place of business might fall under attack. I had mixed feelings over the engineers' decision to stay on. Yes, their work was vital to the war effort, and you couldn't help but admire their dedication and patriotism, but if Alliance crab carriers made planetfall and penetrated our defenses . . .

"Engineers," began Captain Rooslin Halitov, leaning back in his chair and cupping hands behind his head. "It's like God rounded up every boring person in the world and said, you, you, and you? You're going to be engineers. And you over there? The ugly guy playing with the tablet? You, too."

I made a face. "You're an idiot. Every piece of tech you use was designed by an engineer. These people are creative, not boring. And they've saved your life a million times."

"They're still boring. Look at them. Listen to them." He tapped a knuckle on a plasma screen showing a group of engineers looking diminutive as they conferenced below the bowl-shaped innards of a massive tawt drive system suspended by a lattice work of force beams.

Admittedly, their conversation was full of technobabble and devoid of emotion, but they were just doing their jobs.

"Company reports coming in," said Halitov, gesturing to his bank of displays.

I pulled up the text on my own screen:

Captain Katya Jing, Company Commander, Saturn Company
Captain Taris Markland, Company Commander, Turbo Company
Captain Cooch Smith, Company Commander, Ulysses Company
Captain Jenny Zeist, Company Commander, Vega Company

With a quick touch, I chose Jing's report and scanned quickly through the images and data bars. Her people had established the northwest perimeter, and if we came under attack, they would most likely be the first to encounter the enemy. I was not comfortable with assigning her that location, but I knew the rumors about us had filtered all the way down to the privates in her squads and I didn't want to show any favoritism. Moreover, she was the most experienced conditioned soldier in her company, and I needed someone like her spearheading our defenses. I reached the final databar, where a note flashed, indicating that an encrypted comm request awaited. I tapped a button on the tac around my wrist, and my combat skin rippled over me and glowed a phosphorescent green. Communication switched to my skin, and I watched as Halitov made goo-goo eyes at me. I gave him the finger and took the call.

Jing appeared in my HUV. While most people would immediately notice the teardrop-shaped birthmark on her lower left cheek, I saw only a beautiful Asian woman with silky dark hair and wonderfully mysterious eyes. In fact, her birthmark was a welcome reminder of our connection: we were both descendants of those who had suffered from the genetic disorder epineuropathy; we had both survived childhoods full of ridicule; and we had both risen above our second-class colonists' roots to become officers. She had once told me that I knew what it was like to be her. I guess I did.

"Major St. Andrew, sir," she said, snapping off a salute with mock formality. "The captain wishes to speak off the record, sir."

I grinned. "How're you doing out there?"

"It's muggy, the coffee's bitter, and my people think I'm sleeping with the battalion commander. Just another Saturday morning."

"Yeah, well it's stuffy in here. The coffee's just as bitter, and Rooslin's making faces. So, will you have a couple of hours later?" I hoisted my brows.

"You're the CO . . ."

"Right. Rooslin says they have a cafeteria up here, and one of the chefs stayed on. This guy makes some kind of poultry dish thing that's like nothing you've ever tasted."

Her head lowered in disappointment. "Just food? Damn, I was hoping I'd get to sleep with the battalion commander."

In fact, we had never slept together, and all this talk of doing so quickened my pulse. "This battalion commander is already starving. And he's wondering what happened to that shy little captain who used to blush around him."

"There are no atheists or shy people in a foxhole, especially one sitting on the perimeter."

I was about to reply as she turned her head off camera and muttered, "Damn it."

Alarms resounded in my HUV. "Jing!"

A horrific explosion echoed over the channel, and even as she turned back to face me, debris rained down on her—

And the signal cut off.

"Jing? Jing?"

I de-skinned, my gaze intent on the multiple images pouring in from our perimeter cameras. An intense wave of glistening white particle fire formed a weird picket fence of energy that sprouted up along our northwest tarmac and raced toward one of the hangars. I shivered with the urge to abandon my post, use my conditioning to access the quantum bond between particles, and will myself down to Jing's position to whisk her out of there.

"First wave," cried Halitov. "Count nineteen, twenty, twenty-one, twenty-two crab carriers inbound, bearings up. ETA two minutes."

"Where the hell was Diablo?" I asked.

"Yeah, where was he?" Halitov grunted. "Incompetent brass."

I tapped for a link to Lieutenant Colonel Diablo's command post, and the man appeared, stroking his thin mustache. "Sir, we're under attack!"

"That's right. Dig in. Fight."

"What happened to our carriers in orbit? Why didn't they alert us?"

Diablo's eyes glossed over, and he appeared to lose his breath. "That's . . . that's what we're trying to figure out, Major."

"Copy." I broke contact and tried dialing up Jing once more. Tried her private suit channel. Nothing.

"Major, we have multiple enemy contacts," said Captain Taris Markland. I looked at my brother's face on the screen and would never see him as anyone but Jarrett St. Andrew.

"Jarrett, get those shuttles fired up and get those engineers in your sector the hell out of here."

"Scott, man, you have to call me Markland."

"Yeah, right."

"Sounding the evacuation alarm," he said.

My voice cracked. "Jarrett, be careful out there."

He shook his head over the admonishment, then cut the link. Only then did I realize that I had once again called him by his real name. Sure, the Colonial Wardens had staged his death and had recruited him for their elite force, but *Taris Markland*? Did they have to issue him such an awkward name?

I switched to another channel. "Smitty? Zeist? Copy?"

The two captains responded nearly in unison, and their images appeared in my HUV, even as I skinned up again.

"Got those carriers on your scopes?" I asked.

"Got 'em," said Zeist, her already fair complexion growing whiter. "And there's another wing coming in from the south. We've locked their course. Count fourteen, sir."

We were one battalion comprised of six hundred and seventy-one Colonial Wardens. Those crab carri-

ers screaming toward us, their bowls loaded with over
twenty thousand Western Alliance Marines, reminded
me once again that our forces were spread much too
thinly through the seventeen systems. We were out-
gunned, outnumbered, and out of our minds for staying one minute longer than necessary.

Captain Cooch Smith, a brown-haired Warden of
thirty with freckles and a steely resolve that reminded
me of Halitov's, gritted his teeth. "My people are evacuating the engineers, but if those Marines take out our
cannons, we'll have no air support. The transports will
be blown out of the sky."

"Just get them loaded. I'll see if I can get a wing of atmoattacks from Diablo."

"Yes, sir."

"Good luck to you both." I regarded the other
twenty or so support personnel working with us inside
the tower. "All right, people, listen up. We're evacuating
the tower. Purge the records. And I want all of you
out—now!"

With a nervous murmuring but a practiced efficiency,
the personnel erased data, then sprang from their chairs,
heading for the exits. Halitov glanced up to the viewport. "They're in the zone," he cried.

The morning mist gave way to thick columns of
smoke rising from the northwest. Through that smoke
came the first wave of crab carriers, their metallic carapaces flashing, their big clawlike landing gear already
flexing into position. Our rooftop cannon emplacements unleashed salvo after salvo, but those carrier pilots were running defense skins at maximum power.
Our cannons would run out of ammunition long before
they could gnaw away at those shields.

"If we had a little warning, we could've launched the EMP their way," said Halitov. "The pulse wave would've stalled them. We can't use EMP in here without destroying the electronics aboard the shuttles."

"That's right," I said, glancing once more through the viewport at the half dozen crab carriers hovering over the tarmac. "Our intell was corrupt. No one saw this coming. Diablo says stay and fight. I'm making a tactical decision. This place is lost. We'll protect the shuttles. Get those people out. Then we follow. Relay the orders."

He nodded, turned back to his displays, and began speaking rapidly to our company commanders. At the time, I wasn't sure why he gave me a dirty look as I listened in, a dirty look that sent me turning away, but later I would realize that I should have monitored his actions more closely.

I contacted Diablo once more, and his answer to my request for atmoattack jets was anything but promising. "All of our forces are already deployed," he said.

"Very well, then, sir. I've ordered a full evacuation."

"You've done what?"

"Sir, there are over twenty thousand troops hitting the ground as we speak."

He shut his eyes, rubbed his temples. "Very well. Hold them off as long as you can, then get out."

"We will, sir. Have you made contact with our carriers?"

His eyes snapped open, and his voice came through a shudder. "Major, our carriers are gone."

"Sir?"

"It appears, Mr. St. Andrew, that we've been betrayed and ambushed. Now, if you'll excuse me, I've a battle to lose."

I turned away, shocked, then Jing's voice came from one of my panels. "Scott? Copy?"

With a start, I dodged for the display, stared worriedly at her as she crouched in her foxhole, the hazy sky beyond her stitched with particle fire. "I'm here," I said.

"Our civvies are loaded, but my company will be overrun any second. I can't get them out in time."

I swallowed. "I know."

"Scott, I'm staying with them."

I froze, thought about what she was saying, then tried to put my feelings aside in favor of the larger picture. "You're too valuable. I want you out of there. Fall back to Alpha pad. I'll meet you at the drop."

"But Scott—"

I grew rigid, spoke through my teeth. "Jing. Fall back!"

She backhanded a tear from her eye, then my screen went blank.

I tapped for her channel, got the message that she was receiving the call but ignoring. "Jing! Answer me!"

Out of the corner of my eye, I spotted a huge explosion erupting from the south, from the exact hangar where Halitov's "boring" engineers had been working on that tawt drive system.

"Oh, shit," cried Halitov, gaping at one of his plasma screens. "Oh, shit. Oh, shit!"

"What?"

"Got a core leak. The clock's been tripped."

"How long?"

"Give me a second. Pulling up specs. I'll see if I can reach anyone there." He muttered a command, and blueprints of the now shattered tawt drive system popped up on his displays.

I wrung my hands and waited as he scanned the images and spoke rapidly with an engineer. Then he faced me, looking gave. "Three guys are trying to get near that tawt drive. Yeah, they'll try to shut it down, but readings indicate the leak's pretty bad. Clock's reading one hour, twenty-one minutes."

"Blast radius?"

"You want it technical? Or real?"

"Just tell me!"

"Fourteen kilometers."

"Say again?"

"Fourteen kilometers. The whole fucking place."

I stopped, lost my breath, caught it, then thought a moment. "All right, tell those guys to access the situation, and if they can't do anything, then they should evacuate immediately," I said. "Is there anything we can do?"

"I don't know. Maybe I can go sit on it. My fat ass might dull the blast."

I whirled away from him, balled a hand into a fist. "Idiots!" I screamed.

Halitov spoke once more with the engineers, then said, "Yeah, the Marines probably didn't mean to hit that. But hey, at least it wasn't us. I'd hate to think that we decided to blow up this place instead of letting it fall into enemy hands. We've been there before, eh?"

"Think they know about the leak?"

"Don't know. If not, they're about to capture a ticking bomb. At least we get the last laugh."

I huffed. "Twenty-one minutes . . . Skin up. Let's go."

With a sonorous boom, the viewport blew in under the incredible force of a pulse bomb that had impacted just a dozen meters below our level. The blast knocked Halitov and I across the room and sent us skittering toward the back wall. An acrid wind rushed in and howled, attended by the even louder drone of crab carrier turbines and booming particle cannons. The entire pyramid rumbled violently as two more pulse bombs detonated somewhere on the building's west side.

We scrambled to our feet, skinned up, then Halitov smote a fist on the lift's dead control panel. I looked to the shattered viewport, our only exit, the ground some three hundred meters below.

"No, I don't think it's going to happen this time," said Halitov, unclipping a particle rifle from the wall.

"What?" I asked, grabbing my own weapon.

"Making it out alive."

I grinned weakly. "Why do you always get depressed when we're surrounded by twenty thousand troops? What's your problem?"

"I'm not sure," he said. "I usually like being the center of attention." He ventured to the shattered window and stared down at a tiny gray ribbon: the perimeter walkway. "That, Major St. Andrew, is a big drop."

"Yeah, it is."

"If the bond fails, we're going to die."

"That's right."

"Just making sure you knew the odds." With that, he winked, leapt from the sill, and plummeted.

For a second, I glimpsed a long line of Marines flooding out of the nearest crab carrier. While our rooftop cannons punched gaping holes in the surface near them and occasionally took out a grunt or two, for the most part, the enemy advanced routinely on our position. I knew my people would have several surprises waiting for them. However, in all the confusion, I had failed to check my HUV for casualty reports. I didn't realize that nearly half of my people were already dead.

The sill near me exploded with particle fire as several Marines below probed with their beads. I held my breath, reached into the bond, and took to the air.

2 ❯ "I'm still alive," Halitov said over my private channel. "I like that."

With the walkway rushing up at me, I strengthened my connection to the quantum bond, felt the particles within myself, the air, and the surface, then rolled up, brought my boots down, and smack, hit the quickcrete.

"Stay down," Halitov ordered calmly as he spotted something just over my shoulder.

I shot a glance back as he charged a pair of oncoming Marines whose combat skins fluctuated from a mossy green to a deep brown. In a flash barely perceptible to the naked eye, Halitov flung himself into a *biza*, flying headfirst at the soldiers, his particle rifle spewing a glistening hot bead at one while he targeted the second with his free hand. The first Marine crumpled as Halitov's hand penetrated the second Marine's skin and latched onto the guy's throat. The Marine stumbled back, and in that moment of disorientation, Halitov landed on his feet, crossed back, and ripped off the soldier's tac. The combat skin vanished just as Halitov gutted him with a Ka-bar that he had wrenched from his calf sheath.

"Nineteen thousand, nine hundred and ninety-eight to go," he groaned.

"Approximately."

"Yeah. Approximately."

We darted off, keeping close to the tower. While we could will ourselves to evacuation pad Alpha, about a kilometer south of our position, we might lose consciousness from the drain of bridging such a long distance. Neither of us had mastered the technique the way Jing had, and we wouldn't take the risk.

We had reached the tower's southeast corner, where my friend peered around the corner and swore. I got my haunches and stole a glimpse for myself:

Ten crab carriers lined the nearest tarmac, Marines charging out of them as though they had just been given a week's leave at an exotic port. They hooted, hollered, activated their skins, and fired seemingly without cause or direction, just tossing up beads into the sky or at the row of five-story research buildings that lay ahead.

"It's you and me, and we have to get by, what's that? Maybe an entire battalion right there?" Halitov asked.

I glanced to a data bar in my HUV, ordered the computer to make a tactical assessment with troop movement projections relayed via our satellite link. A message flashed: UNABLE TO ESTABLISH EIS. "Eyes In the Sky are gone," I told him.

He chuckled under his breath. "Like that matters?"

"We can still get by these guys."

"Not this many. Not this time."

"What is it with you and this prophet of doom bullshit?" I asked. "I'm tired of it. You want out? I'll relieve you right here and you can go surrender. See if they'll put up with your whining as long as I have."

Abruptly, I streaked off around the corner, reached into the bond, scaled the tower to a height of about ten meters, then dodged right, tipping sideways, defying gravity but feeling none of its effects. The massive swarm of Marines lay off to my right, and though I ran about three, maybe four times as fast as an unconditioned soldier could, I knew the alarms would still wail in their HUVs and they would eventually lock onto me. I noted that Halitov ran about a half dozen meters behind, and over our private channel he muttered something about power going to my head and that he should have taken his own command way back when. Who the hell did I think I was, and where was I going? I grinned. His buttons were way too easy to push.

"They'll get a lock any second," I said. "Soon as we reach the next corner, we hit the *gozt,* drop onto those buildings over there. Roof to roof."

"They already got a loose lock on me," he shouted, then suddenly hustled past me, his combat skin alive with ricocheting rounds of particle fire. If any one of those Marines below managed a steady lock, that fire would penetrate his combat skin.

"Okay, go now!" I cried.

Had we not been under such intense fire, I would have better appreciated our well-timed bullet thrust, arms at our sides, rifles tucked against our legs. We were bizarre, wingless birds, shimmering and arcing across a sky torn apart by the lightning of particle rifles. With our heads coming within just a meter of the first building's rooftop, we broke from the *gozt* and into a perfectly executed roll—or at least I thought mine was until I made contact with my back, then wheeled around as though I were sliding across ice. With a horrible thud, I slammed against the steel housing of an air filtration unit. My right arm tingled, although my skin had absorbed a large portion of the blow.

Halitov had come out of his roll and crawled toward me under a tarpaulin of particle fire hanging less than a meter above his head. "I think we've lost some of them now," he said with mock hope. "Now only about a thousand are after us."

Something hummed. Grew closer. I sat up, craned my head. "Listen!"

The skin protecting his face cleared a little, and his gaze went distant. "I can't right now. Have you checked the casualty reports? The numbers are insane. Three hundred and two KIA so far."

"What?"

"Look at the report."

I called it up in my own HUV, even as that hum grew louder. The names scrolled up one of my databars. I was about to close my eyes and shudder when my brother called. "Scott, you there?"

Though static washed through the image, the dirt and anguish on Jarrett's face were unmistakable. "I'm here, Captain," I said, feeling uncomfortable calling him by rank, but it was still better than *Taris Markland*. "Report."

"First shuttle just launched—and just crashed," he said.

"How many?"

"I'm not sure. At least a couple hundred civvies gone. Prem scan indicates only a few survivors."

"Damn it. And we might lose more. We got a core leak. About seventy minutes left till it blows. Get our ATCs in the sky. We'll run our own cover. Launch the shuttles. And get out of there yourself."

"Easier said than done," he moaned, then muttered a command to his tac computer, widening the image.

His legs were gone. Two corpsmen worked frantically on his stumps and on a gaping laceration across his bicep. I lost my breath.

"Scott, I just want you to know, I, uh—"

"Shut up," I said, staving off the shock and pain. "I want to speak to your XO right now."

His eyelids fluttered, and I thought he might lose consciousness. Before I knew for sure, the image shifted to a squad sergeant, a brunette I recognized as Trina Amitoss, my brother's lover. "Sir, don't worry, sir," she said, her tone a hairsbreadth shy of hysteria. "We're getting him out of here right now."

"Scott, an airjeep just came over the side of the building," Halitov droned, as though he had already agreed to my suggestion of surrender. "And the gunner . . . I think he sees us. He's bringing the cannon around."

"Amitoss, you get my brother out of there," I cried, then broke the link, rose and whirled—

And there it was, the airjeep, about ten meters ahead of us and hovering a meter off the ledge, its pilot tipping the small vehicle's nose down a few degrees, allowing the rear gunner to get a bead.

"Are you thinking what I'm thinking?" asked Halitov.

"I doubt it," I said darkly, then ran straight at the jeep. I figured the gunner would fire, I would dodge his shots, then take him out before the pilot knew what happened. After that, I would hold the pilot hostage, and Halitov and I would hitch a ride all the way back to Alpha pad. It was a grand plan.

However (and in combat there is always a "however"), the gunner's cannon released not a wave of particle fire but a round of swelling blue energy. Even as I launched into the old somersault and kick of the *dirc*, believing I could shift my trajectory to hit the gunner, the round became a scintillating, weblike sphere that dropped over me. I struck one wall of energy, then the others clung to my back, shoulders, arms, and legs. As though composed of a trillion tiny insects, the web began chewing through my skin.

"What the hell is that?" screamed Halitov, sounding as mad as he was surprised by my capture.

"You're out of here," I ordered.

The gunner leveled his weapon on Halitov, who stood there, torn a moment until he opened up with his own rifle, spraying the airjeep's pilot with a vicious bead that drilled into the man's head. I knew that within a few seconds, the pilot would be dead, my skin would dissolve, and Halitov would be captured by the gunner.

So I took a chance and willed myself behind that gunner. The distance was short, the drain not as bad as I imagined it would be. The web of energy that had covered me hung for a moment, a human silhouette devoid of flesh, then it trickled like water to the rooftop. The gunner, a young woman of twenty maybe, with remarkably petite features and a diamond glistening on her finger, sensed my presence and glanced back. I reached up, braced her head in my hands, closed my eyes, listened for the crack.

As she fell out of my grip, the pilot collapsed in his seat, a victim of Halitov's true aim. Realizing that the pilot had died, the airjeep's computer switched to autopilot and brought the vehicle in for a smooth landing on the rooftop, though we could no longer take it since the controls had been set to a user-specific mode. Even then, Halitov made a quick attempt to hack his way into the system, after which he punched the touch screen in failure.

A distant rumble from the north signaled the approach of a squadron of Western Alliance atmoattack jets. They streaked just above the treetops, cleared the perimeter forest, then dove over the nearest row of hangars. The fighters' T-shaped bows and spherical fuselages cast long shadows over the crab carriers parked nearby as pilots zeroed in on our evacuation pads to the south.

I got on the battalion-wide channel. "Listen up, people! Air attack's inbound. I want everyone out now!"

Four of our G21 Endosector Armored Troop Carriers blasted off, turning their beaks toward the inbound atmoattack fighters. Those ATCs were running defense, with four more of the quad-winged craft waiting to launch behind them. I imagined that the pilots and copilots behind those seed-shaped canopies already knew they were dead; it was just a matter of how many enemy pilots they could take with them. What I didn't realize was that the enemy squadron we had just seen was a diversion. As my ATCs opened fire at those incoming ships, a second enemy squadron rose vertically from behind the one of the tawt drive construction facilities. Before those enemy ships even propelled themselves forward, they launched a flurry of multiseeker missiles.

All Halitov and I could do was stand there, listening to the roar of troops below, the sonic booms of turbines, and the high-pitched whistling of those missiles. My pulse raced as three, two, one the ATCs exploded in swelling fireballs that grew long stems of flaming debris racing to take root on the surface.

Another quartet of my ATCs roared over the destruction of their brothers, spitting undulating whips of particle fire on that squadron of atmoattacks. Then one atmoattack from the first squadron broke off, circled back, and began strafing the rooftops.

Suddenly, the building beside our own blew apart as though it had been detonated from within. Colossal hunks of debris hurtled through the air toward us. As the shadow of a tumbling piece of quickcrete darkened the nearest ledge, we leapt from the rooftop, not realizing until we were airborne that a squad of ten Marines waited in the alley. A soldier I figured for the squad sergeant glanced up, shouted something to his troops, and a maw of particle fire opened below. We dropped right into that maw, our skins lightning up like casino signs until we hit the ground, rolled, then dodged back for the wall.

A shit storm of debris rained down on the Marines, taking out two before they even looked up. The rest took our cue and bolted for the wall.

"Lesson," Halitov cried. "Quitunutul arts. *Chak* is the art of the turn." With that, he demonstrated on the nearest soldier, leaping up and whirling in midair while extending his right leg. His boot passed through the Marine's skin and broke the guy's jaw.

"Lesson," I shouted. "*Ai* is the floating kick, counterkick." I ran past Halitov, leapt up two meters, dropkicked one Marine in the head, then rolled, driving my heel into a second Marine's neck. By the time I hit the ground, the sharp blades of my Ka-bars jutted from my fists, as they did from Halitov's.

Though smaller debris continued to fall, we ignored it, shifting fluidly between the rubble to stab one Marine after another. The eight fell, and we looked around, gazes darting through the dust, blood dripping heavily from our knives.

I checked both ends of the alley. Clear. Opted for the rear exit. "This way."

Before I managed a step, twenty, maybe thirty Marines stampeded into the path ahead, their muzzles already winking at us, rounds flashing by or thumping on our skins.

Halitov grabbed my shoulder. An equal number of troops flooded in from the opposite direction. We exchanged a knowing look, one almost sad. A lot of people were about to die.

I thought of every round coming from every rifle directed by every Marine advancing toward us. I thought of the particles that comprised those rounds, those rifles, those Marines. And Halitov did likewise. Together, we found the bond and for a moment just stood there as they fired upon us.

Then, with a precision inspired by our old instructor Major Yokito Yakata, the man who had first demonstrated the technique to us, we turned a hundred brilliant beads of automatic particle fire back on the grunts who had unleashed them. Marines fired wildly as they fell, even striking the soldiers nearest them. Combat skins grew opaque, and as a few dissolved, the utter terror etched on the soldiers' faces chilled me. We wielded an ungodly power given to us by an ancient alien race, a race that might have orchestrated their own demise.

The fire continued to loop, and the dead continued to pile up until shouts of "Cease fire! Fall back!" sent the troops darting off through the steam of sizzling flesh.

Halitov gaped breathlessly at me, then leaned over, placing palms on his hips as though he just run a marathon. Without warning, the drain hit me. The ground turned to water and began rolling. I nearly fell, caught my breath, and finally blinked clear the feeling.

"Oh my god. Please. Help me!"

I craned my head, searching for the woman who had called out, probably a dying Marine.

From behind a bank of tall canisters lining the wall to my left came a frightened looking woman of about thirty, a very attractive woman with striking red hair, fair skin, and icy blue eyes permanently narrowed in her quest for the truth. I knew her, all right. All too well.

"Elise Rainey?" I said, dumbfounded. "Why are you still here? I ordered a full evacuation!"

"I'm just curious why you're not dead," Halitov added, glaring at the woman, whose floatcam hovered at her shoulder, the disk's operational lights flashing and indicating that she was, in fact, recording our conversation.

Her gaze darted past us to the piles of dead troops, then to the fresh Marines taking up positions along the wall. "Just get me out of here."

Halitov grinned ironically at me, then shook his head, took aim at the floatcam, and summarily blew it to smithereens.

"Hey!" cried Rainey.

I leveled my index finger on her. "You promised me."

"I'm a war correspondent," she said. "We get the story. Whatever it takes. I thought you knew I was lying."

"No. But I do know you'll die here."

"No, I won't. You're going to save my ass. Right now. Come on." She swung around and started off, walking straight toward the Marines.

"Screw her," said Halitov. "She comes marching into the tower like she owns the place, tells us she's got access to our entire battalion. Probably slept her way into that."

I lowered my voice. "Doesn't matter. We still have to get her out."

"And the bitch knows that."

"Look, there's no way she could've known we'd be here. She was probably getting ready to surrender, maybe even die. You have to admire that much."

"Well, getting back to the pad should be even more fun now," he said. "Especially with less than an hour on the clock and her slowing us down." With reflexes enhanced by the quantum bond, Halitov suddenly dodged in front of Rainey as particle fire streaked toward her.

With my grumbling XO serving as a human shield, his skin battling off dozens of incoming rounds, I deskinned and came behind them. "Get on my back," I ordered Rainey.

"What?"

"I'm not joking. Just do it."

She toed off her heels and jumped. I staggered forward as she wrapped her arms around my neck and began choking me. I reached up and loosened her grip, then took a deep breath. Was the bond there? Yes. I tucked my arms beneath her legs and began scaling the wall.

She gasped, and I was actually thankful for the twenty or so beads of incoming particle fire that tore up the quickcrete around us. They kept her silent.

We reached the rooftop, and I told her to let go. Thick clouds of brown smoke rose from the shattered building Halitov and I had leapt from and whipped by, stinging our eyes and sending her into a coughing fit.

"Got a plan?" Halitov asked, reaching the ledge and hopping down to join us. " 'Cause I sure as hell don't."

"I think so," I said, then jogged off, out of the smoke and toward the far end of the building. "This way!" I skinned up and called for the blueprints on the building ahead, a broad, rectangular, two-story affair with a half dozen dishes mounted on its roof. SOFTWARE DESIGN OFFICE #4 had at least three subterranean passages leading toward the central hub. From there we could take another series of tunnels back to evacuation pad Alpha. Even though Alliance Marines were probably crawling through those passages like termites, we would only have to contend with them and not air strikes. Once Halitov and Rainey reached me, I shared my idea.

"We can't go back to Alpha. It's already gone," said Halitov.

I tried verifying that fact via my tactical computer, but the Marines had finally decrypted our codes and were jamming all communications. I couldn't even contact my brother or Jing to learn if they had made it out. "We're being jammed," I told Halitov. "How do you know Alpha's gone?"

He made a strange face, almost a grimace, accompanied by a shrug. "I just know."

"I can't go on that."

"Alpha is gone," he insisted, grabbing my wrist. "So are Whiskey and Bravo. Delta's the only pad left."

I didn't like his guilt-stricken tone; no, I didn't like it at all. I ripped my wrist away, grabbed his collar. "How do you know?"

He banged a finger on his tac. "Forty-eight minutes. We don't have time for this."

"If he has a gut feeling, I say we go with it," argued Rainey. "And what's going to happen in forty-eight minutes?"

I ignored her and scrutinized Halitov. "What are you holding back?"

"Just get the fuck away!" he cried, shoving me aside. "We have to go!"

"What did you do, Rooslin?" I raised my voice to a shout. "What did you do?"

He whirled away. "If we don't get to Delta pad, we die." Slowly, he turned back. "You can trust me on that."

I snorted. "And we're not talking about a gut feeling, are we . . ."

His expression said he wouldn't explain further, and the damned clock wasn't just ticking in my ears; it banged like a sledgehammer. I glared at him. "Okay, we'll go to Delta. But if you're wrong . . ." I turned to Rainey, tapped a code into my tac, and removed the bracelet. "Here," I said, handing it to her. "I should've given you this before. The computer will reset for you. You're going to skin up."

"What about you?"

"Just worry about keeping up with us," I said. "Because in about forty-seven minutes, all of this goes bye-bye."

"What do you mean?"

"Forget details. Think big picture. Think big bang." I made sure the tac fit her properly, then activated the skin.

She staggered back as the membrane zipped over her. "This is weird."

"You'll get used to it."

Halitov aimed his particle rifle at a conventional lock on one of three roof access hatches. The hatch blew inward. With his rifle at the ready, he shifted warily inside, down a narrow staircase. I motioned for Rainey to follow him, then hazarded a final glance at the facility my battalion had been charged with protecting. Fires raged from nearly every building within view, and at least a half dozen hangars now lay in twisted, burning piles of steel and quickcrete. To the south, a trio of ATCs jetted away, escorting a pair of civilian shuttles. The ATCs banked steeply to port, evading missile fire. I tensed as they rose higher, higher, then vanished into the clouds. "Go," I whispered. "Go. Go." But an echoing drumroll of multiple explosions made my heart sink, and a second later, fiery ribbons cut across the sky. I started for the hatch, hesitated, kept asking myself why. The Alliances had probably made a deliberate strike on that tawt drive in the hope of a core leak. Why were they wasting a valuable resource that they could have exploited? Later I would learn that all of Columbia Colony was ordered destroyed, including personal residences. The Alliances wanted to ruin our morale, and a massacre on the capitol world was just the ticket.

I hurried down the stairs and came into a wide corridor with a half dozen intersecting passages.

"Somebody said you have two little boys," Halitov called to Rainey.

"That's none of your business," she said, tentatively touching the wall with a finger covered by her combat skin.

"You risked your life for a story?" he asked. "What about your kids? They don't count?"

"Look, you saved my life back there—"

"And I'll save it again," he said.

"Right. So I owe you a thanks. No personal explanations. No insights. That's it."

"We can stay, chat, probably die," I said, shuffling past them.

"I'm walking point," cried Halitov, jogging ahead of me.

He was skinned up. I didn't argue. We charged on, and I played navigator, directing him down the first two corridors toward another stairwell.

It had been a while since he and I had utilized our infantry hand signals, but they had been cerebroed into our memories, and when we reached the stairwell door, he raised a finger for halt. We hugged the wall on either side of the door, and with a start, he swung it open, rolled and pointed his particle rifle into the well.

A flash of light blinded me, and an explosion rattled me to the marrow. Halitov flew past me and collided with the opposite wall, his combat skin alive with tendrils of energy threatening to reach his flesh. Rainey screamed.

I rolled into the doorway, came face to face with an Alliance Marine gripping an unfamiliar weapon not unlike our QQ90 particle rifles but with a much larger muzzle. He was about to fire. I willed myself behind him, my Ka-bar already coming up to penetrate his combat skin, my other hand directing my rifle up to knock his away. Simultaneously, another round exploded from his weapon and hit the ceiling as I thrust my knife into his back and pierced his heart. He dropped as shattered rafters swung down on us. I bolted left, away from the debris, then slipped back into the corridor.

Halitov looked winded but all right, the ghost of his combat skin fading behind him. He had escaped from the weapon the same way I had from the airjeep's cannon. Unconditioned soldiers would not fare as well against that device.

"How did you do that?" Rainey asked him. "I've never seen anything like—"

"That's classified. And if we make it out of here and you do put it in a story, I guess the Wardens might be a little upset over that."

She frowned. "Whoa. I'm threatened."

"You up there?" came an electronically modulated voice from the stairwell. "Abandon your weapons and come down with your hands on your heads."

"That'll be the platoon sergeant," said Halitov.

"Stay here," I told Rainey, then motioned for Halitov to join me in the well.

"You're going to kill them, all of them, aren't you," Rainey called after us.

"Nah, we'll leave one for you," Halitov snapped.

As we shifted stealthily down the stairs, I played a mental game to purge the guilt I was already feeling. I thought of my brother and Jing. I thought of my father, somewhere out there on Kennedy-Centauri. I wanted to see all of them again. And those Marines waiting for us on the next landing stood in my way. I turned myself into a stoic machine, working to the rhythm of my pulse.

"Time?" I asked Halitov.

"Thirty-three minutes, nineteen seconds."

"I want this path clear," I told him. "I want it clear right now."

"Hell yeah," he said, getting pumped up.

"You mean yes, sir!"

"That, too."

Twin pops resounded as we hit the well. Vizi canisters rolled inside, spraying a thick, emerald cloud of the poisonous gas. Halitov's skin would protect him, but Rainey had mine. I remembered the time Halitov and I had been struck unconscious by Losha gas. We had resigned to the defeat. I took a last breath and told myself no, I'm not going to accept this. With that, I tried something new. I manipulated the bond between the particles of that gas, and in doing so, I imagined a combat skin covering my body and protecting my lungs.

"Scott," Halitov shouted, trying to grab my arm—but his hand rebounded.

"I'm all right," I said, grinning in amazement.

"The quantum bond, huh? Whatever works," he said, then vanished into a wall of smoke.

Someone grunted. Sounds of boots shuffling. The gas still hissing. A collapse. Another grunt. Halitov swore.

A Marine came at me from the smoke, a particle pistol blazing. Given the absences of my combat skin, the soldier assumed he had me, then he did a double take as the rounds struck my thought-inspired shield and melted.

I raised my rifle, locked a bead on his head, and held down the trigger until his skin dissolved. I jerked my head away as his scream broke into a gargle, then nothing.

When I turned back, the world darkened around the edges. I couldn't hold out for much longer. I rushed into the smoke, searching wildly for a corridor, someplace, anywhere away from the deadly fumes. I was so intent on finding a sanctuary that the eleven Marines who attacked me fell one after another in a blur of death. I shot them, stabbed them, broke their necks, their backs, drove their noses into their brains. And the blood drenched my utilities as the quantum combat skin faded.

Dizzy, nauseous, my legs wobbling, I staggered into a tunnel marked SUBPASSAGE A7, took a glance at a line of little hovers waiting like golf carts at a club. "Rooslin!" I called. "Over here."

I leaned on one of the small vehicles, then tentatively pulled my thoughts away from the bond and chanced the air. There was something there, something faint. We had to move quickly, but I was exhausted.

After a moment, he came rushing forward, literally dragging Rainey with him.

"Oh, god," she said, wincing at me.

I touched my cheek, and my fingers came up bloody.

"You getting all this," Halitov said to her, his eyes wide, his tone maniacal. "You getting all this okay? You like this, huh? Good story for you?"

"Shut up!" she cried, her eyes swollen with tears. "Just shut up!"

I raised my brows at Halitov. "Time?"

"Twenty-one minutes."

"Can we make it?" Rainey asked.

I just looked at her. "I don't know."

"You don't know. Well can you answer this: How do we know there'll be a ride waiting for us? I mean, you can't contact them, right?"

"Every escape pad has a pair of underground hangars. They're pretty well hidden. We've stowed a half dozen SRTCs in each," I explained. "They're high-speed fighters carrying minimal weapons. They're the best evac craft we have."

"But if the Marines get to them first?"

I hardened my gaze. "Then I hope for your family's sake that you have good life insurance."

"Aw, shit, what now," Halitov groaned as a pair of Alliance Anti-Personnel Drones whirred toward us, their whiskers fluctuating, their spherical shells beaming in the bright tunnel lights.

"They've wised up," I said. "They won't waste troops. They'll wear us down with the drones."

"Wear us down?" Halitov said. "I doubt that."

Before he could launch into his attack, one drone got off a quick shot. My gaze darted around the room, searching for the impact of that round. There was no ricochet. Nothing. Had I not been covered in so much blood, I wouldn't have recognized the obvious. The sting finally came. My mouth fell open. I looked to Rainey, who realized what had happened. "He's been hit," she yelled.

But Halitov was already airborne, sliding toward the drones in a *shoru* that would abruptly take him below then behind them. In the second it would take them to swivel, he would reverse engineer them the hard way. But as he shot below, he craned his head toward Rainey, distracted by her call. The drones exploited the opening and fired pointblank, sending him into a wild tumble toward the rear wall.

With an ominous click, they swiveled their guns around, toward Rainey and I.

"What do I do?" she asked. "What do I do?"

I wanted to answer, but I could barely move through all the pain. My particle rifle lay at my feet. I reached for the bond, but mental fingers grasped nothing. Shit. I would be killed by a soulless automaton. At the very least, I wanted my killer to feel something, anything, over my death.

Rainey lifted her palms and edged back toward me.

The drones glided slowly forward. Halitov came out of his spin and crashed onto the floor. One drone swung toward him, the other kept on us.

"Just stay here," she muttered, then turned and shocked me.

3 ❯ **Clearly, Ms. Elise** Rainey had trouble with the damsel in distress role that Halitov and I had foisted upon her. She was, after all, a war correspondent, had probably seen her share of bloodshed and had escaped from more than one precarious situation. But those facts were easy to forget when you looked at her lithe form and civilian clothes and when you listened to the dread in her voice.

Which was why my mouth fell open as she threw herself in front of me, the drone's cannon expelling so much automatic particle fire that I swore her skin would never hold.

But she understood exactly what was happening, drove herself toward the drone, reached up, and grabbed the thing by its whiskers. The drone took off, carrying Rainey with it. She flew through the air as though gripping a possessed beach ball. The drone carried her toward the wall, then veered sharply, hoping to shake her off. But Rainey threw her legs out, tugging the drone back toward the wall where it smashed violently against the hard steel and heaved a shower of sparks.

Meanwhile, Halitov had made a flying leap toward his drone, and in a display as deadly as it was comical, he gripped the thing between his legs. The drone struggled to remain airborne, even as its cannons directed twin streams of particle fire right into his crotch. Halitov rode that drone as though it were a wild bull, one hand gripping the base of a whisker, the other struggling to jam a particle rifle into a small panel on the drone's face. Even as Halitov fired, Rainey's drone dropped hard and rolled across the floor, shedding more sparks in its wake. Then Halitov blew apart his drone's panel. His mouth opened as he realized that he now plummeted some three meters toward the floor. He could have leapt off the drone, but for some reason he hung on. The drone hit first and blew free of his legs, as he fell off and tumbled onto his side.

Rainey charged over to him, offered her hand, which he ignored, saying, "Take off that tac and give it to him."

"Yeah," I said. "Let me borrow it for a moment."

She hurried to me, and I helped her remove the bracelet. Once I had it around my wrist, I activated the skin, and the tac's computer switched to medical mode to stabilize my wound. I would still need surgery to remove the round, but the skin's lasers would prevent me from bleeding out and protect the wound from infection.

"How long is that going to take?" Halitov asked, glancing warily ahead, expecting more drones to pursue us.

I checked a databar in my HUV. "About forty-five seconds."

He nodded, then shoved Rainey by the shoulder. "Stay behind me."

She leered at him but complied.

"Hey," I called to her. "Thanks."

"Look, to be honest, I really don't give a shit about you. You're just my map out of here. Okay?"

I wasn't offended. In fact, I even smiled. "Okay."

"Come on, come on," Halitov urged, beginning to pace.

"All right," I said, switching off the skin, then return-ing the tac to Rainey. I stood, grimaced over the smol-dering fire in my shoulder, then turned back to the hover I had been leaning on. I climbed into the little transport, bypassed the controls with access codes cerebroed into my brain, then started the engine as Halitov and Rainey climbed into the backseat. The hover had no windows, no roof, no weapons, but it would save us from having to run all the way down to Delta pad.

The whir of more Alliance drones drew closer, and I jammed the accelerator arm forward. Halitov jerked back and leveled his particle rifle on the new pursuers, even as Rainey, who had been gripping my weapon, pointed it over Halitov's shoulder.

"Do I just pull this trigger?" she shouted.

"USM's off," I told Halitov, explaining that anyone could now fire the weapon.

"You want to know how to use that, sweetheart?" Halitov began, hollering over the report of his own weapon. "Hit that button. That's the safety."

"Got it."

"What are you waiting for? Fire!"

She did, but behind us, five drones fanned out, evad-ing our attack as their cannons extended.

An intersection lay ahead, and while the swiftest path to Delta lay beyond it, I opted for a detour in order to lose our mechanical fan club. As we neared the corner, I jerked the control stick left, banking hard. We buzzed around the corner, and Rainey shouted something, though salvos of particle fire stole her words.

"What?" I cried.

"He fell out!" she yelled.

I craned my neck, and there was Halitov, lying on the

floor behind us, the five drones swarming him as though he had rattled their nest. He scrambled to his feet and took off running.

"He can't catch up!" Rainey cried.

"Oh, yes he can," I said. But I knew that if Halitov found the bond, he would rocket right toward us. I eased back on the throttle a bit. He reached us, then threw himself onto the small trunk compartment. As he crawled toward his seat, the drones narrowed the gap, their cannons locked on to the hover.

When I hit the accelerator arm, I thought I had triggered an explosion, but I hadn't. A round of particle fire had blown apart one of our turbines. The control stick felt mushy, and the hover slowed as we reached another intersection, the tunnel cutting thirty-degrees across our path. I fought to bring us around that corner, and once there, I hit the brakes. "This thing is tommyed."

Halitov and Rainey bailed out and took up positions behind the hover, just as the five drones glided around the corner.

Though significantly weakened, I had to do something more than huddle there and turn over my fate to Halitov and Rainey. I imagined myself inside the lead drone, my fingers plucking out the thing's protein CPU. My vision fogged for a moment, but when it cleared that drone fell and skittered across the floor like an errant bowling ball.

With a mild grin, I took on the second drone, but this time when my vision fogged, it grew darker, and, damn it, I passed out.

"Are you all right?"

"I'm terrific. I can't think of another place I'd rather be. How 'bout you?"

"All right, wiseass. You must be tired by now. Come on. We'll stop."

"Sounds great. We can hang around for the last eleven minutes of our lives."

The voices echoed and faded in and out of each other as I grew aware of a strong pressure across my chest. My eyes snapped open, and I found myself slung across Halitov's back. I wasn't sure where we were. The quickcrete was damp, the lighting poor. Had we already reached Delta pad?

"Rooslin," I called softly, barely recognizing my own voice.

He slowed and gingerly slid me off his back. Thankfully, he gripped my shoulders because the ground felt spongy, though it appeared firm, and I nearly fell back, into Rainey. "Time?"

"About ten minutes, but we're almost there," he answered, lifting his chin toward the distance. "The hangars are just past that hatch."

Halitov had taken us in the back way, through maintenance shafts spanned by bundled draperies of pipes and wires. Light filtered in from a huge, open hatch about two hundred meters ahead.

"Can you walk?" Rainey asked.

"Yeah," I said, staggering forward.

She gripped my wrist and tugged me on as Halitov jogged ahead on point. After a moment, she sighed heavily. "I guess there's no way to contact my boys."

"They've cut us off. I'm sorry."

"It's all right. It was my decision to stay behind and cover the attack."

"What were you thinking?"

"I was thinking Pulitzer. Now I'm thinking idiot."

"No, now you're thinking *stay alive*." I reached out

to grab the wall as the floor suddenly shifted, or at least it felt so.

"Major, I, uh, I don't know how to tell you this, but you're looking . . . I don't know. I mean, I figured you for forty, but—"

"Must be the stress," I said, averting my gaze.

"They did something to you, didn't they."

"Who's they?"

"They did something with your conditioning, right? I've heard rumors about Guardsmen and Wardens who've been messed up. Those rumors are true, aren't they."

"Do me a favor and switch out of reporter mode for a moment, okay?"

We neared the hatch, and Halitov appeared from the shadows and came toward us, his eyes glossed with tears, his jaw going slack in surprise? Anger? Suddenly, he cackled like a madman. "Have a look at this!"

Dim, overhead lights picked out a sweeping subterranean hangar. Our sleek fighters were, indeed, waiting for us, save for the fact that they had been reduced to a half dozen mounds of charred wreckage. Around them lay dozens of still burning bodies, most of them members of my battalion who had succumbed to acipalm-three grenades. The stench was beyond unholy, and the sight of limbs strewn all over the tarmac would rob me of many nights' sleep. As we moved farther into the hangar, the full extent of the carnage hit home. There was Jimmy Chico, Mike Blair, Brenda Tax, Simon Kuhns, and Ripley Martin from Turbo Company. And there were, well, parts of Tina James and Billy Fitzgerald. Sure, I had lost people before—but never in such large numbers and never so brutally. At least three platoons had come for the SRTCs. I don't believe a single

Warden made it out. The Alliance Marines took no prisoners.

"Big time ambush," shouted Halitov. "This place was clear. I sensed it. I'm not lying. I swear!"

"I don't understand how they got past our cruisers—unless someone fed them our encryption codes. They knew exactly where to hit us," I said.

"Doesn't matter anymore," Halitov snapped. "Nothing does."

"You said the ships would be here," cried Rainey.

I frowned at her, then realized that she didn't recognize the rubble. "They are here."

She looked at me, looked at the tattered, twisted lumps, then began to hyperventilate.

Halitov threw away his particle rifle and shook his head fiercely. "One minute, thirty seconds."

"We're dead," Rainy said, her eyes bugging out. "We're dead."

I went to Halitov, put a hand on his shoulder. "We're not going out in this hole. Let's head up top, stand tall, and die like soldiers." A chill broke across my shoulders as I uttered the words. I still had trouble accepting defeat, but death . . . I'm not sure why, but I wasn't scared. I wanted to raise my fist in defiance at the enemy, let him know that I cursed him to the bitter end.

Halitov finally regarded me and nodded.

We mounted a pair of ladders, passed through a short conduit, and opened a tarmac hatch. The wind whistled and whipped over us as we pulled ourselves up and onto the broad stretch of pavement, the buildings behind us still burning, some in the process of caving in on themselves. The bodies of my people littered most of the walkways, and I found myself studying their positions and replaying how they had died:

That squad over there had fanned out near the wall. The sergeant had called for the first fire team to move up in an attempt to get the Alliance Marines advancing from behind that fuel depot to push back, falling directly into a crossfire. But there were just too many Marines. And despite losing his first dozen, that enemy platoon leader had ordered his people to press on. They overran my team's position, and those young people—the very best the colonies had to offer—were swatted out of existence. I shut my eyes, but the firefights continued to play out with excruciating clarity until Halitov nudged me.

Crab carrier turbines reverberated in the sky, and there they were, burnished carapaces glinting in the sun and soaring into the heavens in a massive retreat.

"Guess they know about our core leak," said Halitov.

"I think it was intentional." I raised my arm, rolled my wrist, then thought better of shaking a fist. No one would see it anyway.

"Fuck you!" screamed Halitov at the departing troop ships. He turned and had trouble meeting my gaze. "All right, so I didn't have a gut feeling about Delta. I sent our people away from here."

"You did what?"

His tone grew defensive. "I sent them away—because you never listen to me. Because we should've had our own plan to get out of here."

I ran up, got in his face. "We did!"

"What? Leave with the grunts? Part of the code, huh? We're officers! And the grunts are dead!"

I grabbed his shoulders. "So what the fuck did you do?"

"I used our battalion as a diversion so we could get out."

"No, you didn't do that," I said, my eyes feeling as

though they would burst from my head. "You didn't do that. Tell me you didn't do that!"

"I sent everyone to the other pads, leaving this one open. I was hoping the Marines would jump them first. Those troops down below? They've must've figured out what I did and tried to get out, but the Marines beat them to it."

"So you fucked over our people to save yourself."

"Not just me. Us!"

At that moment, we were going to die anyway. I just wanted him to die first. And by my hand. I reared back, about to deliver a punch that would penetrate his combat skin, but he saw it coming, ducked, and delivered a blow to my abdomen, knocking me back.

"I'm sorry, man! I just had to!"

I clutched the fire in my belly and leaned over as Rainey shouted for us to stop.

"You lied to me, Rooslin. You lied! And when you did that, you fucked me over, too. You took everything we've done together, all we've been through, and just threw it out." I was so upset that I couldn't speak anymore.

He closed his eyes. "Nothing matters now."

"How much longer?" asked Rainey.

"It's better we don't know," said Halitov.

She nodded. "What's it going to feel like?"

Halitov switched off his combat skin, then swung around, holding palms out, over the tarmac. "The ground will rumble. Then comes a pulse of light so bright that closing your eyes won't help. Your eyelids will feel like they're melting off. Then, in the next few seconds—"

Rainey waved a hand. "All right, enough."

I lowered my head, thought of doing something,

praying maybe, but I had never been a very religious man, probably because of my father's break from the church, but mostly because I had trouble believing in a higher being that could create a species as violent as us. Instead, I asked questions. What was the point of my life? Had I made a difference? Had I understood what being a soldier really means? Had I lived with honor? Had I forced my best friend to lie to me? I still had no answers, but I did have one regret: I was going to die without ever being a father. And I believe that was the first time in my life that I seriously considered what raising my own family would mean.

"I'm so scared," said Rainey. "I'm so scared. Isn't there anything we can do? Anything?"

"Just make your peace," answered Halitov.

"You guys are Colonial Wardens," she spat. "We're just going to stay here and die in the explosion?"

I glanced up at Halitov, who took a few steps back. He studied her, then gazed knowingly at me. "She's right, Scott. So I have to give it a shot."

He wanted to reach into the bond and attempt to will himself out of the blast zone. The drain could kill him. It would definitely kill me. "Take her," I said, knowing that if he focused hard enough, he could hold onto her, and the two of them could streak along the bond between particles.

"I can't," he said, tapping his temple. "No one comes in here with me." His childhood trauma, the one that involved him being locked in a storage container, once again reared its ugly head.

"What're you talking about?" demanded Rainey.

"Don't you leave without trying to save her," I warned, waving off Rainey's question. "You've already lied to me. Just do this. It's . . . your . . . job."

Halitov took another step back, wearing the face of a man whose world was splintering before his eyes. He visibly trembled as he took another step—

And dematerialized.

"Motherfucker," I said under my breath.

Rainey jolted, then glanced around for Halitov. "Where did he go?"

"If there's a Heaven, he's going to Hell," I said.

She looked at me, then bared her teeth. "You. I have to die with *you*. Why not someone I love?"

"Tell me about it," I said, then went to her, took her hand. "Let's take a walk."

With our backs to the oncoming blast, we started off down the tarmac, our faces lifted into the breeze. After a hundred or so yards, I glanced over my shoulder.

"We should be dead by now, right?" asked Rainey.

I froze. "Yeah."

"What happened?"

"I don't know. I remember some engineers were going in there to contain the leak."

"Well, maybe they did!" she cried, grabbing my shoulders. "Maybe we're going to . . ."

She broke off as the ground quaked.

I grabbed her, pulled her in close. "Just close your eyes."

If I could only reach into the bond and take us out of there . . . I tried, but that warm, comfortable feeling was gone. The bond felt hollow, cold, and distant. I wondered if Halitov had made it out. The son of a bitch had broken my heart.

The ground shuddered even more, knocking us off our feet. Winds of hurricane force roared over us, accompanied by a roar that seemed strangely familiar. I rolled, strained to see anything through the sudden storm.

"Ten seconds!" someone boomed. "Let's move! Let's move!"

Hands snatched my arms, and suddenly I was dragged toward an ATC hovering just a few yards from us. Two Colonial Wardens had grabbed Rainey and were rushing her up the aft loading ramp. Through teary eyes I spotted a shockingly old Halitov, seated in a jumpseat beside three civilian engineers, all of them pale and thoroughly exhausted.

I was led to a jumpseat, collapsed into it, as the ramp whined rapidly up and the ATC's crew exchanged rapid departure commands. I caught the attention of one engineer, a wiry, bearded man with a ruby in his ear. "You shut it down?"

He shook his head, checked a tablet in his lap. "Critical mass is imminent."

"But we picked up a couple more minutes on the clock," added Halitov.

I drew back in surprise. "You helped them?"

He raised his brows. "Figured I'd go down there and sit on the thing, like I told you."

"I don't know how he did it," said the wiry engineer. "But he bought us the time, saved our lives."

The disdain that hardened my expression lifted a little as I stared at Halitov until the ATC's pilot engaged the turbines. We slammed into our jumpseats as the ship climbed in a forty-five degree angle away from the tarmac.

My heart sank, and not from the ride, as I glimpsed LockMar Randall from above. Twenty or more fires heaved great clouds of smoke into the sky, and I couldn't find a single building or hangar that appeared intact.

"Here it goes," said the wiry engineer.

Blinding white light swept over the porthole for a moment, even as our pilot engaged the tawt drive. The light narrowed to a pinpoint as my stomach groaned. The Trans-Accelerated Wave Theory Drive took us back to that moment when all matter was one, then a billionth of a second later—

It was over.

"Major St. Andrew," the pilot called back from the open cockpit. "We've just tawted into the Tau Ceti system, sir. Lieutenant Colonel Diablo will debrief you aboard the *Roger Harrington*. We'll dock and decon in five minutes."

"Very well. Question for you, Lieutenant. Why the hell were you still on site when I ordered a full evacuation?"

"We were never on site, sir. We're Force Recon, operating under your insignia but fully independent, sir. We were sent in to see if you were still alive. The orders came down from the security chief herself."

"Really? Well, I'm not complaining."

"Yes, sir."

"Lieutenant, if you would, I need a tablet linked to satnet, and I need it now," I said, as the sergeant sitting next to me thrust one into my hands. "Never mind. Got one. An efficient crew you have here."

"Yes, sir," replied the pilot, relishing the complement.

With trembling fingers, I punched up Fifth Battalion's casualty and MIA report, which was still being revised as I accessed it. Our escape plan called for the civilian shuttles and our ATCs to tawt out and rendezvous with the *Roger Harrington*. I scanned the list of names of those who had already been checked in, and two names were painfully absent: Captain Taris Markland and Captain Katya Jing. Where the hell were they?

"She make it?" asked Halitov.

"I don't know. My brother hasn't checked in either."

"That doesn't mean anything. There are still ships en route," he said, then took a long breath. "How many did we lose?"

"The number's still unconfirmed," I said, grimacing at the screen. "Five-eleven so far."

His gaze drifted off, and for a few moments all he could do was sit and try to find his breath.

"Some of those people could've used Delta pad to get out," I reminded him.

Halitov bit his lip and just nodded.

"Cut him some slack," Rainey said from across the hold. "He knows."

I smirked at her. "And I hope you understand that the Wardens won't cut you any slack. You broke your media agreement, which now subjects you to a full scan. They'll dig around your head and erase whatever they want. And unfortunately, there's nothing you can do about it."

"They can do that to a civilian?" muttered Halitov.

"They can, but they won't," Rainey said, narrowing her gaze on me. "They're not even going to interrogate me. Because you owe me. I didn't break my agreement. I just wound up in the wrong place at the wrong time."

I considered her request. She had saved my life, and I would be an ungrateful bastard if I threw her to those thought-probing geeks in intell. "I get full approval of all reports you make regarding this incident. Nothing makes satnet without me seeing it first."

"Deal," she said quickly.

I regarded the ATC's crew. "Gentlemen, what you just witnessed never happened."

"No problem, sir," said the sergeant next to me, a round-faced gum-chewer who seemed more bored with than intrigued by our conversation. "I don't exist anyway."

After doctors aboard the *Roger Harrington* patched me up, Halitov and I waited in the small debriefing room adjacent to one of five ward rooms. I kept checking the tablet for news about Jing and my brother. I must have pulled up the report twenty times, and as I called for a twenty-first look, Halitov placed his palm over the screen. "Just let it happen. Don't try to force it."

"What are you talking about?" I asked, prying off his paw.

"You have to pull back. Whatever happens is going to happen, you know?"

"You mean like you lying to me?" I said. "You're my executive officer. I have to trust you. If I can't, then you're gone."

He pursed his lips. "I know."

"Do you know what you said to me by ordering our people away from Delta pad? You said, Scott, I don't trust you. And I won't follow you. And you didn't."

"But I did save your life. I went back there, nearly killed myself tapping into the bond and slowing down that core leak. But that doesn't count for anything, huh? Look at me."

I didn't. He grabbed me by the jaw and pulled my head. I burst from my chair, wrenched out of his grip, and stood, falling into the rest position and ready to launch into any one of the quitunutul arts.

"Just like the old days, huh?" he cried, blasting out of

his own chair and finding his own rest position. "But back then, I always kicked your ass. Ready for another ass-kicking? Let's go. Because I am sick and tired of listening to you and your bullshit honor crap. We *are* more valuable than those grunts. You know that! I heard you say it to Jing! And if that's the case, then why didn't we have our own plan for getting out? But oh, no, you're like the fucking captain of a sinking ship—have to stay on board till the end. We should've been the first ones out and conducted the evacuation from orbit. That's what should've happened. Your plan was shit. The only reason we're standing here is because of me."

"No, you just delayed the inevitable. Ms. Brooks sent down that recon team. She saved us."

"Oh, Jesus. I was expecting a miracle here. Ain't going to happen. You'll never give me any credit."

"Screw credit, Rooslin. I need your trust. But you know what? I'm not sure you're capable of being my XO anymore."

"Oh, you'll fix that, won't you. You'll report every move I made because it's your duty and it wouldn't be honorable if you tried to cover it up," he said in a grating kid's voice.

"The record will show what you did."

"But you can interpret it. You can tell them we ordered those people away from Delta because we thought the Marines had already ambushed the site."

I chuckled over the audacity of his request. "Are you serious? You want me to lie for you now?"

"You don't have the guts to help a friend, do you? You know, if Jing was my girlfriend, I would've saved her myself. I wouldn't have let her rot like you did."

I charged him, wrapped my fingers around his throat before he could respond. I drove him into the wall, found the bond, and held him there. "I didn't leave her to rot!"

His eyes grew wide as he realized that I might very well kill him. He could no longer breathe, and as I drew closer to him, I noticed all the grooves in his face and all the pure white hair around his temples. And my gaze traveled to my own hand, now dappled with age spots, the veins popping. I suddenly released him. He started forward, panting, a hand on his throat, the color returning to his face.

"Stop," I said, putting a hand on my cheek, then touching my crow's feet. "Rooslin, we're dying."

He hesitated, let the fact sink in. We were about to kill each other when, in fact, we might be dead within a week, maybe a month, a year. The aging was unpredictable, and our accelerated fates didn't need any help from us.

"Ms. Brooks says they're working on it," he reminded me. "Well, they'll still be *working on it* after they bury us."

"I'm going to contact her right after this debriefing."

"What's the point? She'll just lie again. The truth is, the conditioning facility on Exeter is tommyed. Beauregard's father blew up the one on Aire Wu, so now we can't be reconditioned. What, you think there's a third facility no one's talking about? It's going to magically appear so our lives can be saved? Maybe you think the Racinians will come back from the dead and build us a new one? Ain't going to happen. What's going to happen is that our teeth will start falling out, and we'll start pissing in our pants."

I had seen him rant that way before, back home when he had discovered that his parents had been killed. But then, there had been time for him to come down, to grieve, to get happy pills. I glanced to the door. At any moment Diablo and his cronies would walk in, and I panicked over what Halitov might say. Oh, he'd give them a piece of his warped mind, all right. A big, fat piece.

4 > **Lieutenant Colonel Jean** Sheffield, our regimental executive officer, entered the debriefing room, quickly returned our salutes, then started for a chair. Sheffield was an excellent officer, even tempered, and despite her twenty plus years of service, she had a limitless well of energy. At that moment, though, she looked pale, a little grayer than usual, and definitely preoccupied.

"I beg your pardon, ma'am, but where is Lieutenant Colonel Diablo?" I asked.

Sheffield blinked off her introspection. "Colonel Diablo? He's been suspended from duty, pending an investigation into the attack on Columbia Colony."

"Ma'am?"

"I won't mince words, Major. The only reason those Marines made planetfall was because they had our encryption codes. They monitored our communications and pinpointed our defenses. When a window opened, they struck. We're still holding on to Rexicity, but Columbia is gone."

"And the other colonies?"

"They didn't touch Govina and Tru Cali like we thought they would, but that doesn't mean they won't. Lincoln and Indicity suffered limited aerial bombing, but no ground troops were deployed. This attack was not about gaining territory—"

"They're sending us a message," I finished.

"That's right. You lost a lot of good people at Lock-Mar Randall, didn't you."

"Yes, ma'am. Most of my battalion. I'm still trying to locate several more MIAs."

"Do you have any idea how many civilians died?"

"I haven't checked the news, I've been so—"

"Over a hundred million."

I glanced to Halitov, whose expression mirrored mine. We just sat there, blankly, unable to comprehend the number.

Sheffield went on. "The media's calling it 'The Columbia Massacre.' We're calling it the worst breach of security in the history of the Wardens and the Seventeen System Guard Corps."

Halitov snorted. "Why don't you just call it the biggest screwup ever?"

"It is," she said, surprising me with her candor. "But we're going to contain this breach. Because if we don't, the war is lost." She faced me, tensing even more. "Major, I'm not here to debrief you. There are two officers from intell waiting outside."

Halitov frowned. "They're going to scan us?"

"We have a traitor, Captain. Maybe a whole group. And even though truth is the first casualty of war, no one defies a scan. We're going to find who did this—no matter what it takes."

"Oh, it's not that you don't trust us, it's just that you . . . don't trust us," Halitov said. "Well nobody's going to poke around my head. Nobody."

"This is a direct order. You don't have a choice. And if you fail to obey it, we'll use drugs, force, whatever it takes to get what we need."

Halitov widened his eyes at me. Yes, if they scanned him they would learn that he had lied to our troops and had kept Delta pad reserved for us. I just shook my head.

Sheffield rose. "Gentlemen, as I said I didn't come here to debrief you. Colonel Ishmar requested that I notify you in person that you are both being relieved of combat duty."

"Until your investigation is complete," I added.

"Negative. If your scans turn up clean, you'll be reassigned as combat consultants to Colonel Beauregard."

I shot to my feet. "Ma'am—"

"I didn't make this decision," she interjected. "But frankly, Major, I do endorse it. At this point, if you and Captain Halitov are not reconditioned, it's in the best interests of the Wardens to remove you from the line."

Halitov punched the table. Hard. "We can't be reconditioned because—"

"I know all about it," said Sheffield. "But the orders are official. They're final. And they've been uploaded to your tablets. Now, let me say for the record that the two of you have sacrificed more than anyone could've asked, and its officers like you that make me proud to be part of this organization. Good luck to you both."

We snapped to, saluted, and watched her go, taking our careers with her.

Once the hatch closed, Halitov swore, picked up his chair, ready to toss it across the room.

"Don't," I said. "It's not worth the effort."

He thought a moment. "You're right." Then he threw the chair anyway. "See, that's what we are now. Fucking furniture."

We stood there another moment until the two dour-looking intell officers came inside and handed us the c-shaped cerebroes. They issued the perfunctory promise that they would search only for military-related activities. Halitov found another chair, sat, held the cerebro in his hands, but wouldn't put it on. I implored him with my gaze.

"Captain Halitov, we're ready to begin," said one officer.

"You're ready to begin?" Halitov shot to his feet and threw the cerebro. It struck the wall and broke into several pieces. "I'm ready to leave."

"Rooslin," I shouted.

But he was already past the hatch.

Less than a minute later, two big corporals dragged a semiconscious Halitov back into the room and dropped him into a chair. He smiled drunkenly at me as one of the intell guys returned with a new cerebro and slid it onto the back of Halitov's head. "They stuck a needle in my neck," Halitov said, slurring his words. "It hurt."

"Always the hard way with you," I sang through a sigh.

He giggled. "Never go down without a fight!"

The scan took nearly an hour and left me exhausted. Afterward, a midshipman directed me to my quarters while Halitov was carried down to the sickbay, where he'd receive more drugs to sober up. I sent off a priority communiqué to Ms. Brooks, who had established her mobile office aboard *Vanguard One*, but the ship had recently made a tawt and the computer was still calculating its location with the satnet computer. The message might not reach her for several days.

Earlier, anxiety had stolen my common sense; I should've set my tablet to automatically alert me if the names Taris Markland or Katya Jing appeared on my battalion's check-in roster instead of repeatedly checking for them manually. I had finally made that adjust-

ment, and when the table beeped the alert, I frantically
read the name Taris Markland and discovered that my
brother's ATC had just arrived. The ship had taken
heavy fire, and after tawting into the system, it had been
towed all the way home. I bolted for my hatch, keyed
open the door, and nearly ran over Ms. Elise Rainey.

"Whoa. Are you rushing off to see me?"

"Oh, no. Sorry," I said, already starting away from
her. "Do you need something? Because I have to go."

"I was just coming to say thanks. And good-bye. After I make my report, they're shipping me out to
Kennedy-Centauri to cover the riots."

I turned back, went to her. "My father's there. If I
give you the information, would you mind checking on
him for me? I've sent several messages, but I haven't
heard back."

"My ride doesn't leave for a couple of hours. Bay
twenty-seven. I'll be at the gate."

"You could just give me your satnet address, and I'll
send you the info."

She looked wounded. "Yeah, I guess I could."

"What's wrong?"

"You really are naïve . . ."

I shrugged. "About what?"

"I was thinking that since I kind of saved your life,
you might like to buy me a drink."

My cheeks grew hot. "I owe you that, don't I . . ."

"Major, I'm not looking for a quick ride on your
bunk, but I'm suddenly thinking that we can keep helping each other. I travel a lot. I might be able to do you a
favor now and again, just like this one with your dad."

She had piqued my interest—and my skepticism.
"What do you want from me?"

"Nothing classified, unless you're volunteering. Just

give me a little data once in a while. A tip from you could put me in the right place at the right time."

"So I have a new satnet pal."

"Exactly."

"All right, I'll meet you down at twenty-seven before you go." I took off running.

"You'd better be there," she hollered after me.

Halitov was just leaving the sickbay when I arrived. "They're going to court-martial me, I know it," he said, rubbing the corners of his eyes.

"They just brought Jarrett in," I reported nervously. "Did you see him?"

"See him? Have you seen the place? It's huge. There are a couple hundred patients in there."

My former XO wasn't kidding. We stepped into a white-walled warren of small exam rooms with curtains instead of hatches. Those rows of curtains stretched out for literally hundreds of meters. We eventually found the triage desk and checked with the nurse there, who, after some checking, found Jarrett's bed number—but not before I mistakenly asked her to search for Jarrett St. Andrew instead of Taris Markland.

"Sir, you can't go in there," said an exhausted young doctor, tapping data into some kind of modified medical tablet strapped to his forearm.

Halitov shifted between me and the doctor. "His brother's in there. And don't you know who we are?"

I glared at Halitov. "I'm sorry about him," I told the doc. "If I could just take a peek. Is he conscious?"

An alarm sounded from the doctor's tablet. He scanned the screen. "Look, just stay here. I'll be right back." He sprinted away, turned a corner.

Halitov reached for the curtain.

"Maybe we shouldn't—"

But it was too late. There was my brother, eyes closed, sitting up on the gurney. I couldn't help but notice how very small he appeared. No legs from the hips down. One arm floating in a tube of bluish-gray solution meant to help his body accept the synthskin field medics had applied to his bicep.

"I told the doctor no visitors," Jarrett said through clenched teeth.

"Oh, shut up," said Halitov. "Your brother's here because he loves you and cares about you."

Jarrett looked at me, but I could only meet his gaze for a moment. The tears were ready to fall, but I had to be strong for him. "They'll get you on nanotech right away. Regrow those legs. Couple months, you'll be back to your company."

"What company?" he groaned. "You mean the four people I have left?"

"Aw, don't worry about that," said Halitov. "They're standing in line to serve with you. You'll have more cherries than you know what to do with. Me, on the other hand? I'm washed up. Just like your bother."

"Would you go?" Jarrett asked Halitov, his tone leaving little room for an answer.

But, of course, Halitov supplied one. "No, I'm staying so you don't turn this into a pity party. You're a Colonial Warden. All right, you got your ass kicked. Lost your legs. But you're not going to lie here and feel sorry for yourself. We don't do that."

"Is that so?" I interjected. "You've been pissing and moaning since I met you at the academy."

"I'm not talking to you," he shot back.

"Look," Jarrett shouted. "I'm *not* feeling sorry for myself. I'm just lying here, fantasizing about the fourteen different ways I can kill this asshole using only one arm." He raised a fist at Halitov, who grinned broadly. An ugly grin.

"Rooslin, outside," I said, then dragged a stool to my brother's bedside.

Halitov rolled his eyes. "I'll catch up with you." Then he yanked open the curtain and strode away.

"He's telling me not to feel sorry for myself?" Jarrett asked incredulously.

"Just ignore him."

"How did you two ever become buddies?"

"Blame it on Sergeant Pope."

"Yeah, Pope. A good man . . ."

"So, how're you feeling? They got you on a lot of meds, huh?"

"Yeah." He pushed up on his elbows.

"No, don't do that. Just rest easy."

"Scott, I want to say something. It isn't easy for me."

"Well, you did lose your legs . . ."

"No, I mean we both have epi, but you've always had to wear yours on your cheek, where everyone can see it. I was the lucky one because my genes figured out a way to hide it. I mean, I really am a gennyboy, but no one knows. I should've been like you. Then I would've understood. It would've made me stronger. And it would've made all of this easier."

"Easier? I don't think so."

He closed his eyes, took in a long, slow breath. "Thanks for coming to see me."

"You want me to go?"

"I'm tired."

"All right. I'll check back in." I rose tentatively from the stool, then glanced once more at him before leaving.

Out in the hall, I met up with his doctor, who wasn't

thrilled I had seen Jarrett. I didn't care and demanded a full report, but since Jarrett's name and DNA signature had been altered, I could not prove that he and I were brothers, and the doctor would not release confidential information to me without official orders.

In the months to come, Jarrett would explain why he wished he wore the mark of our defect. It seems the doctor had told him that nanotech regrowth would not work because of his epineuropathy. Our mutation had finally reared its ugly head in my brother's life, and he had felt lost and utterly unprepared to deal with it. He would not return to the line in a few months, like Halitov had suggested. He would be fitted with prosthetics. He would become a cyborg. And that process could take over a year to complete, after which Jarrett would have to re-qualify for combat duty. My brother was in for a long, frustrating, and painful recovery.

About a half hour later, Halitov and I got drunk in my quarters. It's what you do when you've just been stripped of your command. Jing was still listed MIA, and I had forgotten all about my meeting with Elise Rainey.

"No matter what ship we're on, you always manage to score a bottle of Tau Ceti vodka," I said, then took a long pull on my glass.

"Well, shit, we're in the Tau Ceti system. If I can't score some here, then there's none to be had." He sat cross-legged on the deck, leaning against the bulkhead, shirt off, one hand stroking the bushy gray hair sprouting from his chest. "So tell me, Mr. Scott St. Andrew. What the hell is a combat consultant?"

"Oh, we get to tell Colonel Beauregard that his planning and tactics are good. Because if we don't act supportive, then he brings in other combat consultants who are."

"We're going to be yes men. Furniture." He groaned. "Hey, you hear anything about our scans? At this point I'm looking forward to my court-martial."

"I think intell's still looking at the data. They're supposed to contact Sheffield, then she'll let us know what's going on. All we do now is sit tight."

"And drink."

And we did. For another ten minutes. Then, after a long silence, Halitov asked, "You ever get afraid?"

"You mean of dying?"

"No, I mean about Jing. And hey, back when I said you let her rot—"

"You didn't mean it, I know. Rooslin, I can tell when you really mean something. Don't worry about that. And yeah, I'm scared."

"But you don't love her yet, do you? I mean, you and Dina . . . when you looked at her, man, I could see that whatever was there was a hell of lot stronger than the Guard Corps, the war, all of it. But Jing's different. Maybe even better. She's . . . she's you, man. Like a perfect match. I thought me and Kristi could be like you guys, but deep down I knew the universe would fuck me over and take her away."

"Why do you say that?"

"Because the universe hates me."

"Maybe that's because you hate it back even more. Maybe you should try accepting what it throws at you instead of fighting all the time."

"Okay."

"So, you're going to do it? Just like that?"

"No, but I'll say okay if it'll get us talking about something else. So, do you compare Jing to Dina?"

"You make it sound like Jing and I should have this intense relationship. I'm not sure where it's going with her—if it's going anywhere."

"You need to have sex. I mean everybody thought you guys were rocking the rack anyway."

"Thank you, doctor. I finally realize that sex is definitely the determining factor in a relationship. I'll keep that in mind—if she comes back."

"I wouldn't worry about that," Halitov said, wiggling his brows. "She's standing right behind you."

I craned my head and jolted. There she was, clad in dust-covered utilities, looking as though she had just come off the battlefield. "Oh my god. How long have you—"

"Long enough," she said, then wiped her soiled cheek on her sleeve. "I guess I should've knocked, but I couldn't wait, so I cheated."

I slapped a palm on the bulkhead, stood, started toward her, tripped over one of my boots, and collapsed into her arms.

"Oh, Scott, you are so drunk," she said, pulling me back onto my feet.

"And you're so alive. Thank God."

She trembled, glanced away. "I should be dead. Like them."

"Don't say that." I took her into my arms, hugged her so tightly that I thought I'd break her ribs. "I'm sorry I had to order you away. I'm sorry."

"Me, too." She broke the embrace, brushed hair from her eyes.

It dawned on me then that she had arrived, yet my tablet had remained suspiciously silent. I crossed to the instrument, examined the status panel. No problem there. "Did you check in?" I asked her.

"I haven't had a chance."

"How did you get on board without checking in?"

She tapped her temple.

"Why did you do that?"

"It's a long story. But for now, let's just say I don't want anyone except you guys to know I'm here. Not just yet."

I stroked her cheek. "I want to hear this long story right now."

She started wearily for my latrine. "I need a shower, something to eat, then I have a few things I need to do. Look, I know it sounds all clandestine, but I'll explain everything in a few hours."

Halitov turned a wary glance on me as Jing removed her boots, unzipped her utilities, then padded into the latrine. Once she had turned on the water, he stage-whispered, "She's the traitor!"

I smiled. "Maybe you are."

"I'm serious!"

"Maybe she's helping Sheffield and Ishmar. By manipulating the bond the way she does, she can be a fly on the wall pretty much anywhere. So they're using her as a spy."

"Or maybe that's her cover. She's a traitor. But she lies to us and says she's working for them."

"Or maybe she did something back at Columbia that she doesn't want anyone to know about yet. Sound familiar?"

"We can play these guessing games all night," he said, then finished his drink. "Why don't you slip into the shower with her and find out what's going on—because if you don't, I will." He pried himself up, turned for the latrine.

I steered him toward the hatch. "Go get cleaned up.

Have a cup of coffee or something. I'll call you when we're ready to get a bite."

"I'm telling you, Scott. She's a woman of sinister beauty. Don't trust her."

"A woman of sinister beauty? Where the hell did you read that?"

"In one of my comic books, but I'm telling you, it's true."

"See you, Rooslin," I said, then pushed him into the corridor.

I went to my gelrack, sat, fell back onto the mattress. The sound of running water, the cool comfort of the rack, and the vodka's numbing bliss took me back to my childhood, to quiet nights lying in my bed at home, listening to Jarrett breathe and to my father watching holos in the living room. Soon, the water stopped running. Jing toweled off, came over to the gelrack, and crawled on top of me.

"We have a chance now," she said, leaning over me. "Let's not waste it."

Water dripped from her hair and onto my cheeks. As she reached to wipe it off, I pulled her down and gave her the kiss I should have given her when we were on *Vanguard One*'s OBS deck. I felt neither guilt nor regret. I felt that being with Jing was what Dina wanted for me. I felt a future in that kiss. And, as we began to explore each other's bodies, I couldn't help but smile.

"What?" she asked.

"Nothing."

"Are you sure?"

"I am very sure."

"That's good. I like a man with a purpose."

I could describe in gratuitous and pornographic detail how Jing and I made love—which would no doubt thrill someone like Halitov—but the cries, the dampness of our skin, and the knots we tied ourselves into as we rocked toward climax were not as important as the fact that we had finally exposed those feelings lying deep inside us. We had risked everything with each other. In fact, the moment would have been perfect, were it not for Halitov's warning echoing in my head. *Don't trust her.*

Afterward, we just lay there, staring at the overhead. I hoped she thought I was a good lover. She seemed to enjoy it, but I didn't have the courage to ask. Of course, I didn't have a lot of experience, and it occurred to me then that she had not been taken aback by my aging, nor had it hindered her desire to be with me.

"I'm having sex with the battalion commander," she finally said out of nowhere. "Whoa, I'm a bad girl."

"I'm not exactly the battalion commander anymore."

She rolled over, glanced emphatically. "What exactly are you?"

"Look at me."

"I have. And Rooslin, too. Isn't there anything they can do?"

"Yeah, they've relieved me of my command. Rooslin and I are going to be combat consultants working with Colonel Beauregard. Our days in the field are over."

"No, they can't do that. That's not right. They'll be wasting you. Have you talked to Ms. Brooks?"

"I'm having trouble reaching her."

"That's odd. *Vanguard One's* sitting a couple thousand kilometers off our port bow."

"Then they just got here."

"I think so. But never mind them. I'm thinking about the Minsalo Caves on Exeter. You said the aging reversed itself when you were there."

"It did, but the effect is temporary. What am I supposed to do? Spend the rest of my life living in a cave?"

"I think you and Rooslin have to go back. I think that if there's an answer to this problem, it's there."

"Beauregard was recalled from Exeter. The moon is still controlled by the Alliances. We wouldn't even get close."

"I can get us in there."

"I don't know. Maybe Ms. Brooks has come up with something."

"And if she hasn't? What're you going to do? Play professional victim?"

"No, I just—"

"Oh, no. Here it comes."

"I'm going to do my duty until I can't do it anymore."

She snorted, raked fingers through her hair. "And I'm going to do whatever I can to help you, whether you want the help or not. Because if you don't, then you're being selfish. There are, in fact, other people who care about you."

"I know. Let's get up." And even as I rose, my tablet sounded with an incoming message.

"I'll bet that's her," said Jing.

"And I'm gambling with you," I said, reading the screen.

Ms. Brooks requested that Halitov and I meet with her privately aboard *Vanguard One*. Unfortunately, Halitov had had way too much to drink and had passed out in his quarters. I shared with Ms. Brooks Halitov's "illness," and she said we could delay the meeting for an hour or two, but no more than that. Jing and I dragged Halitov into the shower, where he swore up a storm as the hot spray brought him back from the underworld of

Tau Cetian spirits. While Jing went off to fetch him some coffee, I made sure he got dressed.

"What? You're going to stand there and watch me?" he asked.

"This meeting is important," I said. "That is, if you actually give a shit about your future."

"Oh, I still have one of those? I could've sworn they took that away from me."

"Just get dressed."

He pulled on a pair of boots. "So did you *talk* with Jing?"

"Yeah, we *talked*."

A smile played over his lips. "Did you enjoy the . . . *conversation*?"

"None of your business, all right?"

He winked. "I knew she'd be good. Just look at the body on her. I'm sure you got all the information you need to make your determination. One piece of advice, though. Screw her, yeah. Trust her, no."

"Here's the coffee," Jing said, keying open the hatch. She read our expressions. "What's wrong?"

"Uh, I forget to tell you that I wanted tea," Halitov said as I winced over the lame explanation.

While me and Mr. Tea Drinker caught a shuttle for *Vanguard One*, Jing went off to take care of "some things." I glanced absently through a viewport at the void of space while Halitov rambled on about us walking in there and issuing Ms. Brooks a list of our demands. When he was finished, he asked if I agreed.

I glanced lazily at him. "What're you talking about?"

"You're not listening to me," he said, then shook his head vigorously. "You never do. Why do I bother?"

"Rooslin, I'm sorry. I'm just . . . tired."

"You're not tired. You're old. And we have to do something about this. That's why we have to go in there and make our demands."

I looked at him. The son of a bitch was right. And Jing had been right. I was playing professional victim because I thought it was my duty. It wasn't.

So when we walked into Ms. Brooks's office, where she was just finishing up a conversation with Colonel Beauregard, I approached quickly, saluted the colonel, then turned to her, a heartbeat away from shouting our demands. Then the honorable soldier took over, damn it. "Hello, ma'am. I just wanted to thank you for sending down that Force Recon team. They saved our lives."

"You're very welcome, Major."

"Yes, we appreciate that. But we're tired of being lied to and screwed over by you people."

Ms. Brooks looked aghast. "Major—"

"You promise everything, deliver nothing. You want us to be combat consultants? Unless you can help us get reconditioned, we might be dead in a month."

"Major—"

"I'm hoping you have answers for me, because if you don't, the captain and I are going to walk through that hatch—and we don't care if you arrest us for going AWOL."

"Major, please—"

"At least we won't be used anymore."

Her eyes grew even wider. The colonel's pipe slipped from his lips.

The honorable soldier had finally spoken his peace.

5 ▶ **Halitov looked as** dumbfounded as Ms. Brooks and the colonel. The sheen in his eyes told me that going AWOL had not occurred to him. More than that, his nervousness confused me; after all, wasn't he expecting a general court-martial? That might land him in prison just the same.

"Ma'am, you'll have to excuse him," said Halitov. "We had a rough time at Columbia."

"Don't make excuses for me," I snapped. "And you're calling our op there a 'rough time'? That's the understatement of the year."

"Calm down," ordered Colonel Beauregard, his thick shock of gray hair looking freshly buzzed, his frown lines deepening for a moment before he retrieved his pipe. "I'll have both of you thrown in the brig before you get a chance to go AWOL."

"Sorry, sir," said Halitov.

I gave my former XO an incredulous look, but then I understood: he assumed the colonel and Ms. Brooks had read his scan report and knew about what had happened at LockMar Randall. He had finally come to the realization that insubordination would not help his case. But that realization had come on so quickly that it left me standing there, alone in my fury. He had always been the hothead.

"Major . . . Scott . . ." began Ms. Brooks in a soothing voice. "You've been through a lot, we know. And we promised to help with getting you reconditioned. We're going to keep that promise."

"When?"

"And how?" asked Halitov, though his tone hardly held a challenge. "You've found another conditioning facility?"

"No, but our researchers have developed a series of treatments that should stabilize your aging until we can recover the remaining facility on Exeter."

"But the quake there caused permanent damage," I said, avoiding the fact that the quake had most certainly been created by the Wardens themselves, as part of their plan to kidnap cadets and turn them into Wardens. "Paul said that alliance scientists were trying to get the facility back online, but from what I've read, they haven't. What makes you believe you can repair it when they can't? Was our intell corrupt?"

"That information is classified," said the colonel. "But suffice it to say that we have one new piece of data that the alliances don't have. I was en route to Exeter to launch a new attack when they struck Columbia. We're going back to Exeter. Soon."

"Sir, I suggest that before you do that, you weed out the person or people who gave up our encryption codes at Columbia, otherwise—"

"Major, you cite the obvious, and you know we're working on that."

"I'll tell you who I suspect," began Halitov.

I silenced him with my eyes.

"We're doing everything we can to address that problem," said Ms. Brooks. "Though just a few moments ago we learned some disturbing news. Apparently, some conditioned individuals have developed a new talent for manipulating their long- and short-term memories. Our researchers have confirmed it."

"I thought no one could defy a scan," said Halitov, perking up over that prospect.

"In your case, Captain, you couldn't hide your thoughts," Colonel Beauregard said, aiming his pipe at Halitov. "Technically, you did not disobey orders, but you did misdirect your people. Your actions were selfish, your judgment poor. Perhaps you'll make a few trips to express your condolences to some of the families."

Halitov choked up. "Yes, sir."

"And you, Major," the colonel continued. "You practically volunteered information."

I knew I was blushing, but I couldn't help it. I suddenly remembered when I had been captured aboard the *Rhode Island*. I had been scanned back then, and I had given the enemy everything they had wanted. "Sir, do we know how these soldiers developed the skill? Were they taught it? Or did it occur naturally? And have we found any data in the Racinian ruins regarding this?"

Ms. Brooks picked up her tablet and thumbed through a few electronic pages until she found the one she wanted. "Okay, here it is. Basically, all we know is that the subjects had specific data cerebroed into their long-term memories. We then asked them to concentrate on hiding the data from our scan. Several of them were successful, yet none of them has been able to explain how they did it. They just said, and I quote, 'it's a feeling we have.'"

"What about drugs?" I asked.

"The subjects were able to defy every one we tested on them."

Halitov's face tightened in worry. "So let me get this

straight. We scan everyone, but conditioned soldiers—
we don't know who—will be able to defy the scan."

"That's right," said Ms. Brooks. "And we can't
round up and detain every conditioned soldier we have.
That would leave us vulnerable to attack."

"Then how're we supposed to catch these people?"
Halitov asked. "Do you have any leads? Anything?"

"We're working with the people from satnet and with
our own communications experts to track transmissions
and all chips tawted out prior to the attack," answered
Ms. Brooks. "We have a few other leads—and we'll follow up on those with some good old-fashioned detective
work on the part of officers working closely with conditioned soldiers. It may take time, but we'll resolve this
issue."

"Is Captain Jing working for you?" I asked.

Ms. Brooks hesitated. "We have many operatives
working for us now. I won't confirm or deny whether
the captain is working for us. What makes you suspect
she is?"

I didn't like Ms. Brooks's tone and decided not to
press the issue. "Just a hunch, given her skills."

"I see."

"Gentlemen, despite all of this bad news, something
promising has come out of the massacre at Columbia,"
said the colonel, shifting across the room. "Actually,
two things."

He had my interest. How could something promising
come out of all of that death?

"I suspect you two haven't tuned in to the news feed.
Well, fourteen nations—including the United States—
have just split from the Western Alliance in protest over
the massacre. We're presently negotiating with them."

"You mean we might be able to turn them into allies?" I asked excitedly. "Western Alliance Marines fighting side-by-side with Colonial Wardens?"

"It's a long shot," he replied. "But it could happen. We'll take on what's left of the Western Alliance and the East. We'll finally have a fighting chance."

I glanced at Halitov, who had already brightened. "Sounds good, but you have to wonder if battlefield commanders are going to trust each other—especially now with all of these counterintelligence ops going on."

"We're hoping that the idea of us joining forces will pose enough of a threat to make the enemy stand down and accept our independence," the colonel said. "Whether we'll actually have to run a joint op remains to be seen."

"Even more promising is the fact that we're going to get a majority vote in congress to allow the Wardens to take over the Seventeen System Guard Corps," said Ms. Brooks. "Given the massacre, opposing senators can no longer let alliance bribes dictate their votes. A vote against a restructuring would, in this climate, be political suicide." Her gaze focused on me. "So, Scott, all those worries you had about us planning a coup were for nothing. This is going to happen. And it's going to happen legally."

"Excuse me, but if I'm understanding this correctly, we lost Columbia Colony and those millions of people, but we gained a real chance to win the war," Halitov pointed out. "Which makes me think that our traitor and maybe his buddies anticipated this outcome. He's working for the colonies, but he's willing to sacrifice millions to win the war." Make no mistake. Halitov's gaze burned on Colonel Beauregard.

"Yes, we're already entertaining that possibility," Ms. Brooks said quickly. "And if it makes you feel any better, both the colonel and I have already submitted to scans, the results of which are available to you via the daily jump board."

Colonel Beauregard grinned mildly. "I'm not insulted that you believe I could be a traitor, Captain. These days, I endorse that kind of scrutiny. In fact, when I ordered the crew aboard *Vanguard One* to submit to scans, I insisted that Paul be the first one on line—just to show the crew that I didn't trust anyone, even my own son."

"How's he doing, sir?" I asked.

"After your conditioning treatments, you can ask him yourself."

"Those treatments are going to happen right away?" I asked.

"Deck one-twenty-five, hatch nineteen," the colonel said.

"Sir, if the treatments are successful, will we be reassigned to combat duty?" I asked.

"If that's what you want. But son, haven't you seen your share of blood?"

"Yes, sir. But I'd like to make sure that no one else does. That's why I need to be out there."

"I understand."

"We'll be setting up quarters for you two here," said Ms. Brooks. "You know the transfer drill."

Hatch nineteen slid open, and Halitov and I stepped warily into a chillingly familiar room, though it was much smaller and less elaborate than the chamber it had been designed to imitate. A half dozen black tubes about three meters tall and with diameters of just over a meter stood in a row along one dimly lit bulkhead. Two of the tubes had been peeled back, their skins flapping like metallic rinds. Inside hung scores of gossamer leads that I assumed would be attached to my body. Nearby lay a control panel of sorts, with data scrolling across a bank of touch screens.

"It's just like the conditioning facility on Exeter," Halitov said. "They've re-created our torture chamber in splendid detail."

"Gentlemen," came a husky sounding voice from behind one tube. "These MRSDs are completely safe." The man behind the voice appeared and strode excitedly toward us, his olive drab lab coat whipping behind him, his gray whiskers standing on end as he smiled broadly. "I'm Dr. Jim Vesbesky." He shook our hands as though we were celebrities. "I've been working on your problem ever since Ms. Brooks brought it to my attention." He suddenly chuckled over some private irony. "We've finally made some progress."

"MRSDs?" Halitov asked.

"Mnemosyne Reversion Stabilization Devices," he said, pronouncing the mouthful with utter precision. He had probably created the name. "My assistants will be here momentarily to prepare you for insertion."

"I'm not sure I'm in the mood for insertion today, Doctor," said Halitov.

"Relax. You'll find the experience quite painless. And I must say it's a real honor to finally meet you. I've been waiting for this moment for months."

"Sir, we appreciate all the work you've obviously done," I said, though I had trouble purging the skepticism from my tone. "You really think you can help us?"

"Absolutely. We've studied the effects of premature extraction and pinpointed one cause of the defect lying within the DNA of the mnemosyne themselves." Believing his technobabble was lost on me, he smiled and added, "It seems those little parasites in your brain were not given the proper time to assimilate and subsequently, they developed a mutation. We've developed a multistage treatment that's already proven effective in test subjects."

"Test subjects. You mean other soldiers?" Halitov asked.

Our mad scientist winced. "Not exactly."

"Has this treatment been tested on a human being?" I asked.

"As far as we know, all of the other soldiers whose conditioning was compromised have either been killed or reconditioned. You gentlemen are the last two. That's why this moment is so exciting," he said, shaking his fists.

Halitov swore under his breath. "You know, Doc, I've been slapped, punched, kicked, stabbed, blown up, and shot at. Sounds like shit, I know. Still, every time I walk onto a battlefield, I know what I'm getting into." He pointed at one open chamber. "But I'm not getting in there."

"No one's ordering you," Vesbesky said. "But look at yourself, Captain. Are you even twenty-one yet?"

For a moment, Halitov recoiled self-consciously, then spat, "Doc, I didn't sign on to become a lab rat." He raised his brows. "It's the cheese I can't stand . . ."

"Doctor, is there any chance that we could be harmed, or something could go wrong with this?" I asked. "I mean, how dangerous is it? Exactly?"

Vesbesky hissed with impatience. "I'm doing this as a personal favor to Ms. Brooks. Do you really think I'd want to endanger the lives of two very valuable Colonial Wardens?"

I tensed, hardening my tone. "What are the risks?"

"All right, there's a remote—and I mean *remote*—chance that your brain patterns could become unstable, but we've already developed an emergency response to that. Believe me, you have more to worry about if you're not treated. In this case, the cure won't kill you."

That hatch opened, and in stepped two middle-aged women wearing lab coats and beaming at us with that same silly expression Vesbesky had worn. The brunette, in particular, was quite attractive.

"Ladies," called the doctor. "Major St. Andrew and Captain Halitov have been waiting. Let's get them prepped."

"Whoa, I still haven't agreed to any of this," said Halitov, pulling his wrist from the brunette's grip.

"I don't like this either," I told my former XO. "But I don't like growing old. I don't like it at all."

I left him standing there as the other assistant led me toward an open hatch and a small office beyond. She instructed me to strip down to my boxers, and as I did so, Halitov joined me and furiously undressed.

"I think we're making a big mistake here," he said. "I'm blaming this all on you."

"You always do."

"No, this time I really am," he said, eyeballing me like a gunnery sergeant.

"Hey, that brunette was pretty cute," I said.

"Cute? She's old enough to be my mother."

"Not anymore she's not," I said, wriggling my brows. "You're Mister Mid-life Crisis."

He looked at me. "I get the point. Let's go sniffing for cheese." He trudged off, back toward the tubes.

Within five minutes, tiny, mechanical talons within the tubes had attached over one hundred translucent tubes to our bodies. We didn't feel a thing, since a warm feeling had come up through our feet and had passed through our bodies, numbing us entirely. I wasn't sure how the device had managed that, but I sure as hell was thankful as I stared with a weird fascination and a sense of déjà vu at my body, now an ugly, fleshy vegetable sprouting roots. The C-shaped cerebro extended on a boom from the back of the tube and cupped our heads as the doctor told us to stand by.

"Scott?" Halitov called from his chamber.

"Yeah?"

"They're going to lock us in here, aren't they."

"It'll happen fast. You'll lose consciousness. You won't know it. Just close your eyes."

"It's not helping."

"Then why don't you tell me about, I don't know, what you miss most about home?"

"Nothing. I don't miss a damned thing."

"Are you kidding me?"

"I don't miss a place. I miss a person," he said, his voice cracking.

"Kristi . . ." I replied softly.

"Yeah, and can I tell you something, now that we're about to die—again?"

"We're not going to die, you idiot," I said, dismissing his melodrama.

"I was in love with Dina, too."

I tried to lean out from my tube so I could look at him, but I could barely feel my lips, let alone my legs. "What did you say?"

His reply came slurred and unintelligible. I couldn't work my mouth anymore, either, so I just hung there, contemplating what he had just said. Why had he bothered to share that with me? Was he feeling guilty? I wasn't sure, but as I thought back to our days at the academy, I couldn't remember anything he had said or done that would've betrayed his feelings. I couldn't blame him, though—Dina had been an amazing woman. But she was gone forever. It was time to concentrate on the living, and in my case, on Jing, whose secrets troubled me and tainted the vivid memory of our lovemaking. Somewhere during all of that numbness and hard thought, I lost consciousness.

When the tubes finally whispered open, I shuddered violently and snapped open eyes, anticipating some change in me, perhaps a more youthful appearance and renewed vigor.

Something had changed, all right. But it had nothing to do with me. Dr. Vesbesky and his two assistants lay on the chamber floor. I couldn't tell if they were dead or unconscious, but I saw no blood. Perhaps they had been drugged or their necks broken. Panicking, my gaze flicked to the gossamers still attached to my chest, neck, and limbs. Though sensation was beginning to return, I still couldn't move.

"Rooslin?"

He moaned a reply.

"Wake up, man," I sang ominously.

A flash came from near the control panel, where a figure concealed by the dark phosphorus green of a combat skin stood, working a finger over one touch screen. Judging from the height and build, I assumed he was male.

"Hey!" I shouted, but the figure ignored me, intent on doing something to the machine.

"Who are you?" Halitov cried.

The tube emitted a low hum, and the gossamers tugged at my skin. I could either stand there and perhaps wind up like the doctor and his assistants or make a move, a move I knew depended upon my accessing the bond. I reached into it, and lo and behold, I sensed the energy binding the particles of my body to the gossamers. Concentrating so hard that it hurt, I willed myself away from them, to a point across the room, near the main hatch, where I hoped I could cut off our amateur scientist and potential saboteur.

Before I could bat an eyelash, I stood at the hatch, tingling from the pinpricks where the gossamers had been attached, the deck tipping forty-five degrees as I paid for my magic.

The figure whirled, leveling a pistol on me.

A still middle-aged looking Halitov materialized beside the guy and drove a hand through the guy's skin to latch onto his wrist.

A round exploded from the pistol's muzzle before Halitov could misdirect the fire. That wasn't a particle round but a hiza dart equipped with a drug-filled syringe and onboard computer to control the dose.

I dropped to my stomach, ears ringing, wondering if I'd been hit. I looked up—

Halitov swore and grappled with the figure, his hand still latched on the guy's wrist—even as the assailant booted him in the head and another dart burst from the weapon.

The bulkheads had been designed to capture and dissolve particle, conventional, and even dart fire, and that second hiza round vanished into the overhead as I hauled myself up and felt something wet on my collarbone. My fingers came up bloody. Without time to contemplate the wound, I launched myself into a *dirc*, answering our attacker's dart by turning myself into one. I reached out and grabbed the guy's neck as my momentum wrenched him away from Halitov. We hit the deck, and I lost my grip on the figure as I rolled and turned.

What I didn't realize was that the guy's second dart—the one that had struck the overhead—had tripped alarms and had alerted shipboard security. Those officers were en route and would arrive within a minute. The figure knew, though, because instead of turning the pistol on me he bolted for the hatch and dematerialized before it even opened.

Halitov charged to the hatch panel, keyed open the door, then burst into the corridor as I came up hard at his heels. Far ahead, a couple of midshipmen stared aghast at us, both in our boxers, me bleeding, Halitov screaming for them to make way. Beyond them, our phosphorescent phantom appeared, clutched the wall a moment, dazed, then looked back, spotted us, and took off.

"Stay here! I'll get him," barked Halitov, his gaze locked on my bloody neck for a split second before he reached into the bond and sped off as though surfing a bolt of lightning.

Bullshit, I thought and caught the next bolt, racing madly through the corridor, whipping around the corner, and carrying myself deeper into the ship's bowels. The importance of what we were doing began to take hold. There was a saboteur—maybe even *the* traitor—aboard *Vanguard One*. If this person was operating freely aboard Colonel Beauregard's own vessel, then much more than fleet defenses over a single colony were at stake. This mole could conceivably provide information to the Alliances regarding all major campaigns taking place throughout the entire seventeen systems. The enemy would learn of our troop numbers, ordnance, location, and even our battle plans. This was an inconceivable breach of security. How had the Alliances managed to penetrate our ranks? Had they brainwiped and reconditioned one of our own? I had assumed that something that complicated, that risky, would never work—but apparently it had.

I'm not sure how many officers and crew members Halitov and I veered around, bumped into, shoved, or completely knocked over, but the number rose well into the double digits. Throngs of angry personnel gathered in our wake and began chasing us, even as security team members threaded through them. My friend and I turned deck one-twenty-five into a ward for the exceedingly pissed off, and when I finally caught up with Halitov and we took a moment to catch our breaths, we realized that our attacker was long gone and our new "friends" there on that deck were heated enough to finish our executions. Halitov nearly got into a fistfight with two young second lieutenants that he had shoved against one bulkhead, but the security people arrived.

We returned to Vesbesky's chamber, where military police were already combing over the scene. Vesbesky and his assistants had been stunned into unconsciousness with hiza darts but were still alive. Apparently, our attacker had done nothing to sabotage the controls or our treatment, but had been merely taking us out of stasis.

Back in the sickbay, the doctors shook their heads at the synthskin on my shoulder used to repair the wound I'd received at LockMar Randall, then started work on my neck. "Can you wait until one wound fully heals before you collect another?" one doc asked me.

I grinned at the amiable black man. "Funny thing is, I was just removed from combat duty and given a consultant's job."

"Maybe you ought to go back to the battlefield, where it's safer," he said with a wink.

As the doctor continued his work, Halitov sat nearby, sipping on a cup of tea. He really did like tea. With lemon.

"So if this guy wasn't trying to kill us, then what do you think?" I asked. "Was he trying to kidnap us or what?"

"Maybe. I'm not sure what the Alliances hope to gain by capturing two broken down warhorses. It's not as though we're carrying around that much classified data. Other than being conditioned—and even that doesn't work—we're really not worth much . . ."

"That's where you're wrong, Captain," said Dr. Vesbesky, lying on a stretcher across from mine and recovering from the stun attack he had received. "I said you were the last two that we know of whose conditioning suffered an anomaly. However, we're not certain how many soldiers the Alliances have who are suffering from the same accelerated aging that you are."

"Their conditioned soldiers should be fine," Halitov said. "The conditioning accident happened on Exeter, and it only happened to us cadets, not Alliance people."

"Remember Captain, the Alliances have been trying to get that facility back online for months now. They've been experimenting with it, sending troops in, trying to get them conditioned. I've been told that those troops are now suffering from the same ill effects that you are."

"But you've discovered a treatment," I said. "And if they can't get their hands on data regarding the treatment, then why not grab a few patients and reverse engineer it from there?"

Vesbesky nodded. "The person who stunned me was

trying to get to you—because when it comes to security, I defy even God to get inside my database."

Our personal mad scientist thought he could take on God, but first he had to deal with alien parasites. And the real irony, the irony that left Halitov chuckling like a madman and me stoop-shouldered, came later, after Vesbesky ran diagnostics on us to check for mnemosyne stabilization.

The treatment had done nothing. Absolutely nothing.

6 ⟩ **Ms. Brooks insisted** that we keep the treatment's failure to ourselves. She even suggested that Halitov and I get haircuts, use skin-softening cosmetics, and even darken our hair a little to convey to anyone watching that we were, in fact, being helped by Vesbesky. Neither Halitov nor I would submit to cosmetic surgery, though the option had been discussed. While our faith in Vesbesky had waned considerably, we would give him another chance before making irreversible changes to our bodies. The good doctor, working in a fever pitch, swore he would have the problem solved as soon as possible and urged Colonel Beauregard to keep us close by for another treatment.

I welcomed some R&R and much-needed time to recuperate. That shot had only glanced off my neck and had missed my jugular, but between that wound and the dull ache in my shoulder, I could barely turn without flinching. I returned to my quarters, ordered the supplies I needed, then called over to the *Roger Harrington* in search of Jing. According to the flight boss's log, she had left the ship and had been ordered aboard *Vanguard One* shortly after we had departed. Interesting timing there. Could she have been our attacker? Combat skins could be manipulated to alter one's outline, though you would probably need an engineer to help you do that. No, the figure couldn't be Jing. Why would she turn coat? What did she possibly have to gain? And didn't she have feelings for me? Then again, if she wasn't a traitor, why hadn't she come to visit me? Was she too busy working for Ms. Brooks? I wanted to locate her and demand answers, but the more I thought about it, the more I resigned to the situation. She would come to me when she was ready. She knew where to find me, and you couldn't miss the two MPs standing guard outside my hatch. I lay on my gelrack and switched on the news feed. The menu lit on the bulkhead screen, and I scrolled through the listing until a familiar name struck me cold: Ms. Elise Rainey. Damn it. I had stood her up, and I didn't even have her satnet address. I felt terrible and wondered whether she'd try to contact my father. All I could do was shake my head, sigh, and at least watch her story about Columbia. I was about to ask for it when my tablet beeped and Halitov's mug polluted the screen. "What're you doing?" he asked.

"Just getting ready to watch our friend the war correspondent. She posted her report on Columbia."

"Weren't you supposed to approve that report?"

"Yeah, but she posted it anyway. She's pissed off at me. Let's hope there's nothing classified there."

"Hey, I scored us another bottle of vodka. I'll be there in a minute."

"Rooslin, I just want to lay here and watch this and maybe get a little sleep, all right?"

"Too late," he said. "Me and my personal guard are already on our way." He broke the link. Bastard.

The hatchcomm beeped. That couldn't be him already. "Yes?"

"Sir," began one of the MPs. "Captain Paul Beauregard here to see you, sir?"

I tensed. Beauregard? The colonel's son had actually

fit me into his busy calendar? I pulled myself from the gelrack, checked the video, swore over how young he looked, then opened the hatch.

"Hey, Scott." He wore a wounded expression, and his voice barely rose above a whisper. He offered his hand—

And I just looked at it. "I'll let you in, but I will tell you what a fucking asshole you are."

"Whoa. Nice to see you again, too." He steered his swimmer's frame into my quarters. He carried a small, potted tree under one arm, its pods flat, its flowers pink and vibrant.

"What do you want?"

He cocked a brow, and once more I cursed his youth as he placed the tree near my desk. There was something about him, I wasn't sure what. His self-assurance was gone. He was distracted, even a little choked-up. "I just came to say hi. I mean, we thought we lost you at Columbia."

"You actually give a shit?"

"C'mon, Paul. You know I do. How'd you get out of there?"

"Just got lucky. That's all."

"We make our own luck."

My lip twisted. "Yeah, you're good at that."

He shrugged off the barb. "So what's it been, nearly a month now? The last time was at the service for Breckinridge."

"Yeah. I miss her. I know Jing does."

"How is Jing?"

"I don't know. You tell me."

His frown looked sincere, but he was a good actor. "What? How would I know?"

"Is she working for your father?"

"We all are."

I took a few steps toward him. "You know what I mean."

"Look, if she's running a special op, I couldn't tell you—even if I knew."

I shook my head in disgust, then lifted my chin at the tree. "What're you doing with that?"

"I'm giving it to you. They call it a redbud. Comes all the way from Earth. I thought you could use a little greenery in your life. You know how surrounding yourself with living things makes you—"

"Yeah, I do. Especially when you're fast forwarding through your life." I whirled from him, plopped on the gelrack. "What's wrong with you? You come here with a *tree*?"

"Hey, man, if you don't like it—"

"Fuck it."

Yes, I had shocked him. And, after a moment's contemplation, he finally said, "Look, I didn't mean to go to Exeter alone. It just worked out that way."

"We deserved to go. And what did you do? You went. Without even telling us. Left us hanging. Thanks, *friend*."

"Scott, you know there wasn't time."

"Don't lie to me, Paul. Just don't." He had no idea how important those words were—especially after what Halitov had done.

"I'm not lying. You guys had already been reassigned. I figured you'd be too busy catching up with your brother to worry about recovering Dina's body. Besides, we got recalled anyway. As far as I know, Dina's still hanging in that cave."

"Your father said we're going back."

"Yes, we are. And he's letting us take a small team into the caves to recover Dina's body. You, Halitov, and Jing are all coming."

"Oh, so now we get our chance? Guilt got the best of you?"

He looked away, wouldn't answer.

I sighed. "So how'd you convince your father to let us go? Halitov and I are supposed to be advising from the rear."

He began to answer, but the hatchcomm cut him off. I let the devil and his bottle of vodka inside. "Beauregard," Halitov said with a curt nod, then cast a curious glance at me.

"You mad, too?" Paul asked Halitov.

"Let's see, uh, you fucking shipped off without us . . ." He squinted hard in mock thought. "Yeah!"

"It wasn't my fault. And you guys are blowing this way out of proportion."

"Okay, I believe you," Halitov snapped. "As long as that'll get us drinking." He faced me. "Let's check out Ms. Rainey there. Maybe we'll catch another glimpse of her ass. Bitch, yeah. But she's got a decent ass." Halitov went to one of my lockers set into the bulkhead and retrieved glasses.

"You staying?" I asked Paul in a tone that said I'd rather he not.

But he didn't back down. "Yeah, I am." He tipped his head toward Halitov. "I could use a drink now." The colonel's son took a seat at my desk. "What're we watching?"

I frowned and told the computer to play Rainey's story. After the familiar animation sequence hawking her company, one of the *Roger Harrington*'s busy dock-

ing bays appeared. Rainey stepped into camera view
and began speaking, but her words were lost on me.
Just seeing her brought it all back. We were walking together on that tarmac, death in front of us, at our sides,
at our backs. Images of the attack played on the screen,
accompanied by her solemn narration. No doubt she
had been profoundly affected by what she had seen, and
suddenly, there Halitov and I were, standing inside the
tower and being interviewed by her prior to the attack.

"Major, what can you tell us about your operation
here thus far?" she asked.

"We've secured this facility, and we are prepared to
defend it against anything the Alliances throw at us.
The work being accomplished here is a testament to the
bravery and unselfish spirit of those fortunate enough to
wear the uniform of the Colonial Wardens."

I winced over my prepared answer. It sounded even
more jingoistic than I had originally thought.

"Scott, you look fat, man," Halitov said, then gulped
down the rest of his vodka.

"You look fatter," Paul said, nursing his own drink.
"I won't mention that gray hair."

"Good," said Halitov through a belch.

After we answered a few more questions, the report
switched to Rainey standing back in the bay. "The loss
of life at Columbia Colony is incomprehensible," she
said. "This date will be etched forever in the hearts and
minds of all colonial citizens."

"Oh, man, look at that! We can't even see her ass,"
groaned Halitov.

Suddenly, Paul shushed him angrily.

"What?" he asked.

"I'm just trying to watch." He turned to me. "Hey,

Scott. You hear the numbers but they don't register, you know? I didn't realize it was that bad down there. I really didn't."

Beauregard's voice had cracked, and I suspected that his emotions were honest and barely touched by the vodka. He had let his guard down, and for once I appreciated that, though I couldn't explain it. The report continued, and we watched Wardens load dozens of body bags into ATCs, watched civilians walking aimlessly down pockmarked streets lined by fires, watched a filthy, barefoot man running toward two soldiers with a limp child in his arms. I had seen images of war captured throughout history, and whether they were black-and-white or grainy color or holographic, they were all equally horrifying. We had become more efficient killers and experts at capturing every detail of war. Yet the threat of our own annihilation and the visceral nature of combat thrust directly into our own brains via the cerebro still hadn't put an end to the killing. Maybe we would never stop gathering, never stop hunting. And sitting there, watching it all, made me feel ashamed to be a human. Admittedly, my depression had been fueled by Vesbesky's failure, by Jing's covert activities, and by the mention of Dina's death, but now reminders of the massacre opened a gaping hole in my heart, releasing too many hopes and dreams into the void.

"Well, that made me feel . . ." Halitov trailed off, his tone indicating that he was about to make a bad joke. He lowered his voice. "That made me feel like another drink."

"You're buying, we're drinking," said Paul, thrusting out his empty glass.

I hadn't even touched my vodka, and as I glanced at

Paul, curious over his behavior, jealous over his youth, I remembered what he had told me about leaving the service. "So Paul, I assume you've notified your father that you don't want to be an officer and are ready to resign from the Wardens."

He looked away. I hadn't just struck a nerve; I had ripped it from his body and had stomped on it. "No."

"Why not?"

"Because I can't now. It's too late. And there are other people to think about."

"Fuckin' patriot over here," said Halitov. "Thought he was the rebel."

Paul glanced hard at me. "Why do you bring this up? Because you care? I doubt that."

"Back at South Point, you were the perfect cadet. We all hated you—and wanted to be you."

"So?"

"So I guess it's not easy to find out your hero no longer has his heart in it."

"Believe me, my heart is in this. And I was never your hero. I was your competition. Get it straight."

"But you guys had nothing on me," said Halitov, waving his glass drunkenly. "I loved Dina. I should've had her. Not you guys. She wasted herself on you."

I had been meaning to talk to him about his recent confession, but certainly not in front of Paul, who may very well have loved Dina more than us.

"You loved Dina?" Paul asked incredulously. "Nah. You just wanted her. Now Kristi, on the other hand, maybe you loved her. Which tells me we all have the same shitty luck with women."

I lifted a brow at Paul. "So there's one kind of luck you can't make."

"Doesn't mean you shouldn't try."

I gazed into my glass, my temper subsiding as I thought of Jing. "Yeah."

Halitov slapped a hip. "Well, I hate to be rude, but you two bore the shit out of me, so I'm leaving you the bottle, dismissing myself, and heading down to the officers' club." He stood, staggered over to the hatch, somehow keyed it open, then eyed my plant. "What's with that?"

"See you, Rooslin," I said, urging him out.

He wandered into the hall, where his MP had stood waiting. He draped an arm over the man. "Come on, Frankie. You and me are going to find some young midshipmen and blow the airlocks off this boat."

Once the hatch closed, Paul said, "I overheard my father talking about him. Something about securing an escape route at LockMar. What happened?"

I paused, realized that I could be as tight-lipped as he was. "Just a little miscommunication."

"My father's talking about having him contact some families to apologize."

I just sat there, absently studying my drink.

"Well, I'll let you get some rest." Paul started for the hatch. "And Scott? I just want you to know that . . ."

I didn't look up. "What?"

"That Dina made the right decision when she picked you. You've always been the real soldier. Not me."

"Hey, wait."

"What?"

"Something wrong?"

He looked more uncomfortable than he should. "I'm okay."

The hatch hissed shut after him. I glanced over at that ridiculous tree. Had the war finally chipped into his sanity? Or was he just becoming an eccentric like his father? I set down my glass, shut the lights, and stopped worrying about him, about the war, about everything except my sleep.

About four hours later, the hatchcomm tore me from a deep slumber. I wanted to strangle the idiot who had decided to wake me, but it was my own damned fault. I should've told the guards that I didn't want visitors.

"Captain Katya Jing, sir?" the young MP said.

I fumbled with the keypad and could barely wait for the hatch to open. Jing dragged herself inside, looking pale and covering a deep yawn. "Scott, I'm sorry."

"What's going on?" I asked softly, even sympathetically.

She raked fingers through her unkempt hair, then rubbed her eyes. "Too much. Just . . . too much."

"Come on," I said, leading her to my gelrack.

"You're not going to argue?" she asked. "You're not going to make me tell you where I've been and what I've been doing?"

"Later. I am so tired."

"Me, too." She quickly undressed and slid in beside me. I held her until both of us drifted off.

Vanguard One's skipper, the young Captain Lindemann, cleared his voice, then spoke evenly over the shipwide comm: "Ladies and gentlemen, this is the captain. In one hour, twenty minutes we'll be tawting out to the 70 Virginis B star system, where we'll serve as a command and control vessel for the Third Fleet. Their mission is to destroy all enemy ships orbiting the moon Exeter as well as deploy ground forces to recover South Point Academy and the nearby Racinian ruins. Make no mistake. We're entering a highly volatile zone, and I expect the very best from each and every one of you. Your department heads will brief you regarding the revised CDRs. That is all."

"Who's your department head?" I asked Jing with a feigned look of innocence.

She worked her head deeper into my shoulder as we just lay there, still blinking off our eight hours of blissful sleep. "You are."

"You're not working for the colonel and Ms. Brooks?"

"What makes you say that?"

"I figured you were helping them resolve this security breach."

"Maybe I am, but I can't tell you who I'm working for. It's just too dangerous. You could be scanned, and that would ruin everything."

"Do you know how to fool a scan?" I asked, and I guess my tone was a little too probing.

She jerked away. "I'm lying here with you, and you think I'm a traitor?"

"I never said that."

"Someone set us up at Columbia. You think it was me? You think I sold out my entire company? Do you know how many of them I watched die? God, I thought you were the only one who really understood me."

"I'm sorry. I want to trust you. But you're not helping me here."

She squeezed my wrist. Hard. "I told you. I can't."

"Then what do you expect from me?"

"A little faith."

"If you can't be honest—"

"This isn't about honesty," she said, whirling up to face me. "It's about safety. Yours and mine. Okay? Just deal with it, because it won't change."

I huffed, threw my head back on the pillow. "All right. I'm going to trust you."

"Don't say it like a warning."

"I don't know what to say anymore."

"Scott, I'll tell you everything—when I can." She dropped her head back onto my chest, but I rose abruptly and headed to the latrine. "Scott?"

"I want to see my brother before we leave."

"Can I come?"

"I'll meet you back here."

She smirked and pulled the blanket tightly to her neck.

By no small coincidence, Jarrett was being shipped back to Kennedy-Centauri, to a military hospital in Plymouth Colony, not far from where our father was living.

"How do you know dad's there?" I asked, standing near his bed and dressed in my black combat utilities.

"Remember that news reporter who was running around LockMar, interviewing everyone? Think her name was Rainey? Dad said she contacted him."

I grinned over Ms. Elise Rainey's timeliness and efficiency, although I should remember that she routinely worked under tight deadlines. Still, she must have arrived on planet and had gone straight to work finding my father.

"Did Dad say why he hasn't answered my messages?"

"No, but he did say he's been having problems with the tablet. You know how he is. Probably stepped on it or something. So anyway, maybe your messages got lost. Bottom line is that he's okay. He said he likes the place, and he can't wait to see me."

"That's great."

"No, it's not." His expression grew long. "They're

sending me there as a favor, but now I don't want to go. I don't want him to see me like this."

"C'mon, Jarrett. It's Dad. He can handle it."

"No, he'll cry. And he'll make me cry."

"So what? Think about this—you and me, we could've spent our entire lives rotting away in those mines back home. We would've been there until the numox got us. All right, so we've been messed up pretty badly, but the things we've seen and done . . . the people we've met . . . the people we've helped . . . we never would've had that chance if we had stayed home. And now that you're going back, even though it's not exactly home, you can reflect on this. You've done something extraordinary. And it means something. There are a lot of people who appreciate it—more than you know."

His voice quavered. "Yeah, I guess. And on the bright side, the family jewels are safe and sound."

"And I bet your girlfriend's happy about that."

"She didn't make it."

"I should've asked. I'm sorry."

"It's all right. I fall in love with them, and usually they die. I'm oh for three so far. Maybe I'll meet some nurse or something."

"Yeah, maybe."

"Hey, you know who came by to see me?"

I shook my head.

"Paul Beauregard. That was pretty surprising. I didn't think he cared enough to come."

"What did he have to say?"

"Not much. Apparently the Wardens are issuing me a new crimson star for being wounded in combat. Big deal. Otherwise, he just asked about where I was being shipped and when I was leaving. Then he wished me luck."

"When was this?"

"A couple hours after you came the first time. He said he wanted to talk to you. Did he find you?"

"Yeah, he did. Asshole."

"I don't know. He doesn't seem as in love with himself as usual. I think he finally realizes that he isn't any better than us and a round will kill him just the same."

"Maybe. Anyway, we're tawting out real soon. I have to head off."

We said our good-byes, then I gave him a final hug, doing my best not to choke up. I told him I'd send messages regularly if I could, and he said he'd do the same. We kept our promises, but nearly a year would pass before we would meet in person again.

When I returned to *Vanguard One*, my tablet beeped, and the message was from Mr. Paul Beauregard himself, who said that he, Rooslin, and Jing were waiting for me aboard a G21 in bay 9B. I was already on the bay level, so I wove my way through the crowded corridor, toward them. *Vanguard One* was on Jump Seven, meaning we needed to be battle ready before the tawt and prepared to initiate a rapid-fire deployment of forces the nanosecond we made orbit. Any delay could cost all of us our lives, which was why every tech, pilot, ground troop, and gunner wore the same look of utter intensity, a look and a feeling I found very contagious. I was nearly running by the time I reached our G21, where the troop carrier's flight crew of two was still doing their walk around inspection.

"We'll be checked out in just a minute, sir," said the ship's pilot, a young lieutenant who fired off a crisp salute and shifted with a painfully familiar confidence.

I returned the salute. "When's T-time?"

He consulted his tac. "Eight minutes, sir."

"Very good." I crossed to the aft-loading ramp and mounted the platform.

Inside the hold, Halitov, Jing, and Paul had already climbed into their jumpseats and were hugging the safety bars. Our QQ90 particle rifles stood tall in their deck mounts before the seats. Jing flashed me a strained look as I settled down beside her and lowered the bars over my head. "How's your brother doing?" she asked.

"Better."

"That's good."

I nodded curtly, then glanced to Paul. "Are we it? I figured a small fire team at least."

"Change of plans," he said. "Which I have to say I don't mind. Spec ops rule number one: The larger the force, the greater the chances that we'll be detected."

"You know, I haven't told you how happy I am about returning to Exeter," said Halitov. "I have such fond memories of that piece of shit rock. I almost flunked out of the academy there, got screwed-up alien conditioning, nearly got my ass shot off like what, twenty, thirty times? Last time, if I recall, I took one in the leg, one in the shoulder, and got my forehead slashed up." He ran a finger across the head wound. "And I don't care what they say, synthskin or not, I can tell the difference."

"My memories aren't exactly pleasant either," said Paul. "But it's vital that we recover that facility. And it's vital to me that we recover Dina's body. It's something I have to do. And I appreciate you helping me."

"When did you become a politician?" Halitov said, scrutinizing Paul.

The colonel's son closed his eyes. "You have no idea how hard this is for me."

"Yeah, well you got me along, so it'll all work out," Halitov said, squirming in his jumpseat.

I chanced a quick look at Jing and mouthed, "I'm sorry."

She nodded, but the apology didn't loosen her frown. I was sorry that I had hurt her feelings but not sorry that I had asked her for the truth.

The tawt warning echoed through the bay, and the pilots hustled onboard and fired up their systems. When the tawt finally came on, it clutched my gut and squeezed until I thought I'd pass out. I writhed a moment, blinked, and saw the massive bay doors parting swiftly to unveil a deep, star-dusted field fenced off to port and starboard by hundreds of brilliant blue streaks: our own atmoattack jets spearheading the invasion force.

"Dust Devil Six, ATC five-niner-five in the slot with systems nom, over?" said the pilot to the bay's flight boss.

"Clear on mark," said the boss. "Keep your vector."

"Clear on mark," repeated the pilot as the ATC turbines growled even louder. "Good vector."

"On the count," said the boss. "In four, three, two—"

The turbines wailed at full power as the G-force shoved me hard into Jing, who jerked herself under the pressure. We blew free of *Vanguard One*, the ship shrinking before you could steal a glimpse of her outline. We rocketed along with those blue streaks, became one, and then, through the porthole opposite me, the streaks focused into fighters with cannons jutting menacingly from their wings and bellies. Our pilot banked hard to starboard, slid, then came around, bringing the mottled brown moon of Exeter into view. Behind the little rock hung the great Jovian-like gas giant 70 Virginis b, a protective mother of swirling gas and dust.

Halitov leaned over, glanced through the canopy, and scowled. "Fuckin' place," he muttered.

"All right," said the pilot. "Looks like the Alliance fleet is exactly where we thought they'd be. Diversionary force is kicking on. We'll be riding the planetfall slot in about a minute. I'd skin up, though. We'll take some stray fire on the way down."

I had just finished activating my tac when a particle missile struck us head on, the ship's own skin straining to absorb the energy. Scintillating veins wormed across the canopy, flashed, dissolved, then reappeared as a thunderclap or something similar rang through the hold. I flashed back to the drop I had made on my homeworld of Gatewood-Callista. Our ATC had been shot out of the sky, and I had stared through the shattered canopy as the surface had come up hard.

All of which reminded me that—given my malfunctioning conditioning—I was getting too old for this shit. And so was Halitov, though I suspected he had taken Ms. Brooks's advice regarding our appearance. His hair looked suspiciously darker, and I made a note to ask him about it later.

Cannon fire boomed and reverberated once more as it drummed along our starboard side, and the pilot suddenly dove, the moon scrolling across the canopy with dizzying speed.

"All right, we're in the upper atmosphere," he reported.

"Which means jack," Halitov told us. "We ain't safe till we're on the ground."

Withering salvos came in triplets and took out the

four fighters at our two o'clock, proving his point. The fire grew brighter against Exeter's hundred shades of brown. The canyons, mesas, cliff walls, and great basins materialized rapidly. We were hauling extreme ass, and I was about to question the pilot's decision to take us in so quickly when we rolled to port, cutting through a gauntlet of surface-to-air particle fire that woke a hard shudder in my neck. I glanced at Jing, wanting to ask if she thought we should will ourselves the hell out of there, but my head snapped back as the pilot throttled up and wove sharply away from a missile on our tail. While I couldn't see the projectile, the tactical display flashed red, and that was a color you didn't want to see, ever. Then, without warning, the missile prematurely detonated.

"You see that?" cried the co-pilot.

"I saw it, and I like it," said the pilot. "And look at that. STAs thinning out. We'll make planetfall."

"What happened?" Jing asked.

"They've broken off their attack on our wing," Paul said. "We're overrunning their defenses."

Halitov opened his mouth in mock surprise. "You mean we're actually going to win a battle?"

"We gain air superiority—and he wants to take full credit for it," I said, grinning at Jing.

We streaked in low over Arantara Canyon, then headed west toward the buttes, mesas, and valleys near Virginis Canyon, where we would find the Minsalo Caves and Dina. Crimson rock faces blurred by as off to port, perhaps a kilometer out, our atmoattack jets launched missiles at unseen fighters. If all went well, there would be no dogfights. Jets would annihilate each other from extreme distances, and those pilots would hardly taste war the way all of us had. They were lucky.

"Which entrance are we using?" I asked Paul, realizing that our pilot had just taken us over the cliff we called Whore Face, our old training ground, then we descended sharply toward the caves.

"Found a new entrance while I was living in there," he said. "It'll put us exactly where we need to be."

"Coming up on the DLZ now," our pilot chipped in, then pointed at a broad, flat stretch of Virginis Canyon, where a beacon, a small strobe affixed to the top of a three-meter tall tower and one I assumed was ours, flashed from one small mesa to the east. We zeroed in on that beacon, then the pilot wheeled us around and began his vertical descent. We threw up our safety bars, grabbed our particle rifles, then stood near the aft loading hatch.

"It'd be nice if you told us what kind of resistance we might face down there," Halitov said to Paul. "Call me anal, but I like to know how many bad guys might be shooting at me."

"Probably none," he answered.

"You're kidding me."

"I'm not," he said confidently.

"I hate to sound grim, but Dina's been down there a while," said Jing.

"That's all been taken care of," Paul answered.

"All right, on the ready line," said the pilot as the ATC thumped onto the mesa. "Hatch down."

An achy feeling crept over me as I hustled down the still-lowering ramp. While Halitov had come to despise Exeter, I still held great affection for the rocky little moon. Yes, I knew the academy lay in ruins. I knew that my old barracks was gone. I knew Dina's body lay somewhere below my feet. Yet the ache, a kind of homesickness, made returning seem right, even necessary. We would recover Dina's body, and maybe, just maybe, the Wardens would take back the facility and get it back on-line. Halitov and I would finally be reconditioned.

I turned back as the others jogged away from the ATC and couldn't help but grin as that earthy scent wafted up on the breeze and my combat skin kicked on the polarizers, allowing me to see more clearly in the brilliant sunshine.

"What're you laughing about?" Halitov asked.

"You wouldn't get it." I regarded Paul. "It's your recovery op."

He waved us on past the beacon. I casually spotted a serial number on the tower, and cerebroed data identified that unit as a Western Alliance PX CG Mobile Navigation and Sensory Array Unit. I raised my rifle and cut loose a pair of rounds that struck dead on and shattered both the beacon and its antennae.

"Pilot should've taken this out," I said.

"Encryption jamming is confirmed," Paul argued.

I snorted a little. "*Confirmed* doesn't mean anything anymore."

"So if this thing got off a signal—" Jing began.

"Then the alliances can pinpoint our location," Halitov finished. "Scott's right. That dumb ass pilot should've known that and blew this thing before we got within sensor range."

"Point is moot now," said Paul. "But we'd better de-skin so they can't track our signatures." He swung around, his combat skin rippling off, then he jogged off toward a V-shaped fissure barely two meters across. He reached the opening, set down his rifle, then lowered himself down another meter until he stood on the floor of a subsurface tunnel. "Okay, it's tight in here, but it'll open up in a couple hundred meters." He snatched his rifle, then drew a small light from his tactical vest. "Just stay close."

"Why I'm going along with this, I don't know. I should've stayed onboard and played Vesbesky's games," said Halitov, switching off his own skin. "Same difference, right? I mean now I'm going to shove myself down this little tunnel—just like a rat."

"Can you move your ass?" Jing said, warily studying the sky. "I don't want my last conscious act to be listening to you bitch and moan."

He ducked into the fissure and crawled behind Paul. Jing slid deftly into the tunnel, then I wriggled down after her, nearly forgetting to fetch my rifle and taking a last look at the beacon I had destroyed.

With Paul's light picking out the path, we crawled forward, the tunnel bumpy and damp yet remaining level for the first fifty or so meters. Soon, we began a lazy descent, accompanied by a slight turn east. The tunnel grew no wider, and that concerned me because I knew Halitov would react.

"You okay?" I heard Paul ask, a few meters later. "Come on, Rooslin."

"I'm . . . it's . . . okay," he said, hyperventilating.

"How much farther?" I asked Paul.

"We're about halfway."

"Rooslin, can you close your eyes?" I asked.

"Yeah. Does that mean I'm going to do that now? No."

"You're all right, man. No one's coming inside with you. It's just you. We're out here. And we're all going on together," I said, playing shrink and remembering the night he had almost killed me:

"I'm not going to kill you. I'll just take you real close 'cause that's what you're doing to me every time you

screw up. You gotta know what it's like not to breathe,
to be closed in—I mean really closed in—and there's no
one to help. There's just me, laughing at you, the way
they laughed at me."

"Rooslin, come on," Paul urged him.

Something must have clicked in Halitov, since Jing
suddenly shifted forward, and I followed. We moved
even more quickly, and in what seemed like only a few
minutes we reached a wide chamber whose ceiling
swept up on two sides like a gabled roof. Paul's light cast
a shimmering glow over the alabaster walls, slick and
highly reflective. The familiar stalagmites and stalactites
ringed the perimeter, and as I glanced up I thought I saw
a shadow pass behind one, then reasoned that I had actually seen Paul moving gingerly ahead, rifle leveled, legs
slightly bent in anticipation of an ambush.

"I don't see a way out of here," Jing said, squinting
through the darkness ahead.

"You're right, this is a dead end," said Paul, swinging
back toward us—

As the shuffle of boots sounded from the rear. I gaped
at Paul, then craned my head back. Four Western Alliance Marines haloed by combat skins blocked the tunnel and lifted their particle rifles.

"What the fuck is this?" Halitov cried.

"Oh my god," gasped Jing. "Paul, I trusted you."

"You trusted him?" I asked. "You were working for
him?"

"Yes, but he lied! He lied to me!"

With that, Paul raised his rifle and fired once, twice, a
third time. Something struck me in the neck, and my
hand went reflexively for the wound. A hiza dart had
impaled my jugular, its onboard computer ordering the
syringe to fill my veins with whatever drug Paul had

chosen. "Paul, why?" I asked, eyes bugging, knees beginning to weaken.

Jing, who was tugging on her own dart, vanished a moment, then reappeared. "What are you doing to us?"

"Forget the bond," he said with no malice in his voice. "I've put your mnemosyne to sleep."

The four Marines fanned out as another five, maybe six poured into the chamber, effectively surrounding us.

"Paul, what're you doing?" I asked.

"I don't know, Scott," he said, his voice as shaky as the hand gripping his rifle. "I don't know anymore."

I finally managed to yank the hiza dart from my neck, but the damage had already been done. Besides numbing us to the quantum bond, whatever drug he had used left us lethargic. In fact, Halitov had already fallen to his rump. I lowered myself to the cold, wet floor, then eyed Paul with so much hatred that it scared me. "You gave them our codes at Columbia?"

"I had to."

"Do you know what you've done?"

"I do, Scott," he said softly, painfully. "I do."

PART 2

◀ ▶

Ice Age

18 February, 2322

7 **Over two decades** have passed since that fateful day when Paul Beauregard had told us the truth. He had sold us out at Columbia and was, in fact, the traitor we sought. Every time I consider that revelation, the hairs stand on end. Yes, I had harbored some mistrust for him, but I had never thought he was capable of something so grave, so . . . unimaginable. I could hardly bear to remember it anymore, so I turned to the window and concentrated on the skyline as our shuttle made a final approach.

The first time I had been to Manhattan, I had marveled over the history bound up in all that architecture. I had never seen buildings as ornate. I thought I had heard the centuries-old whispers of those who had lived and worked in the heart of the Western Alliance. I felt rooted to the place. I felt, somehow, that I had come home.

Now, nearly ten years after that first visit, I was returning, and so much had changed. As we landed outside the capitol building, I neither marveled at the buildings nor heard those whispers. I felt as though I were entering a great concrete-and-glass den of wolves and that my true home lay light years away. Security personnel were literally everywhere, posted on rooftops, along perimeter walks, near entrance doors, and, of course, lined up on the tarmac. Although the city's protective energy skin had not been activated, I knew that

on a moment's notice the bubble would go up, and
while it would drain power from the entire island and
cost millions to keep activated, it would effectively
shield the president from a first strike. Consequently,
our cruisers in orbit would not waste their time targeting Manhattan. Their sights would be set on the densely
populated—and unshielded—suburbs of nearly every
North and South American city. Sadly, the three alliances had the technology to shield all of their people,
yet none could fund a project of that magnitude. The
rich would survive a war. Mining kids like I had been
were expendable, and that sad fact underscored the importance of my mission.

A group of five men wearing dark trench coats ran toward our still-humming shuttle, their breaths misty and
trailing, their path marked in a thin layer of snow.

Bren, Tat, Ysarm, and Jiggs were first out, using their
pen scanners to probe the Western Alliance people for
arms, poisons, and other lethal instruments. I held my
head up, into the wind, and felt a few snowflakes strike
my cheeks. I found small consolation in the crispness of
the air and the smell of wood burning in stoves at a
restaurant across the street.

"Sir, we're ready," said Bren, proffering a hand.

I waved off his help and climbed from the jumpseat,
stepped onto the icy tarmac—

And fell flat on my ass.

"Sir, are you all right?" Bren asked, looking shocked
then battling off his grin.

With a groan, I accepted his hand and rose shakily to
my feet. I brushed snow from my own coat and noted
that across the street floatcams had recorded every second of my unceremonious arrival. The journalists
would write quips about me being so humbled by the

power of the alliances that I could not remain on my feet. Still, their remarks would be trivial, given the reason for my visit.

Surrounded by my team, I moved quickly inside, into a private lift, along with several other alliance security people. I switched on my tac for privacy and contacted Davyd, who gave me the latest positions of the alliances' cruisers, then I notified the president's office of my arrival.

"Colonel, we've just received verbal commitments from Ambassador Warring and Ambassador Felice. They're preparing their secession documents now," said President Vinnery, shimmering in my HUV. "Which means, when you go up there, you tell those fools that they've already lost Mars and Jupiter, and any measure they take to prevent their secession will be considered an act of war."

"Madam President, I beg your pardon, but I couldn't help noticing our Eighth Fleet in orbit, and I was unaware that you ordered the spinning up of their tactical nukes. A blockade—I mean a parade—is one thing, but you do realize the message that sends."

"Colonel, they spun up theirs, we spun up ours. It's a little game we play."

"It's a dangerous game, and if I didn't know better, I'd say—with all due respect—that you'd be willing to order that strike."

Her expression grew even more condescending. "It's the order no president ever wants to give, but we will *not* allow innocent civilians to be oppressed."

"We're going to work this out," I said quickly, afraid that I might launch into a philosophical tirade in the hopes that I could prove her wrong. "Please, ma'am, I'm begging you. Don't make another move."

"I'm giving you your chance, Colonel, after which I will negotiate directly with the presidents."

"I understand, ma'am. Just let me speak to them first."

"Good luck," she said darkly.

I switched off my tac and asked Bren for the negotiating team's status. Yes, I would be the primary speaker, but I wouldn't engage in talks without a few tricks up my sleeve.

"Most of the team's already here or en route," he said. "They'll remain in our conference area until you call for them."

"Very good."

He lowered his voice. "Sir, I'm—"

"It's all right, Bren. We're all a little scared."

"No, that's not it. I don't care about dying. That's my job, right? Human shield. I just . . . I don't know. You're a good man, sir. You shouldn't trust anyone."

"Stop worrying."

The lift doors parted. Plush, navy blue carpet swept off toward a broad, wooden receptionist's desk that seemed quite an antique arrangement for a busy president's office. However, the desk was Terran tradition, as were the paintings depicting former Western Alliance dignitaries that lined the walls. As we started forward, we passed through not one but three discreet security scanners whose probing beams emanated from the walls. We went through the motions and were finally granted access to the adjoining waiting area. I shook hands with Ms. Bursa, Holtzman's plainly dressed assistant, who said that the presidents would see me shortly.

"Of course they'll make you wait," said Tat. "You know what they're doing in there right now? Sitting around, talking about how they're making you wait. Petty power."

"Quiet," Bren told the man.

"It's all right, Bren," I said. "He's probably right."

Armed Marines in gray-and-azure utilities stood on either side of a massive, richly carved door bearing the president's seal: a hawk alighting upon a wreath of seventeen stars. I had never been fond of that emblem. To me it implied dominance and subservience, and it hardly reflected the independent status of the seventeen colonized worlds. But that was Terran tradition again, and, ironically, I guessed that the colonial traditions we were establishing would die just as hard.

"They're ready to see you now," said Ms. Bursa, her communications skin vanishing from her eyes and ears. She pointed to the door as the Marines moved sharply aside and one reached for the handle.

I rose, along with my team.

"You must enter alone," Ms. Bursa instructed.

"Negative," said Bren.

"I'm afraid they insist."

Bren shifted to me. "You go in there, they hold you hostage and get the upper hand in the negotiations."

"What's to say I won't go in there and hold them hostage?" I asked. "Bren, I'm a little out of shape, but I'm still a conditioned soldier."

"Sir, don't go in there without us."

"Anything happens to me, don't worry. You won't be held responsible. I'll log this decision so it's legal, okay?"

He shrugged. "It doesn't strike you as odd that they won't let us go in?"

"We're talking about the fate of seventeen colonized

worlds and Sol system. No matter how well they're trained and how loyal they are, we both know that security people eavesdrop. And most of the time, it's a necessary part of their job."

"Yes, it is," he said with a weak grin. "But they know that, too. Which is why this still bothers me."

"I'll keep a line open. If I need you, trust me, I'll call."

He nodded, then motioned for Tat, Ysarm, and Jiggs to take up positions near the door. While none of them were armed, they, like me, were conditioned soldiers, and if I did have a problem, they would will themselves past the guards and into the room, which reminded me that the guards at the door were probably conditioned, too, and the office beyond was most certainly equipped with security and defense systems. Yes, it was a den of wolves.

Taking a deep breath, I started into the president's office, and I'm not sure why, but my thoughts strayed, if only a little, back to that chamber, back to Paul Beauregard. I had a premonition that one answer to my dilemma lay somewhere in the past.

Halitov, Jing, and I lay on the chamber floor, barely able to sit up. Pairs of Marines dragged us back to our feet and held us firmly as Paul discussed something with a young lieutenant who had de-skinned and who wore a horrible grin. At least Paul maintained his anguished look. I don't know that I could have born his gloating. He came forward, rubbed his eyes, then just stared at us.

"Was that you in Vesbesky's chamber?" I asked him.

He nodded slowly. "I didn't want to turn you over to them. I thought I could just get the data, but I couldn't."

"You rat fuck!" Halitov said through his teeth. "Selling us out. Come over here. I want you to look in my eyes and tell me what you did."

Paul took a deep breath. For a second, I thought he would meet Halitov's gaze. Instead, he just looked away.

"How long have you been working for them?" Jing asked.

"Not long," he answered, then added quickly, "Listen. They're not going to brainwipe you. I have that promise in writing. They just want to observe you. Study you. Look, the war's winding down. We're not going to win."

"Not now, we're not!" Halitov shouted.

"Paul, how could you do this to us, to your father, to your homeworld?" I asked, still unable to comprehend his motivation.

"They have my mother."

"What?" barked Halitov.

"They've had her ever since my father began his little operation to take over the Seventeen. They've been trying to blackmail him, using her as the bait." He chuckled low and scary, walking the razor's edge of a breakdown. "My old man played the good soldier, told them they could kill my mother, that he wouldn't betray the colonies. But he doesn't care about the colonies. All he gives a shit about is himself and his reputation and his fucking ego. Do you know what he said to me when I told him Dina was dead? He didn't say he was sorry or that she was a good soldier or that she had given her life for something greater than all of us. Do you know what he said? Nothing. He wasn't even listening."

I slowly realized what had happened to Paul. Dina's death had sent Paul into a deep depression, and, vulnerable, he had succumbed to the temptation to save his mother and punish his father. Only after going to the Alliances had he realized the full extent of his treachery, but then it was too late to change anything. I thought of our conversation back in my quarters; the signs had all been there, but who would've thought to listen?

We make our own luck.

I didn't realize it was that bad down there. I really didn't.

It's too late. And there are other people to think about.

"So all of that digging I did for you was really for them," Jing said. "You turned me into a traitor."

"It doesn't matter anymore," Paul said. "The Alliances outnumber and outgun us, and they have a new weapon against conditioned soldiers—the drug that's inside you right now."

"After you hand over the colonies, do you really think they'll hand over your mother?" Halitov asked.

"I'm not giving them the colonies. The colonies were theirs in the first place. None of us would be here if it weren't for them."

"Yeah, they brainwashed you good, didn't they," snapped Halitov.

"And those encryption codes at Columbia?" Paul said, unfazed by Halitov's remark, "Yeah, I had to give them up, but I only made their job easier. They would've attacked anyway and still beaten us."

"Does that make you feel better?" Jing asked, seething.

"Paul, do you remember when we were just cadets? Remember that night in our billet?" I asked. "The night we had to choose sides? Do you remember what you said?"

"I don't know."

"Well, I remember it exactly. You said the articles of the Code of Conduct are no longer valid. 'We're not alliance citizens anymore. We're colonists, and that's where our loyalties should lie. We've been exploited for long enough. Maybe history is repeating itself here, but if it doesn't, then our families are doomed. I want to know right now who will stand with me.'" I paused to let the memory sink in. "That's exactly what you said."

He sighed in disgust. "And I can thank your cerebroed brain for that guilt trip down memory lane, huh?"

"Don't turn your back on us."

Halitov snorted loudly. "Are you kidding? He's not turning his back—he's stabbing ours!"

The colonel's son glared at Halitov, then he looked to me, his fury fading. "Scott, you've always lived by the code. What would you have done? Would you have abandoned your mother?"

At the moment, I would have rather taken a round of particle fire than consider that question. He was reminding me that my own mother had abandoned Jarrett and I. Her lack of loyalty was why I never turned my back on the code. Sure, when I had agreed to join the Wardens, I accepted the fact that the code was being rewritten, but at its heart still lay the same principles that made me proud to be a Colonial Warden. Paul had disregarded those principles in favor of the love and loyalty he had for his mother.

"That's a stupid question to ask him," said Halitov. "You know how he is. He would've done the same thing your old man did. The colonies are more important than one woman."

"Is that right?" Paul asked me.

"I wouldn't have abandoned her," I answered slowly. "But I wouldn't have made deals with the devil to get her back."

"Yeah, well you have no idea how it is out there. You don't know. You just don't."

"Maybe not. But I do know one thing. You're going to die for this."

"Probably, but you won't have the pleasure of seeing it."

"There's no pleasure involved. Right now, I hate you, Paul. But I pity you even more. You could've come to us, told us what was happening. We could've formed a little commando unit, gone in wherever they have her, and busted her out. You could've done that."

"You're saying that now, but you wouldn't have helped. You would've done what Rooslin said. You three are soldiers. You think like soldiers. I can play the part, but inside, that's not me." He threw up his hands. "All of this is not me."

"Fuck the psychobabble," said Halitov. "You ratted us out. And I'm blaming you. And you know what's worse? You soiled Dina's memory by using her as an excuse to get us down here. Did you realize that?"

Paul tensed and grew flush. "Dina's going to get a proper funeral. That's already been taken care of."

"You had them recover her body?" I asked, tipping my head toward the Marines.

"No, I'm going to get her now."

Halitov threw a madman's glare at Paul. "Have fun."

"And after that?" Jing asked. "You're not going to keep feeding them data, are you?"

"There's a mission coming up. It'll be the last thing I have to do."

Jing winced and glanced away. "Oh, God."

"So what're you going to tell Daddy about us?" Halitov asked.

"The truth. You were taken prisoner. I managed to escape."

"And even if they scan you, they won't get anything different, will they?" I said.

"No, they won't."

"And who would suspect the colonel's son?" Halitov said.

"Not us," Jing added darkly.

Paul turned and headed back for the young lieutenant.

"What? No fucking good-bye?" yelled Halitov.

The colonel's son paused, threw us a sidelong glance, then kept on.

"All right, let's move out," said the lieutenant. "Jing goes on A-6. St. Andrew and Halitov with the others on A-7."

Jing glanced worriedly at me. "Guess I'm heading out on a different transport."

"Why are you separating us?" I called to the lieutenant.

"Shut up," he hollered.

"I might never see you again," Jing said.

"I know. Would you like to get married?"

"What?"

"I mean, you know, if we live through this."

"You picked some time for a marriage proposal."

"I never said I had good timing."

"Hey, if he doesn't want to marry you, I will," said Halitov. "We could learn to like each other."

"I said shut up," the lieutenant barked once more. You just knew the kid was days out of the academy, and we were his first big mission. "Okay, I'm going to read to you the conventions regarding prisoners of war."

"Listen, boy," began Halitov. "We've done this before. You obviously haven't. You shut the fuck up and take us to wherever we're going."

The lieutenant marched up to Halitov and grabbed him by the throat. "Old man, you're a POW. If you open your mouth again, I'm going to fill it with dirt, then tape it shut. After a while, you'll wind up swallowing that dirt. And that's just nasty. And unnecessary, right?"

Halitov nodded. The lieutenant released him.

And that's when my former XO fired a huge glob of phlegm into the lieutenant's face. The spittle struck a direct hit and hung from the young man's nose. Yes, that was my partner—a man of great courage and fierce loyalty and no class.

The lieutenant tripped Halitov to the cave floor, and even as the two Marines holding him gathered dirt in their palms, Jing cried out as they hauled her away.

I wanted to shout, "I love you!" because I meant it. But even as I opened my mouth, the words seemed cheap and desperate, not unlike my marriage proposal, which she had never answered.

But then she did. "I'll marry you, Scott. I will."

Before I could reply, they shoved her into the tunnel.

The Marines forced dirt into Halitov's mouth, wrapped him with tape, then hauled him back to his feet. My own Marines shoved me on, my limbs still numb. By the time we made it outside, onto the mesa, the Alliance ATC carrying Jing—a boxy, broad-shouldered aircraft—was already blasting off, its exhaust so violent that it threatened to blow us off the cliff. As we leaned into the wind, eyes narrowed and growing teary, our own ship settled down. They shoved us up the ramp, into the hold—

Where we took in a remarkable sight.

Looking as though they had spent the past year or so on a deserted island, or, in fact, roaming the canyons and caves of Exeter, three long-haired and bearded men sat in jumpseats, their clothes sun-bleached and tattered but unmistakably South Point Academy cadet uniforms.

"Who are you guys?" I asked, still astounded as the Marines lowered me into my own seat.

One man, a blond, lazily raised his head. "You, you're that gennyboy who was a first year. You had a brother. And you got so old."

"That's right. I'm Scott St. Andrew. What happened to you guys?"

"When the academy was first attacked, we went to the other side of the moon, met up with a few others, then stayed there. A few more of us came, and some tried to escape and got killed or captured."

"You know we came back and took this moon from the Alliances."

"Yeah, we found out only after the Alliances took it back again. Fucking game."

"Do you know Paul Beauregard? He was in the Minsalo Caves for a while with a few people."

"We made it a point to stay out of there. That place was always heavily occupied."

"How'd you get caught?"

"Long story," said another cadet, his dark hair thinning at the crown, his beard matted with dirt. "None of your business, though."

"Don't mind him," said the blond. "By the way, I'm Tim Coris. He's Ric Santorman, and he's Brandon Tai." The last guy, perhaps the leanest and frailest, glanced up to reveal tear-stained cheeks.

"This is Rooslin Halitov," I said. "He's usually pretty talkative."

Halitov fought against the dirt and tape. He was cursing me, all right.

Once the Marines had locked us into our seats, the ramp cycled shut, and the shuttle pivoted west as it rose, the landing skids chinking into their bays. My bravery had not faltered thus far, but as we lifted off, the reality of the situation struck a solid blow; while I'd been a POW before, you never knew what to expect. I felt scared, breathless, and furious at myself for putting so much trust in Paul. I lay my head on the jumpseat, about to close my eyes. The two Marines who had stayed aboard to escort us sat up near the cockpit, just behind the pilot and co-pilot. Something flashed. Both slumped in their seats.

A fourth long-haired, bearded man, this one also blond, exceedingly thin, but with strikingly familiar eyes, put a finger to his lips, the Ka-bar in his hand still dripping with blood. He had willed himself into the ATC, and his gaze widened on me and Halitov before he whirled toward the cockpit, raising the knife.

8 >   While Halitov and I typically had bad timing and worse luck, we had stumbled our way into someone else's rescue attempt. Perhaps the universe's guilty conscience had something to do with that. No matter. We would happily allow ourselves to be saved. Trouble was, our "rescuer" had other plans.

The wild-haired blond with those familiar eyes stormed into the cockpit, slit the co-pilot's throat, then held the knife at the pilot's sternum and cried, "Get the tawt computer online. I'm going to feed you new coordinates."

Our pilot, a man no older than the lieutenant, had a decision to make: life or loyalty. He turned his head, eyed his dead comrade, then simply said, "Roger that." He reached forward, glided his finger over a touch screen. "Ready."

As the knife-wielding blond rattled off the coordinates, I concentrated on the numbers and searched through cerebroed data in my head for a location, and, as usual found more than I needed. Star system: Procyon A/B. White dwarf. 11.4 light-years from Earth. Satellite: Icillica, sole moon of Procyon C. Surface gravity: .787. Atmosphere: hydrogen, with traces of oxygen and nitrogen. Terrain: craters covered by frozen water and methane. Primary colonies: Regal, Victory, Augusta, Wintadia, and Colyad, all mining operations. Chief exports: nickel, iron ore, apatite. The data was complete, though it failed to explain why we were heading to a dirty snowball in the middle of nowhere.

"Coordinates locked," reported the pilot.

"Hey!" I cried. "We can't tawt yet. I have to contact Colonel Beauregard and Ms. Brooks. This is urgent. It can't wait."

"It'll have to, Scotty boy. Because you have no idea how long I've been waiting for this moment. You don't recognize me, do you?"

Oh my god. I did know him. Private Eugene Val d'Or, Kilo Company, Twenty-seventh Platoon, Eightieth Squad. We had been first years together at the academy. I remembered reading his name on that Racinian Conditioning Fatality Report, the same report that listed my brother dead, and while Jarrett had been kidnapped by the Wardens and given a new identity, Val d'Or had obviously met a different fate, one he was trying to revise before my eyes.

"I know who you are," I told him.

"And I'm sure Halitov over there remembers me cutting his rope out on old Whore Face, don't you, big guy?"

Halitov emitted a muffled scream and fought against the locked bars.

"Eugene, please," I said. "Let me get off that signal."

"Scope's full. Atmoattacks everywhere," he replied, then regarded the pilot. "Tawt. Now!"

"Tawt clock is active," said the pilot. "Stand by."

"If you don't let me contact them, we could—"

I began my sentence in Exeter's atmosphere, felt my stomach drop, then finished that sentence over sixty light-years away:

"—lose the war . . ."

"Tawt complete," reported the pilot, furiously working his touch screen to shut down the drive system.

Dim white light filtered through the canopy as the system panned into view. We streaked toward a bluish white fleck burning on the fringe of the white dwarf's glow.

"Unlock us now," said Tim Coris.

Val d'Or nodded and ordered the pilot out of the cockpit. They passed into the hold, then the pilot took a jumpseat and locked himself down. Only then did Val d'Or unlock his comrades' safety bars, leaving Halitov and I trapped in our seats.

Halitov, whose hands had been bound by standard-issue force cuffs, groaned for Val d'Or to remove the tape from his mouth. Our old rival complied, and Halitov whined and leaned over to heave a disgusting mud pile.

"Is he puking?" asked Ric Santorman.

Halitov looked up, mud dripping from his chin. "What's it look like, asshole?"

"How long till we make orbit?" Coris asked Val d'Or.

"Clock said fourteen minutes. Autopilot will put us right in the slot. See, you sonsabitches! I told you it'd work. You just had to trust me."

"Eugene, you have no idea what's going on out there," I said. "I have to contact the colonel and Ms. Brooks."

"No, you don't." He dematerialized. I craned my head to find him standing beside me. "You're the last person in all the colonies I'd expect to find here."

I faced him. "Likewise. Now, you're going to walk over to the cockpit, and you're going to get the pilot to activate the emergency beacon so we can tawt out a chip to Exeter."

"I'm not giving up our location."

"Why not? You worried about being caught? Being drafted back into the Guard Corps? They think you're dead. You probably smashed your tac. They can't get to you."

"Unless someone tells them who I am, and they confirm via DNA analysis. But to tell you the truth, I'm worried more about my colleagues here, who are still classified MIA and have no desire to fight in this fucking war anymore. They're going home with me. And we'll figure it out from there."

"Let me ask you a question. While you were planning this big rescue and tawt out to Icillica, did it occur to you that your home might be enemy-occupied territory?"

"Of course it did," he answered, his voice faltering a little.

"Well, it didn't occur to me!" shouted Brandon Tai. "Eugene, did you dump us back into the shit hole!"

Val d'Or hustled toward the cockpit, and, forgetting that the controls were user-specific, attempted to pull up long-range sensor reports from the system. He swore, raced back into the hold and fetched the pilot. After a moment's work at his touch screen, the pilot looked back at Val d'Or and said, "Looks like two cruisers in polar orbit, and I'm betting they've been there for a while, which means they're supporting ground forces. Garrisons have been established. There's a pair of atmoattacks en route. They've tagged us, read our log, and one of those pilots is hailing. What do you want me to say?"

"No reply yet. Calculate a close quarters tawt into the lower atmosphere over Colyad."

"Our drive's a twenty-one twenty. The computer's not equipped to handle a tawt that precise."

Val d'Or threw his head back, whipping hair out of his eyes, then slammed a fist on the pilot's console. "We can't tawt? Then make up some bullshit excuse and get us past those fighters and on the ground—or I'm going to slit your throat."

"I have no authorization codes to be operating in this system and no good reason to support why I tawted in. I can't lie about a tawt malfunction because they've already read the log. Why don't I tell them the truth?"

"The truth?" asked Val d'Or.

"Yeah. They might attempt to negotiate if they realize we're carrying two Colonial Wardens. That'll buy you some time."

"Forget all that. I got a better plan. I'm going to take out those fighters, and you're going to make a run for it." Val d'Or turned back to the hold. "Timmy? Get over here."

Tim Coris bounded forward and accepted the knife from Val d'Or, who gave his fellow highjacker a hard look and said, "Don't let me down."

Coris nodded, even as Val d'Or closed his eyes and dissolved.

"All right," Coris began, placing the knife on the pilot's neck. "When you see those fighters blow, you punch us a hole down there."

"I'll try," answered the pilot. "But I'm just wondering whether getting my throat slit is a better way to go than getting blown out of the sky."

"Stop wondering. Start flying," said Coris.

I leaned over and squinted through the canopy. A glimmer shone at our two o'clock, then dove suddenly. That would be the first fighter. Val d'Or had probably rendered the pilot unconscious and had destroyed the onboard computer. The jet broke into a flat spin and fell out of view.

"There's one," Coris told the pilot. "Wait now. Wait . . ."

A pair of heartbeats later, the second fighter simply dove ninety degrees, dropping like a missile toward the ice.

"Okay, now! Go!" Coris shouted.

Our necks snapped sideways as the thrusters drop-kicked us forward and the pilot plotted a course between the two clouds of tumbling debris. Val d'Or returned, gripped the bulkhead, then hunched over, tanking down air. He paid the same price for that little trick that we did, though his skill seemed comparable to Jing's. And it was then that I remembered his conditioning should be as problematic as ours was. He had been through the same accident, yet his skin, though darkened by the sun, remained fairly smooth, and his hair, long and unruly, was untouched by gray. Perhaps those were just temporary effects. Perhaps he had spent time in the Minsalo caves and his body had rejuvenated, a process that wouldn't last long, though.

"Well, that woke them up," said the pilot, pointing toward one of his displays. "Now we got four more in pursuit, weapons hot. Guess your work's not finished."

"Launch countermeasures," cried Val d'Or, clearly too drained to will himself within those enemy cockpits. "Evade! Evade!"

The ATC slid right, darted forward, then banked hard as though riding a great breaker. The drug Paul had given us still numbed Halitov and I to the bond. I dreamed of willing myself all the way back to *Vanguard One*, where I could tell Colonel Beauregard to his face that his son was a traitor.

"Insertion calculations complete," the pilot said. "Get ready for the burn—if they don't kill us first."

Before he finished, particle fire boomed hard against our aft skin. A few more direct hits like that would weaken the energy barrier. Once it came down, so would we.

"Ten seconds!" announced the pilot.

A needling, scraping sound erupted from the loading ramp, and I knew exactly what was happening. "Skin up!" I told Halitov.

We hit our tacs, the membranes flowing from our wrists and quick-sealing us against the sudden loss of pressure as a carefully placed round of particle fire blew a jagged gash in the ramp's surface.

Coris, Santorman, and Tai, who were not strapped down, flew across the hold and slammed against the ramp, ribs crunching, eyes pleading as they gasped for air. Halitov and I had front row seats for their slow and untimely deaths. I couldn't look at them anymore and glanced to the cockpit, where Val d'Or gripped the co-pilot's seat and banged his fist on a panel, activating the cockpit's emergency bubble. An opaque wall shimmered at the pit's entrance. He and the pilot were now protected by the bubble, though a couple more hits might take out the drive and batteries, killing power to the bubble and leaving them to the merciless vacuum.

Indeed, another round did strike, though it spared the drive and batteries and tore the loading ramp's gash even wider. An already unconscious and probably dead Tim Coris passed through the gap, but his feet stuck. I could only imagine what he looked like from the outside, flapping and trailing us like a banner of human misery before the heat of our entry burst him into flames. Santorman rolled into the gash, then plunged away sans grotesque drama. Tai's body lay across the hole, and unless he turned, he would hang there until we were destroyed, reached the ground, or another round blew him into space.

We couldn't hear the pilot's voice from behind the bubble, and a quick scan of his channel said he was not in contact with our pursuers. With only our own senses to inform us, I felt even more helpless. "I could use a good joke about now," I told Halitov over our private channel.

"Okay, a priest, a rabbi, and two Colonial Wardens walk into a bar, see. And the priest says—"

"I know what the priest says. You told me that one already."

"Shit. All right. Let me think."

One, two, three rounds sledge-hammered the living hell out of our aft quarter, tearing the entire loading ramp away, along with Tai. I gazed at the surreal ring of fire behind us as the ramp tumbled into the nothingness at the ring's core, followed by a tiny, limp form. Our combat skins strained to protect us from the extreme heat, but they couldn't work miracles. I activated my HUV and read a databar confirming the inevitable. We would burn up in less than a minute.

"Okay, I got another one," said Halitov. "It's about this old staff sergeant who's trying to get into the officers' club, right?"

"Heard it."

"You know, for someone who's about to die, you're a demanding bastard, you know that?" said Halitov.

"Were you really in love with Dina?" I asked, knowing the question came out of nowhere, yet knowing we might be burned to cinders before it was answered.

"Yeah, I was."

"Why didn't you ever do anything about it?"

"Because . . . God, it's hot . . . because she never liked me."

I blinked sweat from my eyes. "You could've worked on her. I did."

"Maybe there was too much competition. Maybe, maybe, maybe. Who cares anymore? Damn, my EC's tapping out. How 'bout yours?"

The ENVIRONMENT CONTROL databar glowing in my HUV showed all bars in the red. "We'll probably pass out soon. Oh, man. I didn't want to go this way."

"Yeah, I was hoping I'd get a heart attack while having sex. I've had a couple dreams of that happening."

"You would."

He swore through a deep sigh. "You know, I'm tired of this shit. I really am. Nothing ever goes our way. What did we do to deserve this? You know, maybe it's something we never thought about, like that time when I was ten and I pulled up Linda Haspel's dress then pulled down her panties and everyone could see her. Yeah, maybe my whole life's about paying that back."

While he continued to ramble, I noticed that the flames behind us had become smoky wisps of exhaust and that the temperature now rapidly plummeted. We had reached the upper atmosphere, and as the ATC leveled off, the moon's gradual curve rolled up, revealing great plains of silvery white broken by tiny lines, like the veins in a leaf.

". . . and there it is. My whole life is totally screwed up because I hurt that little girl's feelings. Yeah, they made me apologize to her, but I didn't mean it. If I had, we wouldn't be here right now."

"You're right," I said. "You're absolutely right."

"Hey, it's getting cold!"

"Yes, it is." I peered beyond the tattered rim where the loading ramp had been attached, and my combat skin's targeting computer zeroed in on three fighters narrowing the gap behind us. "I'm glad we're not going to burn up. Getting blown out of the sky is much better."

Salvos of particle fire streaked by, and as Halitov damned those pilots and all of their descendants, I braced myself as our portside thruster gulped a round and burst free from the fuselage. Tremors ripped through the bulkhead and deck with such violence that the locks securing my safety bars broke. The bar came loose in my hands, but I kept it down. Where else was I going to go? A jump at that altitude would've resulted in my rebounding halfway across the moon, turning me into a mushy sack of broken bones.

Shedding metal, varicolored liquids, and black smoke, we plunged at a sixty, probably even a seventy degree angle toward the surface, our remaining thruster wailing against the added burden as winds buffeted hard, knocking us against the seats. Dim flashes appeared far behind us, then blossomed into a half dozen rounds that exploded from our pursuers' underwing cannons. A quartet of booms caught my attention as the pilot released four self-guided mines, clusters of pyramids trailing sensor antennae some six meters long. The antennae sprang to life, tilting their globulous heads back toward the fighters as the mines jetted off, carried by miniature jets.

Two of those incoming rounds struck glancing blows to the starboard wing, while the others fell a mere meter wide as an explosion thundered behind us. And there, fading fast, hung the expanding fireball of what had once been a mine and an atmoattack fighter. I suddenly liked our pilot. I would shake his hand if we survived.

"I've tapped into a GPS satellite," said Halitov. "We're heading toward Colyad. About eight hundred kilometers northeast of the primary pad and entrance."

"But if Eugene's smart he won't take us in the front door."

"Like I said, that's where we're headed."

"Yeah, you're right. He's anything but smart."

Our only thruster flamed out, even as the two remaining fighters barreled toward us. Had I been able to see through the cockpit, I would've been holding my breath. We were gliding straight for a massive, ice-covered crater whose base lay nearly a kilometer below the surface. The crater would not have startled me. The six batteries of anti-aircraft guns positioned along its rim, however, cannons jutting up like black slashes against all that ice, would have done the trick.

However, Halitov and I sat blithely unaware of all that firepower—

Until the first round blew with an unholy rumble and came within a couple meters, displacing so much air that we suddenly rolled to port, as though evading some incorporeal missile.

And that's when Halitov ordered up satellite images of our location and announced the obvious: "Six batteries down there, set up along Rinca-Mushara Crater."

"Only six?" I asked.

He gave me a look. "If those artillery guys can't shoot one gliding ATC out of the sky, then they don't belong in the Marine Corps. And what's really pissing me off is that the fucking universe can't decide which way to kill us."

"Listen," I said. "Listen."

"What?"

"They're not firing."

"Yeah, that was a warning round. They're waiting. The next one will finish us."

"Maybe our pilot's sweet-talking them," I said.

"Or maybe Eugene got his energy back and is working a little Racinian magic on them."

"Check the GPS for our altitude," I said.

"Checking. Oh, this is wonderful. Twelve hundred meters and falling fast."

The crater's rim wiped by then rose as we plunged into the great belly of bluish-white ice hanging above an oppressive gray sky that seemed to crush the landscape. I forced the safety bars up, then stood, pulling myself weakly yet steadily toward Halitov. I worked the keypad above his jumpseat once, twice, a third time, but the lock had been damaged.

"Come on, man!" he cried.

"It's not working."

"Then you jump. I'll ride it out," he said.

I crawled back toward one of the dead Marines, still locked into his seat, and withdrew a Ka-bar from his calf sheath. I brought the knife back to Halitov and jammed it into the main lock mechanism above the bars. Sparks jumped. The bars held fast. Somewhere, light-years away, Linda Haspel smiled.

Desperate and without thinking, I straddled Halitov, took the bars in both hands, and tried pulling. The drug Paul had given us still robbed me of most of my strength—not that I could have freed Halitov, but at least my attempt would have been valiant.

"Get off of me, you ass. That won't work!"

A tingle in my neck said look up, and there, framed by a ragged rhombus of steel, lay the slick and bumpy surface, unfurling just meters below. At any second we would strike that sheet of ice and slide uncontrollably toward the crater's opposite rim, where we would strike the wall. If the collision didn't get us, the fire would. Of course, any other obstruction along the way, say a ten meter tall hill of ice rising at a sharp enough angle, would render us just as dead, though more expeditiously so.

"We're going to touch down!" cried Halitov. "Jump!"

I hung on to his safety bars.

"Jump, you ass!"

Particle fire burrowed into the ice and frozen methane behind us, blasting up an astonishing barrage of fragments that flew into the hold and rained like flaming hail onto the fuselage. Tiny fires outlined each strike, appearing like the navigation lights on a tarmac as the methane burned a moment before dying. My skin rippled as more fragments caromed off, then—with a double *thwack*!—we met the surface and began fishtailing to port.

"Oh, shit, here we go!" Halitov shouted.

We rolled onto our side, still spinning, still headed God knew where. I dangled from Halitov's safety bars, while he looked down at me, pinned himself against the bars. Suddenly, we rolled again, onto the ATC's back, then once more, onto the starboard side, even as I lost my grip and went crashing into the portside seats. Ahead, the cockpit bubble faltered a moment, then winked out. Val d'Or clambered into the hold, heading toward the aft exit conveniently opened for us by those fighters. Surprisingly, he was skinned up. I glanced to the cockpit, where the pilot sat slumped in his chair, yet he still wore his tac. I figured Val d'Or would've used the pilot's override codes so he could "borrow" the tac. Perhaps our old rival had never smashed his own tac. He had hidden it while on Exeter, only to fetch it moments before his escape. He was a lot smarter than I had thought.

"Rooslin's trapped," I called to him. "How 'bout a little help?"

"I'm out of here!"

"You were training to become a Guardsman! We're your brothers. You don't leave us behind!"

Val d'Or picked his way past us, fighting against the shimmying hull as we screeched over the ice. He reached the edge of the hold as I struggled to my feet.

"No one gets left behind!" I cried.

And I'm unsure whether the steel in my voice or his guilty conscience won out, but he gazed across the crater at the jagged runway we were cutting, then scrutinized us. His expression remained as frosty as the crater. Still, he charged for Halitov, leapt up, grabbed the safety bars.

"Come on, give!" he shouted. "Give! Give!"

I shifted toward him, fell onto my side, pulled myself back up, as the terrain grew more ragged and that ATC rattled even louder but failed to drown out the particle fire booming from somewhere outside. It wouldn't be long. The wall or those fighters would finish us if we didn't abandon ship. I jumped up and gripped the bars, dangling from them with Val d'Or. We screamed in unison, and during that scream, an idea chilled me.

"Let go," I told Val d'Or. "I'm going to brace myself in there, then turn up the power on my skin. Maybe the rebound will blow the bars."

"I'll do the same," said Halitov.

"You take right, I'll take left," Val d'Or told me, then swung his feet up so that he could jam himself between the bulkhead and the bars.

I did likewise, straining despite Icillica's weaker gravity. "All right, we'll reduce power then roll up to full on three," I said. "Ready?"

Neither Halitov nor Val d'Or responded. And I wouldn't have been able to hear them if they had. The cockpit took a direct hit, and, amid fountains of sparks and arcs of flames, it tore away from the rest of the ship and booted us upright for a moment before the jagged edges of the forward hull bored into the ice, driving us down one meter, two, three until we stopped so abruptly that Val d'Or and I sailed across the hold and collided with the rising ice mound behind us. Through dust clouds of ice, I saw Halitov was still locked into his jumpseat, yet the seat itself had detached from the bulkhead and had fallen forward, pinning Halitov between it and the deck.

"Rooslin, you all right?" I called.

"Shit. Do I look all right?"

Shadows wiped across the ice outside, accompanied by the tinny drone of thrusters. I couldn't tell if they were approaching or not. Maybe they were circling, getting ready for the final kill.

"Come on, let's get him," I told Val d'Or, but when I looked over at him, he lay there, unconscious. He must have turned down his skin power so much that the collision had knocked him out. Damn. I could've used his help. I crawled over to Halitov, seized the jumpseat's edge, then pushed him onto his side.

"Wait a minute," said Halitov. "Son of a bitch." He drove his forearms against the bars, and they gave.

I grabbed his wrist and pulled him from the seat, then started back for Val d'Or.

"To hell with him," said Halitov. "Let's go."

"No one gets left behind."

"Only the dead." His gaze darted over the hold. "Where's that Ka-bar?"

"He was going to help you."

"I don't care. Never liked him. Never will."

"You can kill him later." I didn't mean that, and Halitov knew it as he glanced dubiously at me, then stormed forward, picked up Val d'Or, and slung the man over his shoulders as I retrieved the Ka-bar and tucked it into my calf sheath.

We kept tight to the bulkhead, reached the edge, then I scanned the sky. Those fighters were still up there, but they banked away as great tracers of particle fire rose from the crater's rim behind us, the angle of those streams growing tighter as the jets dove and finally disappeared on the horizon.

"Locals putting up a fight?" asked Halitov.

"Let's find out."

We hopped down from the hold, crossing tentatively onto the ice until our skins created enough friction to help us stick while also accounting for the lower temperature and surface pressure. We had forgotten to set our tacs for autoenvironment, but the computer recognized that error. Sans our footsteps, the crater remained eerily silent. Out there, far behind us, lay our cockpit, a toothy hunk of silver smoldering at the end of a bluish-white trench, otherwise the crater floor remained flat, with the occasional shallow depression. We trudged off toward the rim about a half kilometer away, minding our steps but even more mindful of the sky and the looming walls of ice whose pockets could hold any number of Alliance Marines posted as snipers or sentries.

"Okay, got another one for you," Halitov said.

"Seems this captain was having a hard time getting his unit motivated. So he goes to his XO and says . . ."

"Says what?" I asked.

"You mean you haven't heard this one?"

"No."

He chuckled under his breath. "Well, I'm not going to share it with you because you're an ungrateful bastard who can't sit politely through an old joke."

"I thought I was a demanding bastard."

"That too."

Something glimmered near the foothills ahead. "What do we have there?"

The glimmer darkened into a definite form, a boxy ground vehicle that my tac identified as an SS MORROW A1 TRACKED TROOP CARRIER.

"After all that, we get to walk right into the enemy's hands." Halitov lifted his glare to the heavens. "I'm sorry, Linda Haspel. I'm sorry!"

9 ❯ **There was no** point in running. We would stand our ground against whatever emerged from that transport. We had experience. We had a knife. We had seriously bad attitudes.

Halitov set Val d'Or onto the ice, then waved his hands.

"What the hell are you doing?" I asked.

"Giving them a bigger target. Maybe we'll die quick."

I stood there, dumbfounded, then resigned to the absurdity of the moment and began waving myself.

The tracked vehicle rolled right up to us, a metallic beast with a heavily armored snout, domed back, and rows of cannon ports along its flanks. It was not unlike the tracked vehicles of centuries' past and was far cheaper to manufacture and operate than a hovercraft of equal size. Since Icillica wasn't the most valuable of the Seventeen Worlds, the Alliances spent the least amount of money to equip the garrison while still maintaining control. But cheap or not, the SS *Morrow* could easily intimidate two poorly armed officers carrying an unconscious man across the vast plains of an ice-covered crater.

A rear hatch rolled open, and out leapt four civilian miners wearing bright blue Exxo-Tally standard-issue environment suits with transparent helmets that fit tightly around their heads. I knew they were miners because in addition to the company's logo on their breasts, mining identitags common to every mine, including those back home on Gatewood-Callista, dangled from collar clips. The miners held QQ90 particle rifles at the ready, and they fanned out and confronted us like a small team of well-trained Wardens.

One miner, a man towering a full head above us, stepped forward and raised his rifle. Beads of sweat dappled his pale, shaven head, and he studied us with green eyes so bright, so inhuman that they startled me. "What is your calling?" he asked, his voice amplified by the suit's external speakers.

"I'm Major Scott St. Andrew. This is Captain Rooslin Halitov. We're with the Fifth Battalion, Eighth Regiment, Colonial Wardens." That wasn't exactly the truth. We'd been removed from the battalion, but force of habit prevailed. "We were taken prisoner on Exeter, tawted out here, and technically speaking, made a pretty half-assed escape attempt."

The man stared unblinkingly, then, for a moment, I thought a wave of sadness passed over his expression. "I didn't ask *who you are*. I asked what your calling is."

"I'm sorry, I don't understand. But you people are civilians, right? Was that you on that artillery fire?"

"Yes, it was."

I proffered a hand. "You saved our lives. Thank you."

He took the hand, didn't shake, just squeezed. "You're not really alive. Not yet, anyway."

I withdrew. "Maybe you're right. So what's happening here?"

Cocking his brow, the miner shook his head, saying, "You have a lot of questions because you are a man without a calling."

"Uh, Scott?" said Halitov. "I think we got a neovic. He fits the profile."

Before I could dip into all of those records the Guard Corps and Wardens had dumped into my brain, the bald miner gestured that two of his team retrieve Val d'Or. As they did, he said, "Come with us. We have a calling for you."

"You can skip the calling with me," said Halitov. "A little food, a little shelter, and a big ticket off this rock. That's what I'm about."

"You have no idea what you're about," the miner warned. "Everyone aboard. Now."

We fell in behind two women loading Val d'Or into the SS *Morrow,* then reached the crimson-lit hold, settling heavily into jumpseats as the driver, hidden behind his broad seat, abruptly kicked the vehicle into gear.

"What's your name?" I asked the bald miner, who had taken a seat beside me.

"Hardeson Poe. And the captain is right. I was born a neovic."

At that instant, everything I never wanted to know about the moon's predominant and fringe religions flashed through my head. The neovics existed on the periphery of religious circles, and while some of their philosophy had been borrowed liberally from Buddhism, Hinduism, and even the Colonial Church of Christ, their beliefs rested most heavily on data recovered from the Racinian ruins on Drummer Fire. The primary concepts were easy to grasp: the universe is alive, experiencing itself, and our minds are the universe. All power, all matter, all particles are within our minds, our spirits, if you will. They worshiped the power of the human mind and strove to reach a tantric state so they could tap into the bond between particles without the aid of the Racinian conditioning that Halitov and I had received and had learned to love and hate. They wanted to achieve the power Halitov and I had been artificially given, and the first step toward experiencing the universe on a quantum level was to understand your calling, your natural, pre-ordained place in the universe. I didn't bother to skim the records anymore. While I appreciated the connection between physics and mysticism, and, for the most part, kept an open mind, I seriously doubted that the neovics could tap into the quantum bond without the aid of mnemosyne parasites introduced into their brains. The human body had simply not evolved enough to do something like that.

"I respect whatever religion you choose to practice," I told Poe.

"It's not a religion," he said. "It's life."

"All right. No debate. Because right now I really need to contact some people with the Wardens. It's imperative that I get a chip out to them immediately."

"All long-range communications are being disrupted," Poe said. "And that includes the signals from your tacs. The only way to get a comm drone out is to divert their orbital support."

"You mean those two cruisers up there in polar orbit."

"Exactly."

"So if you control the artillery here around the crater, we can use it to create that diversion. How many people are with you?"

Poe smiled, his weird eyes going distant.

"How many?"

"Major, you need to slow down, assume nothing, and consider the fact that another calling may await you."

"With all due respect, sir, if I don't get a message out, the Alliances could very well win the war, and your home here will revert right back to the days of Alliance discrimination and oppression."

"Major, we're being occupied by the enemy. We're already there . . ."

"And you'll stay there if you don't help me."

"There's a lot you don't know about what's happening here. There's a lot you need to see. You, Halitov, and the other man there, you're conditioned, is that correct?"

As he finished the question, something quaked in my thoughts, the barest tremor at first, than a full-on reverberation as the quantum bond between particles revealed itself once more. Paul's drug was wearing off. I breathed a sigh. If Poe became a problem, at least Halitov and I would be better equipped to handle him.

"Are you all right, Major?" Poe asked.

"Sorry."

"Are you conditioned?"

"That's classified."

"That birthmark on your cheek . . . you have epineuropathy. We've heard rumors about a few like you who got conditioned and became more powerful than any other soldiers."

I forced a grin. "Just rumors."

"We also heard that the Seventeen System Guard Corps is being replaced by the Wardens."

"Now that'll probably happen."

He closed his eyes, took in a long breath. "Do you think the Wardens will send help?"

I could lie to him, but he struck me as a man who could face the truth with his head held high. "Both sides have spread their forces too thinly. The Alliances can't afford to send reinforcements here."

"I wasn't asking about them."

"I know. But if they can barely hold this world, do you think the Wardens can?"

"Then no one's coming," he said gravely. "They've left us to the wolves. Two hundred million people, spread across five subterranean colonies, forced to live out our lives under the guns from above and the garrisons holding our capitols."

"I've been a POW. And I've fought on my own world against Alliance Marines. I know what it's like to have them come into your home."

"And you know what it's like to drive them out."

"Yes, but as part of a strike force, not a ragtag miners' rebellion. Did the Alliances wipe out the Seventeen's command post here?"

"They did, and within the first hour of the attack. The soldiers they captured were hauled off, probably brainwiped and measured for enemy uniforms. Since then, the Marines have been raiding our towns and searching for soldiers who are hiding among us. And since then, we've been collecting weapons, organizing ourselves, and in the last week we managed to secure the artillery on this side of the crater."

"They're letting you have it, you know that," I said. "Otherwise, they would've taken you out from orbit."

"Don't be so sure."

"I am. They're setting you up for a massive offensive,

letting as many of you as possible gather in a central location, probably near these guns, so they can make one fell swoop."

Halitov, who had been listening quietly—an amazing feat for him, though he was exhausted—finally looked up. "Yeah, so they've set up a trap. And our new buddies are driving us right into it. Uh, this is where I get off, if you don't mind." He rose.

"Sit down," I ordered him, then regarded Poe. "Look, if you need our help, we'll give it, but right now my only goal in life is sending that message." Even as the words left my mouth, I realized the lie. I wanted to contact the colonel and Ms. Brooks, yes, but I wanted just as badly to recover Jing. If we could tap into satnet, break an alliance code or two, we could find her prisoner transfer orders.

"Right now, Major, your goal in life is survival," Poe said. "Which is why we're going to take back the capitol building from the garrison holding it. And you and your friends are going to lead us to victory."

Had his words not been uttered so seriously, so sincerely, I would have laughed in his face. And then he looked at me with those eyes, eyes tinted permanently green as part of some ancient Racinian ritual, according to my cerebroed data.

Halitov turned up the charge on his skin, then lowered his head and called me over the private channel: "Look, these miners don't have a prayer. We're not going to help them. We're going to use them to stay alive, get that message to Ms. Brooks, and figure out a way to get back to *Vanguard One*. Do me a favor? Lie to them. Tell them anything they want to hear, so long as we know what we have to do."

I weighed that, then turned to Poe. "As I said, we'll help, but my duty is to get out a message to my superiors. That has to come first."

His eyes narrowed to slits. I waited for his nod, but none came. "The universe did not place the three of you here by accident."

"No, us getting shot down was very deliberate," Halitov said with a snort.

"Before we do anything else," Poe began softly. "Let me show you my world."

Halitov tossed a silly look my way, but I ignored him.

"All right," I told Poe.

The bumpy ride suddenly softened as the SS *Morrow* broke onto smooth pavement. Although we couldn't see outside, I assumed we had passed into one of thousands of mining access tunnels leading to the subterranean colony.

We traveled for about another thirty minutes, with me repeatedly asking how long the ride would take and where we were going. Poe remained irritatingly cryptic. Twice Halitov threatened the man, and I had to intervene.

Finally, after nearly a full hour, the transport came to a gradual halt, brakes squeaking a bit then dying off into the engine's idling hum. Poe instructed us to remain seated while the driver spoke over the comm.

In the meantime, Val d'Or was coming around, and Halitov grabbed the hairy cadet by the shoulders. "Hey, asshole. Wake up so I can beat you back into another nightmare."

"Fuck you, Halitov," Val d'Or moaned, then rubbed the back of his head, and glanced around. "Whoa. This is an Alliance track."

"That's right. We're prisoners," Halitov lied.

"Shut up," I said, crossing to the man. "These miners picked us up. They're organizing a rebellion." My tone darkened. "Lucky for us, huh?"

"I don't believe it," said Val d'Or, his gaze locked solid on Hardeson Poe. "It's you. The guide. *The* guide."

Poe came over and helped Val d'Or to his feet. "Are you from Colyad?"

"Yeah, I was born here. The calling took me way out to Exeter, but now I've finally come home. I can't believe it's you, standing here. I've only seen you on holos and from a distance during the *trovakas*. I just . . . I can't believe it."

The hatch opened automatically, revealing diffuse blue light and an icy tunnel bearing the groove marks of the original drillers. Halitov shoved his way past us. "Sorry to break up your fanatic family reunion, but I'd like to see where the hell we are."

"Some would call you the fanatics," said Poe. "And Captain, we've passed through the airlock, so you can de-skin." Poe turned, reached out, and touched Val d'Or's wild hair. "You've some stories to tell. Come on."

I followed them out of the SS *Morrow*, de-skinning as I leapt from the hold. When my boots hit the ice, they gave, and I suddenly dropped flat onto my ass. I suspected even then that me and icy surfaces would never get along.

"You sure he's the guy you want leading your people?" Halitov asked Poe, then smiled tightly.

Poe broke away from Val d'Or and offered his hand. "It's his experience as a tactician that I'm interested in, not his ability to walk on ice . . . or water."

"Thank you," I said, taking his hand, rising, then

brushing off my rump. I spotted a pathway a few meters to the left, one that Poe's people had chosen.

We entered a nondescript hub in the railway station, and miners were posted at the four major corners, all wielding rifles confiscated from the Alliances. Clearly, Poe and his people had already organized the citizenry, and that became entirely evident as we entered the station proper. I gazed out across a broad, bustling platform where literally thousands of people boarded or exited from fifteen to twenty trains. Our railway system on Gatewood-Callista seemed rudimentary by comparison. Armed miners stood at every gangway, and big particle cannons jutted from circular, perimeter bunkers whose armor resembled metallic scales. A half dozen airjeeps manned by still more miners zoomed overhead through the vast chamber carved into the ice, their pilots carefully monitoring the hustle and bustle below.

"You've done a fine job securing this position," I told Poe, though I still felt the heat on my neck from those cruisers in orbit.

"A few guardsmen helped train these people. Every man and woman here will die for our freedom. But you need to see more. We're taking a train to Noe Providence. First, we need to get you out of those uniforms."

Poe led us up, onto a catwalk running parallel to a row of offices. As we walked, Val d'Or rushed up beside me. "Scott, now that we're here—"

"To be honest, Mr. Val d'Or, I don't want to hear anything from you at this moment." I glared. "You got your wish. Your home. Aren't you going to run off and find your family?"

"I already have."

"These people?"

"I'm a neovic, and so are my parents. I'll meet up with them, but first this is my calling."

"Incredible," said Halitov, who'd been walking behind us. "One minute he's a backstabbing opportunist, the next he's a religious nut. At least he never commanded troops."

"No, but I will now," Val d'Or retorted.

"Eugene," I began, tempering myself a bit because I realized I wanted something from him. "You were in the same conditioning accident with us. Same one as my brother, too, only he and some others were kidnapped by the Wardens while you escaped. Since then, Rooslin and I have been aging abnormally."

"Obviously."

"Hey, I still get laid more than you," barked Halitov, whom I silenced with a look.

"What do you want to know?" asked Val d'Or. "Why I'm not aging as fast?"

"If the exact same thing happened to you, then you should be suffering from the same effects as us."

"Remember the caves?" Halitov asked. "Remember how Paul's aging was temporarily halted and reverted?"

I grabbed Val d'Or's arm. "Do you spend time inside Minsalo?"

"I kept my people out of there. Look, I wish I could tell you why. But I can't. Sorry." He pulled away.

"You're not sorry," spat Halitov. "You're laughing your ass off right now. But karma's going to come back and bite you like a *shraxi*, trust me."

"Here we are," called Poe, pausing before an office door he had just opened.

Inside, the former insurance firm's offices had become a makeshift warehouse for stolen military supplies.

Rows of everything from old-fashioned sandbags to uniforms to crates of weapons rose over our heads and stretched off into the shadows. Poe led us down one dark aisle to a rack of Exxo-Tally mining uniforms. There, he told us to find our sizes and change.

"Clean skivvies," said Halitov, reaching into a box and holding up a pair. His gaze went skyward. "Thank you, Linda."

"Who?" asked Val d'Or.

"The woman who controls his fate," I answered, as though it were obvious.

"You two are weird."

"Listen to this," cried Halitov, dropping his drawers. "Mr. Neovic over here. You ever tell anybody at the academy that you were one of them?"

"You make it sound like we're fundamentalist freaks. What we are is dedicated to the sheer beauty and power of the human mind."

"You ever tell anybody about your *dedication*?" Halitov said, probing on.

Val d'Or shrugged. "They would've called me a hypocrite."

Halitov chuckled under his breath. "And they would've been right. You got conditioned to tap into the bond. But isn't your entire religion based upon the idea of doing that naturally, without the mnemosyne?"

"I followed my calling. I did what was right. If it meant getting conditioned, then that's what I had to do. My people understand. They just want what we have, and they know one way to obtain it is through prayer and meditation and total focus. Once you connect to the bond through sheer force of will, you'll have a more intimate relationship with the universe. The mnemosyne act as a filter, dulling some of our awareness."

"You know that for a fact?" Halitov asked dubiously.

"I've never experienced it myself, but I've witnessed others who have."

Halitov caught my gaze and made an exaggerated frown. I gave a little shrug and kept dressing.

"Let me have your uniforms," said Poe, returning with an empty shipping container. "We're going to burn them."

"Excuse me, but that's the property of the Colonial Wardens," said Halitov.

"And if the garrisons find out we're here," I reminded him, "there will be a serious manhunt." I nodded to Poe. "Burn them."

Halitov unpinned his captain's gon from his uniform, then resignedly handed the uniform to Poe. "I earned this," he said, holding up the gon. "And no one's burning it."

"I wouldn't carry that," said Poe. "If you're caught with it—"

"If we get caught, they'll run DNA," I told Poe. "They'll find out soon enough who we are."

His phosphorescent eyes widened. "Then let's not get caught." He left with the uniforms.

I tucked my own major's angle, a gold triangle impaled by a small ruby, into my palm, squeezed it, then squeezed it again. *I should be doing what I've been trained to do: lead troops. God damn you, Paul Beauregard. Damn you to hell . . .*

Once we were zipped into our blue mining jumpsuits and had donned our black boots, Halitov threw out his arms and said, "Can you appreciate the irony of this or what?"

"Irony?" I asked.

"We shipped out to Exeter, got trained, got conditioned, got attacked, got taken prisoner, got shot at, beat up, fucked over—all so we wouldn't have to stay home and become miners like the rest of the poor blue collar slobs on Gatewood. And after all that shit, here we are, light years from home, putting on the blue."

"What's with him and the drama?" asked Val d'Or.

I rolled my eyes at Halitov. "Get over it."

"Oh, I'm over it. And the sad part is, I look pretty good in this thing. Still a man in uniform, and the women are still going to swoon. Lead me to the miners' daughters."

"Ask my ghost," I told him. "Because I'm going to kill myself now."

"Scott, my boy, cheer up." He slapped an arm over my shoulders. "So what if we lose the war? So what if we die before our time?" He looked at me, puckered his lips. "At least we have each other."

"Yeah, the curse continues . . ."

Poe, Val d'Or, Halitov, and myself, along with four of Poe's recruits, took a train to Noe Providence, one of Colyad's most productive mining towns and its seediest, with robbery, gambling, prostitution, and smuggling running rampant. Hard-working miners engaged in rowdy and visceral activities, and most colos came to expect that, as did law enforcement officials, who policed with a forgiving hand. On the train, Poe explained that production had slowed, since miners knew that their efforts now helped the Alliance war effort, and tension crackled like electricity between workers and Marines.

Unarmed, we reached Noe Station, and Poe got us by security scanners with a few nods to his contacts. We headed out on foot through a tunnel that emptied into a

broad coliseum of ice under which stood a shanty town
of Quonset huts and other prefab structures serving as
homes to several hundred miners. As we shifted stealthily between the buildings, our boots crunching over
sand or some other substance that been spread over the
ice, I noted that some of the miners were in their teens,
and, in fact, a few of them could be no more than ten or
twelve.

After crossing through several alleys, we reached a
main avenue, where a pathetic little bazaar lined both
sides of the street. Vendors worked from the backs of
dilapidated hovers and sold barbecued beef and
chicken, along with personal hygiene items and music
or film holos, games, and a few of the newer virtual reality headsets. To the sudden halt of my heart, Alliance
Marines shuffled everywhere, rifles shouldered but
gazes keen and darting through smoke wafting from the
grills.

"Holy shit," Halitov whispered. "That beef smells
good, but get me the hell out of here."

I shifted up to Poe and couldn't help speaking
through my teeth. "You didn't say we'd be getting so
close. And I told you, I don't have time for this. If you're
not going to help me get my message out, then I'll do it
myself."

"Just give me another moment," he said, withdrawing a small earpiece and translucent microphone from
his hip pocket. "They'll be making a demonstration
soon." He donned the communications gear, said, "Status? All right, then."

Ignoring my frown, Poe led us on, through the marketplace, and toward a great octagonal hole in the far
wall with lights flashing along its perimeter.

"That's the main entrance to the network," Halitov

said, aghast. "We'd better not be going in there—unless we're being double-crossed."

I put a finger to my lips. "Just be ready."

Poe darted between a pair of parked airjeeps, then hunkered down behind a third. We joined him there, then peered cautiously over the side panels at a long line of children in mining uniforms, some of them just eight or nine, marching out of the entrance, escorted by a half dozen screaming Marines.

"What's this?" I asked Poe.

He looked at me, eyes glassy, lips tight. "Just watch."

"They can't force kids to work," said Halitov. "It's ridiculous."

The parade of children came to a halt, all fifty or sixty of them. One gunnery sergeant eyeballed the group, then began his inspection, scrutinizing them as though they were green cadets in boot camp, but they were kids, for God's sake, and one little girl near the end of the line, a petite angel with curly blonde hair, stood there, whimpering a moment before her face knotted and she cried hysterically.

"Do you hear that, ladies and gentlemen," shouted the sergeant. "What's that noise?" He ran up to the little girl. "What's that noise coming out of your mouth?"

"Oh, I want him," said Halitov. "First I'm going to break his arms and let him stare at the bones popping through his skin, then—"

"Shut up," I told him, tensing as a hundred or more adult miners flooded in from the main entrance, the group held at bay by a full platoon of Marines jogging alongside.

"Whose child is going to die today?" The sergeant whirled to face the adults. "Whose child is going to pay the ultimate price because Mommy and Daddy have chosen to slow production?" The sergeant snatched up the crying girl into his arms and raised her before the crowd. "Will it be her?"

"This is insane," I whispered.

"We've found the deepest level of Hell," Halitov added.

Poe glanced hard at me. "That sergeant will kill her."

"He's bluffing," I said.

Poe shook his head.

"I won't sit here and watch this," said Halitov, sizing up the distance between the airjeep and the sergeant.

"Yes, you will," said Poe, grabbing Halitov's wrist. "There's an entire company inside."

Halitov's cheeks flushed. "That makes the casualty report higher."

I balled my own hands into fists, staring intently at the sergeant, who pulled the girl tight into his chest, then jammed a QQ60 particle pistol into her head. "This little girl is going to sacrifice her young heart because you people have chosen to resist. Now, think about it. I'm going to stand here before all of you, and I'm going to kill her. And you can't blame me for this. You can blame yourselves."

"Rooslin," I began, sharing a very familiar and knowing look with him, a look we repeatedly wore during combat, one that reminded us of the ultimate sacrifice we were prepared to make. "Ready?"

"I didn't bring you here to save her," Poe said quickly. "She's already dead. I brought you here to show you what we're fighting for. You can help us save thousands more. But if you blow our cover, nothing changes. Nothing."

He was right, but I couldn't take my gaze from that

poor little girl, her cries like daggers in my heart, the gun pressed to her soft flesh, the sergeant's voice coming in a psychotic lilt, "Oh, Sweet Jesus, this little one has to die. Oh my god, she has to die!"

10 > **They were killing** children.

Even the most detached, most dispassionate Colonial Warden among us would have had a problem with that.

Still, trying to save one little girl might result in us getting captured—again. We would fail to send off that message and ultimately lose the war because Paul Beauregard would feed the enemy everything they wanted to know in an effort to save his mother. We had to think long term, but doing that was hard when you were watching a sadistic sergeant jabbing a pistol into a little girl's head.

Sometimes when I speak to cadets at the academy, I ask what they would have done, given the identical situation. Some say matter-of-factly that they would have let the girl die. Others, guided more by their outrage over Alliance Marines engaging in such heinous activity and by their personal convictions, would have tried to save the girl. After much heated debate, the floor inevitably becomes mine, because they always ask, "So, what did you do?"

The truth is, Halitov stole the decision from me. One second he huddled with us behind the airjeep, nodding that he was ready, and in the next second he was gone—without having waited for my order. Admittedly, my tone indicated that I had made up my mind; however, I was still weighing the consequences, and Halitov couldn't have known that. In any event, he should have waited.

The air beside the sergeant fluctuated like a heat haze, and from those waves Halitov emerged. I expected all bug eyes and brutality from him, but to my surprise he worked like a thief instead of an assassin. Even as the sergeant jolted at the specter materializing before his eyes, Halitov tore the pistol out of the man's grip, threw it away, then snatched the child and dematerialized with her. He reappeared beside us, the screaming girl in his arms, her cries muffled by his big palm.

"Aw, hell, what'd you do that for?" asked Val d'Or.

Halitov's fiery gaze was answer enough.

"You neovics can play your little games," cried the sergeant. "If not her, then another child. Makes no difference to me." He dashed to the line and grabbed a small boy, who began kicking and screaming.

Judging from the sergeant's response, some neovics were able to connect with the bond; the sergeant had obviously seen them do that before. I made a mental note to ask Poe about that, then closed my eyes and said, "We lose this one, Rooslin. But we make sure we win the next. Let her go." Suddenly, a round of particle fire reverberated through the chamber and struck a blow harder than if it had actually hit me.

The little boy fell silent. I tried, but I couldn't look up. Every muscle tensed. I shuddered. Hard.

"Oh, no," gasped Halitov. "This can't be happening."

"This happens almost every day, all over this moon," said Poe. "We believe the lieutenant colonel who's running the show has gone insane. He's the one who gave these orders. But we'll talk more later. Let's move now."

"What about her?" Halitov asked, still holding the

little girl, whose bright eyes would soften even the hardest heart. "Those Marines will find her."

"Her parents are back there in that crowd," said Poe. "I hate to say this, but she's their responsibility."

"They can't help now," argued Halitov. "Better she lives—even without her parents."

"You're an asshole, Halitov," said Val d'Or. "You shouldn't have played God in the first place. Leave her."

"Scott?" Halitov called, looking to me for a decision I didn't want to make.

Then I stole a look at that dead little boy, his parents hovering over him, the sergeant droning on about how someone else's kid would get shot tomorrow if the miners failed to increase production.

"She comes."

Val d'Or swore. Poe thought a moment, drew in a deep breath, nodded, then slipped off, with the rest of us dropping quickly into his path.

"Don't worry, sweetheart," Halitov told the little girl. "You're going to be safe."

"But what about my mommy and daddy?" she asked.

"You'll meet up with them. Don't worry." Halitov pushed his captain's gon into the girl's palm. "Hold on to this for me. Okay?"

"Okay," she said, distracted by the gleaming badge.

Despite the occasional stare, we crossed the marketplace without incident and reached the station. There, Poe instructed Halitov to hand off the little girl to an operative who would deliver her to a shelter for war orphans. She could remain there until she was reunited with her parents.

"Here," the girl said, proffering Halitov the captain's gon.

"No, sweetheart. You take it."

She smiled. "Thank you."

Poe nodded to the operative, who scooped up the girl and vanished into the crowd. We shifted quickly aboard the next outbound train, and fell into our seats.

"She would've died, just like that little boy," said Halitov, glancing through me as I studied him from an opposite seat. "I can't get him out of my head."

"There have been dozens more just like him, and hundreds more throughout the colonies," said Poe. "But we can take back Noe and the other provinces. Seizing the capitol will be our rallying cry. Once we do that, the others will move."

"Sounds like you're ready," I told Poe. "And so are your people. You don't need us. Just help me get access to a communications database. I need the location of the nearest tawt-capable transmitter."

"One did survive the invasion," said Poe. "But I told you, long-range communications are impossible. Any unauthorized probe trying to tawt out of here will have its nav system jammed."

"But if that probe issues the correct authorization codes, it'll be allowed through," I said. "And there's a long list of those codes in my head. We'll input all of them and have the computer initiate a rapid-fire relay. One of them has to work. We have to give it a try."

"If you help us seize the capitol, I'll get you to that transmitter." Poe narrowed his gaze. "You saw them kill that boy. You know what you have to do. You know your calling."

"Of course he does," Halitov said, then cocked a brow at me. "Did you think it wasn't coming to this? At least we're still fighting the same bad guys."

I considered Poe's offer, then banged a fist on my knee. "We don't have time for this," I said. "I need to get that message out—now!"

"Unfortunately, Major, in order to do that, you'll have to get inside the capitol—because that's where the surviving transmitter is located."

"Of course it is," muttered Halitov. "That's the universe flipping us the bird."

Poe went on, "That transmitter, along with the rest of the compound, has been secured by a full battalion."

My shoulders slumped even more as Poe leaned over and widened his eyes. "I know that willing yourself there will cause a considerable drain, so I suggest you stick with us, help us plan this attack, and once we're in there, you can attempt to send word to your friends." Poe's tone waxed sarcastic. "You might even save a few children along the way."

"Count us in," said Halitov.

Poe looked to me.

"I want the location of every transmitter within ten kilometers, and along with it, I want security holos that indicate those transmitters have been destroyed."

Poe's expression darkened. "I've been honest with you, Major."

"Then you'll get me what I want."

"Not a problem."

"Shit, Scott, even if there is another transmitter, we'll still have to get to it, launch our own attack without their help, and maybe get off that message," Halitov said. "This way we kill two birds with one stone."

"Or maybe we're the birds, and they have the stone."

"Just get him the maps and holos," Halitov told Poe. "He gets cranky like this. It'll pass."

* * *

Four standard hours later, Halitov and I were back at Colyad's main station, seated in a conference room just off the catwalk. While we waited for the guardsmen who had been working with Poe to arrive, we brainstormed some ideas for our attack plan and studied the maps and holos of the other transmitters, noting that the information was recent and difficult to forge. Those transmitters were gone. Poe had been honest with us.

"Satisfied?" asked Halitov.

"For now."

Poe joined us and explained that his entire force numbered about three thousand, but less than half of those miners would be armed. He also explained why the Marines had not launched a counterattack to win back the main station, a question that had been gnawing at me.

"Bribery, gentlemen. We've paid off the battalion commander so that he reports our numbers as far greater than they are. He also reports that while we're occupying this territory and controlling it with confiscated weapons, we pose no real threat to the overall operation and occupation of this colony."

"This battalion commander," I began. "Can we count on him to back off or misdirect his forces when we attack the capitol?"

"I wish we could, but while he'll take our money, our drugs, and our women, he won't walk away from a fight," explained Poe. "He's already warned me about that."

"So you've got about three thousand miners ready to go. How many are neovics? And how many of them can access the quantum bond?" I asked.

"You were listening very carefully back there," said Poe, now beaming at me. "Unfortunately, several of us have revealed our skill to them. I wanted that to be our greatest element of surprise."

"You mean you people can actually tap into the quantum bond without Racinian conditioning?" asked Halitov. "I thought that was a colonial legend."

"There are ten of us, including myself, who possess the skill and focus. Those ten individuals will be arriving shortly, along with the guardsmen."

"How many guardsmen?" I asked.

"Just seven, I'm afraid."

"And they're all conditioned," concluded Halitov.

"No, they're not," Poe corrected. "But neither are the Alliance Marines. Yes, we're heavily outnumbered, but I'm hoping our access to the bond will make up for that."

A knock came from the door, and Poe answered, allowing the people we were just discussing to file into the room. Ten miners, four males, six females, ranging in age from about fifteen to a woman well into her sixties, shuffled in and stood along the wall, followed by the seven guardsmen, who, despite their mining outfits, moved with that familiar deportment and keen-eyed mistrust characteristic of Guard Corps troops. Val d'Or returned as well, having shaven, cut his hair, and appearing exactly the way I remembered him from our academy days. I trembled with the desire to learn why he was not aging the way Halitov and I were.

"All right, ladies and gentlemen," Poe said, crossing to the front of the room. "At zero nine-fifty, we're going to attack the capitol. This is the major offensive we've all been waiting for. And it seems that the universe is on our side. Major Scott St. Andrew, Captain Rooslin Halitov, and Second Lieutenant Eugene Val d'Or were shot down over Rinca-Mushara Crater, and they've volunteered to help." Poe hoisted his brows at me. "Major St. Andrew will lead the attack, and in return we'll do everything we can to help him launch a comm drone so he can get off word to his people. Major St. Andrew?"

I rose from my seat, then leaned over and worked a touch screen on the desk. The holoplayer's overhead projector winked on, and a 3D simulacrum of the capitol building beamed overhead, rotating slowly to reveal a five-story, U-shaped structure with a pair of hexagonal towers jutting up nearly one hundred meters from the north wing's roof. Between those towers lay the broad, flat dispatch pad for communications probes, a disk with a diameter of several hundred meters and ringed by scores of miniature launch platforms atop which sat the missile-like probes and message drones. An enormous metallic conduit attached to the great ceiling of ice hung above the disk, and probes would blast up from the building, rocket into the tube, then rise to the surface and launch. Though I had yet to study the building's schematics, I assumed the communications command center lay somewhere, just under that pad; however, getting to it via a conventional attack would be impossible. A force fence like the ones I'd seen on Mars encompassed the grounds, and I noted that the sentry towers had all been destroyed, replaced by a dozen airjeeps positioned at equidistant points down the perimeter. Moreover, Marine snipers had strung out along the rooftops and walkways, as well as above and below the elevated maglev train bridge running behind the building, adjacent to the modest-sized governor's mansion, where still more Marines kept watch on that building's domed roof.

I cleared my throat. "Ladies and gentlemen, you're all familiar with the target and realize that a conventional attack would be a waste of time and resources. That's why Captain Halitov and I have devised something, well, much more unconventional . . ."

About an hour after the briefing, Poe, Halitov, and I, walked through the station, pausing before a small Italian restaurant, a mom-and-pop operation with the age-old checkered tablecloths and bottles of vino. We had a few hours before we took up our posts and began the attack.

"You know what this place is saying to me?" asked Halitov.

"No, Rooslin," I moaned. "What's it saying to you?"

"Come inside for spaghetti and meatballs, because this might be your last meal."

Poe drew in a long breath through his nose. "Smells really good. My treat."

Halitov practically leapt into the place. We asked for a table in the back and settled down to salads and fresh bread, my stomach groaning in anticipation of the pasta to come.

"So you like spaghetti and meatballs?" Poe asked Halitov.

My former XO closed his eyes in ecstasy. "Eating spaghetti and meatballs is not a matter of life and death. It's more important than that."

Poe grinned. "I see."

I made a face at my comrade. "Everywhere we go, that's all he orders. You'd never know he has Russian blood in him, though he does take to the Tau Ceti vodka pretty well."

"What's it matter?" asked Halitov, jabbing a black olive and a huge hunk of hydroponic lettuce into his mouth. "When you got no woman, only food is left."

After rolling my eyes, I regarded Poe. "So, you think it'll work?"

"I think it's the best chance we have," he said. "We would have never come up with a plan like that. Thank you."

"Don't thank me yet. Anyway, there's something else I've been wanting to discuss. Rooslin and I were involved in an accident. There are problems with our conditioning, and as you can probably tell, we've been aging at an accelerated rate. But Eugene was involved in the same accident."

"Only he hasn't aged," said Poe, with a knowing gleam in his eyes. "He told me about that. And this may come as a surprise, but he asked if I could help."

"No shit?" said Halitov. "Guess he's only two-thirds the asshole I thought he was."

I shushed Halitov, then said, "Can we get Eugene to a doctor or some medical facility? Maybe run some tests? Figure out what's different? Our lives literally depend on it."

"Running tests won't help," said Poe. "Eugene is a neovic—and that's the difference."

"Whoa. Hold on a second." Halitov aimed his fork at Poe. "You're going to sit there and tell me that he's not aging because of his religion?"

"I just did."

"Bullshit. There's something physical here, and we can pinpoint the difference."

"Good luck trying." Poe straightened as the waitress delivered our entrees.

"What is it about being a neovic that helps him?" I asked.

Poe shrugged. "It's everything."

"Well, this is easy," began Halitov, his sarcasm not

missing a beat. "All we have to do is convert, turn over our worldly possessions, and start talking vague and mysterious."

Poe fixed Halitov with a solemn stare. "Captain, we are *not* a cult. I wouldn't even call us an organized religion. We're simply people trying to make connections."

"Through prayer and meditation," I muttered, thinking aloud. "Maybe Eugene's always prayed, always meditated, and he's more in control of his thoughts and his body than we are."

"Or maybe his genes shielded him from the accident," suggested Halitov. "And all this metaphysical mystic crap is exactly that."

"Make no mistake," said Poe. "You were placed here for a reason—to save us—and, perhaps, save yourselves."

"Know what? These are the best meatballs I've ever tasted, but you two are ruining them." Halitov grimaced at his plate. "Can we all shut up and eat?"

I waved him off, leaned toward Poe. "Tell me more about the way you meditate."

"After we eat, I'll let you try it for yourself."

"What is this place?" I asked Poe as we ventured into a narrow cavern that had taken us twenty minutes via airjeep to reach. "Narrow" was being generous. I had to turn sideways to follow him inside, and Halitov said that his meatball-laden gut would not stand for such abuse, so he waited for us in the tunnel.

"We discovered it a few years ago," said Poe. "Just follow me."

I hesitated. "First, you tell me why you dragged us out here."

"I told you, to help."

"How?"

"You'll see. Come on."

He left me behind, and I stood there, shaking with indecision. Finally, I swore and hurried after him.

The passage grew a meter or so wider, yet we remained hunched over for another few minutes until we abruptly reached a ledge overlooking a perfectly spherical chamber of translucent ice cast in the orange glow of Poe's searchlight. The opposite wall stood some fifty meters away and swept seamlessly upward without signs of drilling or the melting techniques I had seen elsewhere in the colony.

"Racinian?" I asked, imagining those ancient aliens manipulating the quantum bond to construct the place in such flawless detail.

"We think so," said Poe. "And we think this moon is a companion world to Exeter. In the center of this chamber is a perforation in the space-time continuum, one the Racinians discovered. They built this chamber around it, and it's a safe bet that they harnessed its power."

I squinted toward a point in the middle of the chamber, where, for a split-second, a tiny blue flash erupted. "I've seen something like this on Exeter, though it was more a rift, with these blue orbs that shot from the ground and rose into space. And when I got near it—"

"What?" Poe asked intently.

"I saw something."

"Yes, you did," he said gravely, then regarded the chamber. "I believe the Racinians were also trying to protect themselves from this perforation, and the chamber here is all that's left of their efforts."

"Why do you say that?"

"Because when we found this place, I reached into the bond and jumped to the center."

"Then you saw it, like I did. The beginning of . . . everything."

"You went back?"

"I saw the universe collapse on itself, moving to a point when all matter was one."

Poe looked away a moment, his breath racing. Then he said quickly, "I went forward through my own life. I saw the exact time, place, and hour of my death."

One look into the man's eyes told me that he firmly believed what he had seen, and I'm unsure if I was trying to cheer him up or whether I doubted his vision, but I said, "Maybe you only glimpsed a single thread. One possible future."

"What I saw was like a billion trillion images, each one slightly different, but in all of them I was trying to manipulate my own fate—because I had seen it—and in all of them, I died at the same time, place, and hour."

I drew my brows together. "How were you able to comprehend a billion trillion images?"

"The same way you were able to comprehend the beginning of everything."

I shrugged. "There could be a scientific explanation for what we saw. Maybe they're just hallucinations coming from our subconsciousness and somehow heightened by this seam or perforation or what have you."

"You know they're not. You know they're real."

I sighed loudly. "Why did you show me this? Are you looking for sympathy? Is there something I should know that'll help us with the attack?"

"You want to know how to solve your aging problem," he replied, then pointed at chamber's center. "There's one way to find out."

I snickered. "No, thanks. I'll leave the paradox to rest and take my chances the old-fashioned way."

"Good."

"What?"

"I said good. You'd rather trust in yourself. I should have done the same. Because that's the first step."

"Toward what?"

"Listen carefully, Major. Right now, standing beside this perforation, we're as close to the bond as we can get without using our minds. This is the place where I've trained those neovics who can touch the bond. And this is the place where I can train you."

"Train me? For what?"

"I don't believe you can make yourself young again through sheer force of will, but you *can* stop this accelerated aging. You need to make a connection with the bond that is much more intimate than what you know. When you do that, you'll be able to control what's happening, just as Eugene has done."

"But he told me he doesn't know what's happening."

"That's right. For him, that control occurs naturally, unconsciously. He has always been a neovic."

"Mr. Poe, I'm intrigued by this place and these ideas, but there's a Dr. Vesbesky on board the Wardens' command ship who thinks he has this all figured out. And if we ever get back, I'm going to give him another chance."

"That's fine. Trust in science. But right now, just take a moment. Close your eyes, reach toward the center of yourself, toward what you believe is your burning core. Go there for a moment, and tell me what you see."

Trying not to make a face, I sighed deeply, was about to close my eyes, when Halitov burst onto the ledge. "Excuse me, but we got a big problem," he cried.

"What is it?" Poe asked.

"One of your people just called. Something's going on at the capitol."

"I'm sorry, Major," said Poe, sounding calm despite the news. "Another time. Come on."

Back at the main station conference room, we patched into the security holo images and watched as Alliance Marines tightened their stranglehold on the capitol. Air-jeep patrols were doubled, as were sniper nests and artillery bunkers. You could've received an F in your recon intelligence course and still easily conclude that the enemy had been tipped off.

"Mr. Poe, we need to get off a message so we can warn our CO of a traitor," Halitov sang bitterly. "Seems we share a common problem."

"If there's a traitor among us, it's me," said Poe. "I leaked the information. They know we're going to attack, and they know exactly when. They're waiting for us."

"I knew it," hollered Halitov. "I just knew it!"

"You did not, asshole," I said. "You knew nothing."

Poe swallowed and took a long breath. "Gentlemen, our attack on the capitol is part of a moon-wide assault that myself and the other miners in all five colonies have been organizing for months." Poe directed his attention to me. "Major, you weren't far off the mark when you said that the Marines were herding us into one place so they could launch a major attack. Actually, we're doing that to them. We need as many as possible near the capitol when the bombing begins."

"You set us up for a suicide mission," said Halitov. "Well, guess what? I ain't playing."

"I thought we were the rallying cry," I told Poe.

"Now you're saying we're the diversion? Why didn't you tell us?"

"I told you everything I knew. I wasn't sure of the extent of our role until only a few hours ago."

"Prove it," challenged Halitov.

Poe gripped my shoulder. "Major, you know how military operations work. Flexibility, maneuverability, and misinformation work hand-in-hand."

"But now our people outside won't stand a chance," I said. "Unless you have an alternate plan."

Poe's gaze fell to his boots. "I have nothing."

11 ◆ Miners across five major colonies on Icillica had organized themselves into a resistance and had planned and coordinated a major assault with the help of but a few hundred guardsmen and retired military folks. The simultaneous attack on Marines occupying their cities and provinces would be recorded in history as the single greatest civilian uprising of the entire war. Years later, Halitov and I would say we were proud to have been a part of it, but secretly, we both knew that being a part meant that we'd had front row seats to yet another massacre, with the defeat at Columbia Colony still fresh in our thoughts.

As we hunkered down on the rooftop of a small machine shop about a quarter klick south of the capitol, waiting for our signal, Halitov looked at me and said, "We should've been on Jing's ride."

"When we get in there—"

"You mean *if* we get in there . . ."

"*When* we get in there, I'll launch the drone while you're hacking into their POW records. I want everything you can get on Jing."

"I knew you'd say that. I shouldn't have brought her up. And you know, even if we find out where she is, we still have no ride off this rock. And even if we find one, what's to say those cruisers don't blow us into a navigational nightmare?"

"You're right. You'd better start thinking about that. I'll expect your report within the hour."

"I'll give you my report right now: We are—"

"Don't say it. Let's use reverse psychology and think positively."

"What do you mean?"

"I mean this is going to be one of the easiest ops we've ever run. We're going to stroll right in there, get off the message, find out where Jing is, commandeer a ride out of here, go stop Paul, save Jing, then eat pasta and drink vodka."

"My God, you're right. What was I thinking? And this particle rifle they gave me? I don't even need it. I should throw it away."

"Oh, just hang on to it as a souvenir. Maybe you can test fire it a little bit, once we get down there."

"Yeah, that sounds good."

An unsettling moment of silence passed between us.

"Scott? This is bullshit."

"Yeah, I know."

"I have to say it."

"Go ahead."

He sighed loudly. "We're fucked."

"But maybe that's good, because if someone wrote the story of your life, it wouldn't be boring."

"It'd be a horror story."

I forced a smile, skinned up, activated my HUV, and zoomed in on the capitol building. I panned from sniper's nest to sniper's nest, from airjeep to airjeep, from cannon bunker to cannon bunker. A little over three thousand miners would, according to the Alliance Marines, storm the building, with only about thirteen hundred of them armed with particle weapons. In the

Marines' minds, the battle would resemble something ripped from a text on medieval warfare, with Saxons laying siege to a Celtic fortress. Of course, we had something slightly different in mind.

"Major, we're ready," came Poe's voice over my private channel. "On your signal."

"On my signal. Initiate Alpha Zulu. Mark!"

I had great respect for those civilian miners; they had as much courage as any guardsman or Warden I had ever served with. They came running out of buildings and access tunnels and subway entrances surrounding the capitol. They were the group armed only with conventional pistols, lead pipes, and—believe it or not—rocks. They crowded along the perimeter force fence, firing lead rounds and hurling those rocks, and all the Marines could do was remain in position and stare in disbelief at the amazingly pathetic assault on their position. As Halitov and I used the bond to double-time sideways down our building, we shouldered our rifles, then hit the ground, de-skinned, and charged into the crowd. We needed to get as close as possible to that fence.

With our heads low, we wove into the riot, fists and voices raised around us. I wanted to skin up and glance at my HUV to be sure Poe's ten neovics were doing likewise, but then I'd alert the Marines. I could only hope the others had reached the fence.

"This is your attack?" cried the lieutenant colonel, a portly, unkempt man in his fifties, skinned up and standing in the rear seat of an airjeep hovering over the crowd. His voice came harsh and amplified via his suit. "Are you the only brave souls who dare defy Marines of the Eastern and Western Alliances? Where are your friends? I want them to bear witness as we mow you down like Sunday grass gone too long in the rain."

"Well, Poe didn't lie about him," muttered Halitov over the channel. "Mow them down like Sunday grass? Guy's a nut."

We reached the edge of the crowd, coming as close to the capitol building as we could. I glanced to Halitov, nodded, then spoke over the command channel to our guardsman. "Clock starts at T-minus five minutes. Mark!"

In case our conditioning failed—as it was wont to do—Halitov and I had devised a backup plan. But one look at him told me he was all right, and I already felt the familiar and welcoming tingle. I reached out, willed myself inside the building, into the lobby, bridging the shortest distance that I could. We hoped that doing so would temper the drain on our bodies. I arrived with a chill, and it all hit me at once:

The dizzying backlash of my effort . . .

The Moorish-Gothic architecture of the high-ceilinged and ornate entrance . . .

And the two Marines pivoting to face me, their rifles coming to bear . . .

I threw myself forward into a *biza*, driving myself headfirst toward them, even as I skinned up and wrenched my rifle from my shoulder.

But Halitov had materialized just a few meters to my left and had reacted a half-second more quickly. He had catapulted himself in an *Ai*—the floating kick, counter-kick—and booted the first Marine with one foot, the second with the other. As their heads lolled back, he hit the ground and did a reverse somersault while withdrawing a pair of Ka-bars Poe had given him. He spun and slashed the Marines' throats before they saw him coming. I hit the ground, turned.

Three streams of particle fire struck Halitov, even as a fourth and a fifth caught me in the abdomen, all of them originating from a small bunker constructed at the foot of the broad, main staircase. The bunker, a circular nest of alloy blast plates attached to a titanium frame, stood about two meters tall and provided good horizontal cover for those troops guarding the stairwell, but it hardly protected them from a vertical assault.

In unison, Halitov and I leapt up, shooting a full ten meters to the ceiling, where we turned, struck boots-first, and hung there, inverted, leveling our particle rifles. All five Marines fell under our spray and could not react in time. Their combat skins succumbed, and our rounds chewed into them.

Remaining on the ceiling and exploiting that improbable advance, we darted to the stairwell, taking the walls around, passing the second floor, where the house and senate chambers were located, forging on to the third-floor governor's offices, then passing long halls leading to the executive offices on the fourth. As we ascended, I contacted Poe, who told me his neovics had reached the security bunkers and were working to take down the force fence. They had three minutes before the armed miners outside would launch their attack amid the riotous diversion of the rock-throwers and name-callers.

We had three minutes to seize control of the communications command center and disrupt local transmissions. With that done, I'd be free to launch my comm drone, and Halitov could probe their records for news about Jing. Even then, we only had a few minutes more until we needed to evacuate. According to Poe, miners in Wintadia Colony, along with a dozen or so colonial pilots, were gaining control of a squadron of atmoattack bombers fitted with ice-burrowing missiles that would penetrate the surface and reach the capitol. The blast would level everything within a half kilometer radius and take out perhaps seventy or eighty percent of the garrison. The civilian population in the area was already quietly evacuating, but those three thousand miners would remain until the very last minute.

All of which meant that Halitov and I had a pair of ticking clocks ringing so loudly in our ears that we could barely think straight. But we had to. Those bombers were en route, and I imagined the faint whine of their turbines in the distance.

Panting, we reached the fifth floor, and for a moment I turned my head and was lost in images displayed on a long bank of stained glass windows. The first expedition to Icillica unfolded in striking detail, and the visual narrative continued all the way to the founding of the moon's first colony, Colyad. Abruptly, particle fire turned the magnificent scene into a shower of tumbling glass. We dodged from the spray, toward an inverted sign ahead:

COMMUNICATIONS COMMAND CENTER
LEVEL FIVE CLEARANCE

We streaked down one wall, glanced furtively around the corner, as the power suddenly went out and backup generators kicked in. All right. We had to get past four Marines crouching along both sides of the entrance, two hallways spanned by force beams, and a spacecraft-like hatch of alloy as thick as my fist. Make that five Marines. No, six, seven, eight . . .

"What the hell?" Halitov thought aloud. "They're diverting people up here."

"Doesn't matter. It's all about the clock. They're all going down. Now!" I vaulted down from the wall, hit the floor, then I screamed like a maniac and ran toward the Marines, whipping myself into a killing frenzy. So much particle fire exploded toward me that the world became flashes of white light and booming and the beating of my heart. My tactical computer issued multiple warnings about the drain on my skin: sixty percent, fifty percent, forty-two, as I fired point-blank at the first Marine, held the bead until he collapsed, then spun and fired at the second Marine, as my skin plunged to twenty-two percent power.

Jerking like a man suddenly electrified, I shouldered my weapon and launched myself over the second pair of Marines, withdrawing my Ka-bars as I did so. With the blade tips held between my thumb and forefingers, I flicked my wrists and sent the blades tumbling. Even as they flew, I reached into the bond and guided each of them through the air, feeling the connection between the particles in them, in the air, in the Marines' skins, and even in their heads—which is exactly where they struck. One man got it in the cheek; the other woman blinked as my blade struck her left eye. And it all happened in a flicker of death that drove me on.

In fact, I had no idea where Halitov was or what he was doing. I reached the first row of force beams, willed myself to the other side, then hesitated. *Oh, shit.* I felt as though I just been pistol-whipped. I glanced back at the force beams. The drain should not have been that strong. My eyes felt very heavy, and for some reason, all I could see in my head was a page from the *Chronology of Important Events in Galactic Expansion:*

2284
First convention of business and political leaders

*from all extrasolar and solar colonies held in Columbia
Colony, on planet Rexi-Calhoon. Informal assembly
created. Negotiations begin to establish a new Colonial
Alliance. Two high-ranking officials from 12 System
Guard Corps attend convention to listen to arguments
why they should break from alliances and become new
colonial military.*

"You all right?" Halitov asked, materializing beside
me. "Come on!"

I just looked at him. Who was he? And I felt com-
pelled to read aloud the page in my head: "By mid-year,
nearly one million Exxo-Tally employees killed on frigid
world of Icillica in Procyon Binary star system. Akin to
old Russian Arctic and yielding similar deposits of
nickel, iron ore, and apatite, Icillica predicted to become
next Gatewood-Callista and geologic cash cow for
colonies. Life-support systems in forty-seven of fifty-one
mining facilities go offline, as do all three redundancy
systems. Corporate investigators declare malfunction an
act of sabotage but cannot gather enough evidence to
formally indict alliance military."

"What're you talking about?" he screamed, then
shook me by the shoulders. "We have to go!"

I stared blankly at him, the page flashing over and
over.

And then you could almost hear the click in his head
as he remembered something Kristi Breckinridge had
told us: "*We have learned that as the aging progresses,
there's a long-term memory imbalance that interferes
with the short-term. You can't remember if you shut off
the vid, and you can't stop reciting some obscure data
cerebroed into the deepest parts of your mind.*"

"Oh my god," Halitov muttered. "Oh my god!
Scott!" He slapped me across the face. "You're not go-

ing to let this happen. You're stronger than this. Come on!"

I narrowed my gaze on this person who had just struck me, my hand going to the flame in my cheek, my mind screaming against the mental thumbing through thousands of records. Many hours later, Halitov would tell me that he had never seen such a lost look on my face. I had to believe him, because I didn't remember anything that happened until we were on the other side of the command room hatch, Halitov dragging me inside, my combat skin fully depleted, my right arm throbbing from a superficial wound to my bicep.

Groaning, Halitov lay me on the floor, then shut the hatch, just as more particle fire tied ribbons of lightning across it. "See that, you old bastard?" he asked. "I, Captain Rooslin Halitov, am a hero. You remember that first before you remember Columbia." His gaze went vacant as he glanced at a display in his HUV. "Shit, we're running out of time. We have to move!"

"We're inside already?" I asked, wincing over the needles in my arm. "And what happened to my combat skin?"

"You could ask them," Halitov said, pointing to the fourteen dead communications specialists slumped at their terminals. Some had their throats slit; others had swallowed particle fire or had had their necks broken. Halitov's signature was everywhere.

"What happened to me?"

"Uh, you were just a little drained, blacked out or something," he lied (later he would tell me the truth). "You jam their comm and get off that probe, I'll work on finding Jing." He seized my wrist, dragged me to my feet, then led me to a chair before a myriad of touch screens with a remarkably familiar layout that matched cerebroed data in my head.

"Okay," I told him. "I got this."

While his fingers danced over the screens at a terminal behind me, I hacked into their system using encryption codes confiscated during a black op on Mars. Nineteen Wardens had given their lives to obtain the data, and I felt a sense of reverence as the computer accepted the codes, granted me access, and I immediately disrupted all Alliance local communications by broadcasting a pulse signal on their channels. Of course, they could switch to some of ours, but that would take time and be a logistical nightmare. The disruption was temporary, but it would be enough. "Poe, copy?" I said over our channel.

"Copy. Comm is down," he reported, particle fire echoing behind him. "They're already skinning and deskinning to get it back up. Good work, Major."

"How's it coming on that fence?"

"Shutting down now. With ten seconds to spare. See you outside."

"Copy." I spun to face Halitov. "Anything?"

"Not yet."

"Well, you'd better move."

"What do you think I'm doing?"

With my hands beginning to tremble, I typed in an encrypted text message addressed to Ms. Brooks. I kept it short and fragmentary: *Captured on Exeter. Shot down over Icillica. At Colyad now. Rebellion in progress. Need extraction. Priority note: Paul Beauregard is our traitor. Confirm: Paul Beauregard is our traitor. Detain immediately.* I switched on the camera and spoke rapidly: "Ms. Brooks, Paul sold us out the Alliances because he's trying to save his mother. They got Jing, sent her off somewhere else. We desperately need your help. But no matter what, you have to detain Paul immediately. He gave up the encryption codes at Columbia. All of those people died because of him. He admitted that to me. You have to stop him. St. Andrew, out."

The text, audio, and video automatically saved to the chip under separate files, and the comm drone was already spun up, its engines engaged. I spoke rapidly with the drone's onboard computer, feeding it every authorization code in my head, the numbers and letters pouring from my lips with a machine-like precision that startled me. With that done, I banged a floating button on the screen and watched the monitor as the drone burst from its pad. "Message is away!" I cried, breathing a huge sigh of relief. I remembered that if those codes failed, the drone would be blown out of space before it tawted. I called up the local satnet and watched radar images of the probe as it left Icillica, rising high enough into the upper atmosphere to make the jump. "Come on, baby," I whispered. "Take the codes. Take the codes."

COMM DRONE TAWTING OUT OF RANGE reported a databar hovering near the green blip on my screen. I burst from my seat. "Yeah! It's out of the system!"

The little probe would tawt back to Exeter, and even if *Vanguard One* had already left the system, the drone would automatically access the satnet to find out where the ship had gone, then it would tawt again and again to complete its mission. Once it came within range, it would broadcast both the audio/video message and the text version on all emergency channels. At least one message had to get through.

"Still nothing on Jing yet," said Halitov. "They got

those records behind so many walls it's ridiculous."

Sparks shot from a small hole in the hatch, then grew into a broad fountain. "Just keep trying," I told him, not bothering to mention that the Marines outside were cutting through. He would notice the sparks in a moment anyway. I took a deep breath and opened the command channel. "All right, Poe, my message is away. Evac is on your command. What's the status on our birds?"

"Nine minutes, thirty seconds to drop," he answered, his voice burred by exertion. "And Major, we . . . we . . . we need you outside."

I swung back to the terminal, pulled up images from the security cameras, and gasped.

Once the force fence had come down, those poorly armed miners were supposed to retreat, allowing our armed forces—led by guardsmen—to launch their assault. I can only speculate on why they did what they did, but, perhaps, driven into a killing rage by the lieutenant colonel, those people had stormed the compound, waving their feeble pipes and pistols at Marines with fingers poised over the triggers of their big particle cannons. They had run just a few meters past the fence when the Marines had opened up on the mob, shredding them into piles of flesh and blood. Hundreds of bodies lay strewn along the fence line, with armed miners and guardsmen crouching behind them and trading fire with the Marines. Viewing it all on the screen made it seem less real, and comprehending the full extent of that carnage would take me years of reflection.

"Anything, Rooslin?"

"Just got into the records now."

"They're getting slaughtered outside. We have to go help."

"No problem. Our buddies outside that hatch are going to cut through and roll out the red carpet for us."

I stared at the glowing, meter-long seam in the hatch. "I know."

Halitov drew his head closer to one screen, then banged a knuckle on it. "Got her. Sol system. She's in the Nereid Research and Testing Facility."

I closed my eyes, braced myself. "Any record of a brainwipe?"

"None here, but you know that doesn't mean anything."

"Any transfer orders pending?"

"Negative. But she's definitely there."

"All right," I said, turning toward the hatch and wondering just how many Marines waited on the other side. "We can't chance this. We need to be outside. Now."

"I'm with you," Halitov said. "North Wing bunker?"

"That's the one."

"Hey, Scott?" he called as I was about to close my eyes and find the bond. "Stay close, okay?"

I frowned. "Yeah, sure."

And with that, we willed ourselves behind two Marines operating a particle cannon near the north wing. Halitov plunged his blade into the back of the first operator, while I gave the second one a headache from which he would never recover. We shot up the cannon's control panel, then, fighting against the weariness of exploiting the bond, we fled along the wall, toward the next bunker.

"That's it," said Poe over our command channel. "Major, let's get everybody out. Now!"

Miners broke from cover and charged away from the fence line. The enemy reaction was equally swift. Airjeeps swooped down, mercilessly strafing those miners, as the lieutenant colonel lorded over the scene from his own airjeep, shouting, "That's right, run! But you can't escape from the iron fist of the Alliance Marine Corps!"

"That asshole killed children," said Halitov as we ran.

"Rooslin, I know what you're thinking."

"I'll do it with or without you."

"I know. So I'm coming."

"I thought you weren't about revenge."

"I'm not. But sometimes justice needs a little help."

As the lieutenant colonels' airjeep passed overhead, we crouched down then sprang up, rocketing through the air two stories until we reached the side doors, clutched them, then hung from the jeep, our boots dangling. With a solid jerk, I pulled myself up and dropped into the backseat.

The lieutenant colonel raised his QQ60 particle pistol at me, craned his neck, saw Halitov, gaped, then returned his attention to me as Halitov took the man's fat head in his hands. I winced as the colonel's head twisted at a bizarre angle. At least I couldn't hear the bones crack over the battle's din. The colonel fell limp, and, with a sudden flood of rage, I threw him over the side. As his body dropped, miners whirled back and fired upon it, broad beams of particle fire ripping it apart before it thumped on the quickcrete. From somewhere in the distance, a cheer erupted.

The airjeep's pilot, a young second lieutenant, turned back and raised his hands. "I have a little boy."

"Yeah? What about all the little boys and girls you've been killing here, huh? Huh? HUH?"

Before I could stop him, Halitov raised his rifle and literally blew the pilot's head off.

"Rooslin!" I screamed.

He just looked at me, then dropped over the side. I followed, plummeting through his wake.

On the ground, we bolted for the fence line, fire still whizzing overhead and thumping hard into the bodies we veered around and threaded between and jumped over. I checked my HUV. Skin power at only thirty percent but rising. If we didn't reach cover soon, a few well-directed and sustained beads would revert my skin to zero power and leave me vulnerable. Halitov knew that, and he placed himself near me, letting his skin take most of the fire as we charged toward an airjeep waiting for us near the great marble columns of the Colyad Museum of Natural History. A bead locked onto my back, drove my skin down to five percent, four, three—

Halitov shoved me onto the ground, turned back, and stood there, taking all the fire himself while unleashing his own bead toward the airjeep targeting us from above. His skin flickered out, even as the jeep soared by and the incoming ceased as smoke poured from its turbines. I scrambled to my feet, and together, we rode a wave of life-saving adrenaline as we ran to the jeep, reached it, hopped in the back, and the pilot, one of our guardsmen, took off, the wind whipping so hard that my eyes began to tear.

"ETA on our birds?" I called to Poe, but he didn't answer.

Instead, Val d'Or's voice came over the channel. "It's Eugene, Scott. We're just under a minute. Get out of there."

"Yeah, thanks for the tip. Where's Poe?"

"He got shot up pretty bad, but he's with us. We'll meet you at Point Victory."

"We're on our way."

"You know, if those bombers don't get through . . ." Halitov began over the rumbling engines.

"Don't jinx us," I hollered. "They'll make it."

We turned back as the airjeep blasted over the city, coming within mere meters of rooftops, small communications dishes, and suspended walkways. In the distance, hugged by those massive walls of ice within the even larger chamber that held the entire colony, sat the capitol building, waiting innocently. Some miners, mostly the older folks and a few vets, remained behind to fight the good fight until they were either shot and killed or disintegrated by the bombs. Their whole lives had been coming to it, and as muzzle flashes shone like glitter and larger explosions cast flickering shadows across the ice, I imagined that beneath all of the chaos, those good people were dying by the minute, yet they hit the ground feeling proud of themselves, their brothers, their colony.

With that image still crystallizing, my attention lifted to the far off ceiling as a rumble so loud that our airjeep's engine seemed to whisper emanated from the ice. The ceiling splintered into hundreds of narrow fissures as pieces of ice rained down in a bizarre subterranean hailstorm. Our pilot swore and banked hard to port, narrowly missing a fragment larger than our ride as the smaller pieces pinged on the hull.

"Jesus . . ." shouted Halitov, leaning forward and reflexively covering his head despite his regenerating combat skin.

I did likewise. "Poe didn't tell us about this!"

Amazingly, the rumble grew even louder, and I couldn't help but steal a look back as, in the bat of an eye, the bombs, four of them to be precise, blew through the ceiling, hit the capitol building, and tossed up a swelling blue-gray cloud backlit by hundreds of fireballs.

"Holy shit," was all Halitov could say, and I thought he was referring to the blast, but when I looked up, I realized that our pilot lay slumped in his seat, a sharp-edged ice fragment jutting from his shoulder. The airjeep suddenly dove toward a row of buildings. A proximity alarm wailed from the cockpit controls, along with the computer's monotone warning: "Impact in four seconds."

12 ❯   **With no time** to wrestle the pilot out of his seat and seize the controls (which were set to user-specific mode anyway), Halitov and I abandoned ship as the airjeep plowed into the nearest building, shattering windows and pulverizing stone before it vanished into a network of offices.

As multiple explosions resounded from above, I found the bond and hit the ground with but a second to spare. While my conditioning saved me from the full impact of the ten-plus meter fall, the sudden connection was jarring. I fell on my stomach as yet another explosion sent debris jetting from the gaping hole in the building.

Halitov took my wrist, hauled me up, then pulled me away from the shower of glass and stone and shattered office furniture. We sprinted off into the eeriness of the deserted city street, the icy rain diminishing as the ceiling creaked and began to settle. For a moment I imagined that great mantle of ice collapsing on the entire colony, burying forty square kilometers and quick-sealing our fates.

"We're still within the blast radius," Halitov said, reading a databar in his HUV. "And we're still about a full kilometer away from the rendezvous."

"And I'm still waiting for the good news."

"Hey, man. We're still alive. But if that's something you're fond of, you'd best haul ass and not look back."

I complied but still ordered my tactical computer to display an image of the street behind us. A massive dust cloud swallowed the buildings and pavement, and the damned thing's hunger drove it much faster than we were running.

One block, two, three, a right down a street lined with mining hovers, a left down another lined with cargo containers, and the cloud still came. Even as it touched our shoulders, we found an alcove and charged beneath. Halitov shot open a door ahead, and we rode out the wave inside a small building, not realizing until the dust settled that we were standing in, of all places, yet another small Italian restaurant, the menu posted on the front door. Either the universe was trying to urge me to eat more pasta or Halitov just had a knack for finding good Italian food and saving our lives. He ran a finger over the menu and paused on spaghetti and meatballs. "We have to come back here," he said.

"I figured."

"How's your skin?"

"About fifty now."

"Yeah, that's where I'm at," he said, shoving open the door, then reflexively waving the dust from his eyes despite the combat skin's protection.

"Hey, Rooslin?"

"What?"

"I won't forget what you did back there."

"If you do, I'll remind you."

"I know you will."

"Hey, the way our luck runs, I'm sure you'll get your chance to repay me." He trotted off.

I started after him, stopped, locked up.

2285

Construction begins on agricultural domes of Tau Ceti XI. No other planet has soil more fertile and adaptable to Terran-based crops. With grain production on Aire-Wu cut in half by an unknown disease, Tau Ceti XI becomes leading producer of grain, forage, fruit, nut, vegetable, and nonfood crops, as well as leader in development of new chemicals from organic raw materials. Inte-Micro and Exxo-Tally begin formal and covert negotiations with 12 System Guard Corps representatives who favor colonial secession. Construction begins on first colonial military base within Tau Ceti's agricultural domes.

Someone pried open my left eyelid, directed a small light into it, then did the same to my right. "Pupils equal and reactive to light."

I jolted, snapped open my eyes, and an old man's face came into focus. Bald, gray beard, soft blue eyes. If he wasn't a doctor or medic, he ought to play one in films and holos.

"Easy there, Major. You're all right. I'm Dr. Roshmu, and you're in Casa Province, Point Victory. Your friend brought you here."

I slowly sat up, blinked hard. A makeshift medical ward had been established inside a high school gymnasium, with hundreds of miners lying in cots and attended to by doctors roaming the aisles. I'd seen treatment sectors for Mass Casualty Incidents before, but nothing as large or as well-staffed as Point Victory's.

"I'll call your friend," the doc said.

"Thanks. And, uh, did you examine me?"

"Major, I tried. But whatever's happening to you is way beyond anything I've ever seen. I can't even describe your brain activity. I'm not sure what I was looking at."

"What you were looking at is classified. And those records? You'll need to destroy all copies. Can I trust you on this?"

"My son is a guardsman, Second Battalion, Sirius Company." The doc spoke rapidly into a translucent boom mike at his lips, then winked at me. "It's done." He excused himself.

I lay back on the pillow, trying to remember what had happened. We had been inside the restaurant, and then I had seen that image, that page from—

A chill struck me. Was my memory misfiring like that old woman I had encountered in the Minsalo Caves? Would my life finally end the way hers had?

"Look at this guy, lying around while I do all the work," Halitov said as he loped down the aisle. "Yeah, here he is, saved once again by my capable hands."

"Capable, if not modest."

He grinned. "In war, modesty will get you killed."

"All right, seriously now. I want you to tell me exactly what happened. Don't pull any punches."

"You know what's happening," he began slowly. "But if you want to hear it from me . . ."

We spent about fifteen minutes talking. He described my "blackout" inside the capitol and the second one inside the restaurant. He had carried me on his back all the way to Point Victory, nearly a full kilometer. In point of fact, during the entire journey I had been reciting colonial history and a parts list from a J229 endo/exo military cargo transport. There were 151,971 parts on that list, and Halitov found the conversation anything but entertaining.

"I'm scared, Scott," he finally said. "Really scared.

Because if it's happening to you, then it'll happen to me. And I don't know when or where."

"Then we stay together. And we help each other."

"What if it happens to us at the same time?"

I just looked away, then lifted my tone. "Hey, have you seen Poe? Did he make it?"

"He's here, but I haven't seen him. I know he was in surgery for a long time. He left Eugene in charge of his group, and I have to say, that asshole's been doing a pretty good job coordinating with the miners in the other colonies. Word has it these people are actually winning. They gained control of the capitol in Wintadia, and the garrisons in the other colos are about to fall. Pretty amazing, huh?"

"Yeah, but what about those cruisers in orbit? They'll send down more air and ground support."

"They haven't so far. Maybe they've exhausted their personnel. And with just two ships, they're barely hanging on to the system."

"I hope you're right. Because it won't be rain falling on this colony's parade." He glanced up and nodded.

"I'd like to see Eugene. Maybe we can help."

"You mean you want to mop up, too?"

"He'll need a Blast Damage Assessment, and it's part of our jobs."

"Oh, so we work here now? No one's told me where I can pick up my paycheck."

"They don't issue checks that small." I rolled off the cot and started shakily down the aisle.

Halitov arrived at my shoulder and reluctantly led us through the treatment sector, through a long corridor, and into a bare-bones communications center established inside one of the school's computer labs. Miners serving security detail scanned our tacs then allowed us inside. Halitov remarked that several Alliance suicide bombers had already tried to gain entry, but their attempts had been quickly thwarted.

Val d'Or glanced up, spotted us, then detached himself from a terminal where he'd been studying a long bank of displays. He glanced quizzically at me. "Scott, you don't look good."

"This was never about beauty, huh?"

"No doubt. One look at Halitov confirms that." Val d'Or smiled broadly at my former XO, who returned a lopsided grin and scratched his eye with his middle finger.

"How can we help?" I asked. "You know, you could put us on BDA back at the capitol."

"That's already done. Reports coming in now. We knocked the garrison down to about twenty percent, and they've fallen back into the mines. We're rooting them out now."

"See? He doesn't need us," Halitov said, elbowing me. "Let's go back to that restaurant."

I elbowed him back, faced Val d'Or. "What else can we do?"

"Two things. You can listen to a bit of good news, then you can go see Poe. He's been asking for you, Scott."

"How is he?"

Val d'Or sighed loudly. "He's dying."

I shuddered, remembering Poe's story about seeing his death. "How long?"

"Could be anytime now."

"Does he know?"

"No one's told him. But he knows."

Of course he does.

Halitov took a few steps away, clearly uneasy with the conversation. "You said you have some news?"

"A colonial battle group just tawted into the system. I haven't been able to raise them yet, but maybe your message got through."

That woke my frown. "Even if it did, they couldn't send help this quickly."

"Then maybe Poe's word got out."

"What're you talking about?"

"A few months ago, his people hijacked an ore barge and got off a short-range transmission. They thought that if the signal reached satnet, then even ships just skipping through the system would pick it up. Maybe one did. Or maybe the brass have been monitoring Alliance communications and are aware of the attack. Who knows. But I'm not arguing. I'll take the miracle, thank you."

"As soon as you raise one of those ships, I'd like to speak with its skipper."

"I knew you would."

"And Eugene?" I extended my hand. "You've done a lot here. You could've gone AWOL, but you made the right decision. You helped save a lot of lives."

"But not all of them. It was Poe who helped me understand my calling."

I nodded. "We'll go see him now."

Inside a small classroom converted into an intensive care ward, Poe lay on a gurney, eyes closed, his pale cheeks haloed by the flickering light of a half dozen touchscreens suspended behind him.

"I'll be here," Halitov said, hesitating in the doorway.

"What's the matter?"

"I don't know. The battlefield and all that death? I know how to turn it off. But it's this . . . this is what gets to me now."

"Okay." I crossed the room, passing several other patients connected to wires and tubes, and reached Poe, whose chest was wrapped into a translucent bandage filled with neoanticiline, a fluid meant to prevent infection. "Mr. Poe," I said softly.

His eyelids flickered open, his lips already forming a smile. "Major. Thanks for coming."

I took his hand in my own. "We did it."

"Yes. They called. We answered."

Poe and I grinned at each other, until my grin faded. "I have to ask you something."

"You want to know if this is the vision I had back in the chamber."

"Yes."

"In that vision, you come to me here, and you ask me if this is the vision, and I say exactly what I'm saying now."

"I'm sorry."

"Don't be. It's true that since I found out I've been anticipating—and dreading—your arrival. Yet I've realized something. I was meant to help my people, but I was also placed here to help you, because you're going to help millions more. Go back to the perforation. Meditate there. Take your thoughts beyond the mnemosyne and find the bond on your own. The results will surprise you. Now promise me you'll do that."

"I promise."

"Use my airjeep. The coordinates are set. But first send your friend over here."

"He's a little, uh—"

"I know. Send him."

After a brief argument with Halitov, I persuaded him to speak with Poe. I watched as Poe whispered something in my friend's ear, then gestured him off.

"What did he say?" I asked as we left the classroom.

Halitov gave me a strange look. "Nothing."

Out in the hallway, my tac beeped, and I took a message from Val d'Or, who said he had established a link with the *Thomas Krieger*, one of our long-range destroyers spearheading the battle group. Poe's message had, indeed, been received, and for a moment, I wondered if Poe had foreseen everything that had happened. Maybe he had known all along that the battle group would arrive and help ensure the colonists' victory. I could have easily driven myself mad with suppositions, so I took Val d'Or's lead and didn't argue with the miracle. I spoke with the ship's skipper, who told me that he'd have troops on the ground within two hours and would dispatch a dropshuttle for us. I told him that I had sent word to Ms. Brooks and Colonel Beauregard, but he said his orders had not come through them but through Fleet Command.

"So we don't have much time to eat and get ready to go," said Halitov. "So screw getting ready. Let's eat."

"I want to go somewhere else first."

"Then I'll meet up with you."

"No, you have to come."

His lip twisted. "Are we going back to that chamber?"

"I just want to try something. And Rooslin, what did Poe say to you?"

"Just some unbelievable bullshit."

My gaze said I wasn't letting him off the hook.

He squirmed then added, "I just don't believe how he knew."

"About what?"

"When we were inside the capitol and I was running a search for Jing, I ran a concurrent search for my sister. I found her, all right. She's serving aboard the *Mao Triggor*. They're part of a security flotilla around Neptune. Bottom line? If you want to get to Jing, you'll have to go through my sister first. Fuckin' small universe . . ."

"Yeah, it is. So Poe knew you ran the search?"

"Yup. And he told me that my calling would first be with her, then with you."

"What did he mean by that?"

Halitov threw up his hands. "I don't have any plans to join the Alliance Navy, I can tell you that. So maybe the old guy's just drugged up and delusional."

"Or maybe, somehow, he's right."

With a wave of his hand, Halitov dismissed the thought and quickened his pace.

Outside the school, I explained to Poe's people that he had allowed me to borrow his airjeep. They confirmed that with him, and in short order, Halitov and I were whirring above the still-deserted streets, the dusty stench of the capitol bombing strong enough to warrant skinning up. We reached the entrance to the perforation in about thirty minutes, and within a few minutes after that, we stood on the ledge overlooking the sphere of translucent ice, with the perforation tossing up azure flashes at its core.

"So what the hell are we looking at?" Halitov asked.

I began to explain. He balked.

"Okay, Rooslin. You tell me what we're looking at and how it got here."

"I can't. And I won't. Because I don't care!"

"Listen, Rooslin. Poe said we're as close to the bond as we can be. He trained his people here, and there's no doubt that they can manipulate the bond without having been conditioned."

"Okay, so we got the tour. Can we go now?"

"This place can help us. Poe told me to close my eyes and reach toward the center of myself. He said we can tap into the bond naturally, and if we learn to do that, we'll be able to control our aging, like Eugene has."

"We don't know if he's doing that."

"Shouldn't we at least try? You would like to get laid some time in the near future, wouldn't you?"

Halitov saw his whole sex life flash before his eyes, or at least that's what his far off expression seemed to indicate. "Point taken. What do we have to do?"

I repeated Poe's instructions, then followed them, closing my eyes and focusing my energy on an imaginary point, a point burning a brilliant white. Within the penumbra I saw two images of myself: one solid, fleshy, quite real; the other ghostly, incorporeal, with arms spreading like wings. I willed myself toward that specter and found myself enveloped in it, tingling with that familiar sensation as I felt the particles within myself, the ice, and even those within Halitov standing nearby. "I think I've done it," I said. "It's different here. It's like I can choose either path, one through my body, and one through my thoughts."

"I see it, too," he said. "A body. A ghost. And the ghost takes me to the bond. This is weird, man! Maybe this is where science and the spiritual collide."

"But what now? How do we heal ourselves? Poe never told me that."

"Let's go back. Maybe he can tell us."

I opened my eyes, and a voice inside told me that it was already too late. I broke Halitov from his trancelike state, and as we wriggled through the tunnel exit, I called Val d'Or, whose somber words echoed that inner voice. Poe was gone.

"Of course he dies without telling us," Halitov said. "Linda Haspel is *still* not through with me."

"We'll just have to keep trying," I said. "We have to find the bond without the mnemosyne and somehow gain control over them. We don't have a choice."

"Oh, there's always a choice. Unfortunately, death is always one of them."

We boarded the airjeep and headed back to the school, where Eugene told us that the driver of an SS *Morrow* waited to transport us to the surface.

"Man, it seems like only yesterday that we were just cadets and I was watching you cut Halitov's rope on old Whore Face," I told Val d'Or.

"Yeah, we've grown up a lot since then, huh?"

I shook his hand. "My report will reflect everything you've done here."

"I appreciate that. Thank you." He faced Halitov and spoke in a falsetto. "And you, Mr. Halitov, *you* I'll miss the most . . ."

Halitov, who had been proffering his hand, withdrew it quickly. "Have a nice life, asshole."

"You, too."

Once inside the SS *Morrow*, something occurred to Halitov, and he swore loudly.

"What?"

"You rushed me out of there, and we forgot to eat!"

"We'll get something on board the *Krieger*."

"You think that shit'll be half as good as this local stuff? You're dreaming, man."

"Now I know this aging problem is really getting to you. Our lives are all about planning to eat, eating, then planning to eat again."

Halitov just leaned forward, elbows on his hips, chin pressed squarely on a palm. "If they get the sauce right, then even if the pasta is undercooked, it'll still be okay . . ."

I left him to his imaginary meal and threw my head back, realizing that I finally had a chance to breathe and turn all of my thoughts to Jing. I imagined her lying on an examine table and being probed like a laboratory animal. Then I imagined myself exploding into that lab to sweep her away from it all. But deep down I knew her rescue, if one ever came, would never be that romantic or easy.

Once on the surface, we met up with the dropshuttle and were summarily ferried back to the battle group. Our dropshuttle pilot reported that the Alliance cruisers had tawted out of the system instead of engaging. The system was ours.

Captain James W. Callahan, a luminous figure with a snowy white widow's peak and the build of an athlete half his age, greeted us on the *Thomas Krieger*'s bridge with a salute and hearty handshakes. "Gentlemen, your reputation precedes you, and it's a distinct pleasure to have you on board my ship."

"Meaning no disrespect, Captain," I began. "But we'd like to leave as quickly as possible."

He smiled knowingly. "That second chip to Ms.

Brooks and Colonel Beauregard has already tawted out. All we can do is hope that they contact us before we get new orders—otherwise you'll be coming with us or heading back down to the moon."

"Let's hope it doesn't come to that. You'll contact us the minute you hear something?"

"Of course. Now then, I'll have my XO show you to your quarters. You'll have access to satnet there, and I've given you authorization to the encrypted logs per your request. You'll find war news there as well."

"Thank you, Captain. I appreciate it."

"And Captain?" Halitov asked. "I have a request."

My cheeks warmed. I figured he was about to ask for his spaghetti and meatballs, but he surprised me by wanting to speak with the ship's psychiatrist. The captain would arrange an appointment.

We opted to dine in my quarters, and there we stuffed ourselves with pasta glossed with a thin layer of marinara. Halitov ate the meal but spent the entire time cursing the chef. And worse, he had tried to score a bottle of Tau Ceti vodka, but no one would even admit to having one.

I glued myself to the terminal and stared repeatedly at the schematics of Nereid Research and Testing Facility where Jing was being held. I split the image and considered the flotilla, though the data I had on it was over a week old. The Alliances could have increased their defenses, and for all I knew, Jing could have already been moved since we last accessed the database. The uncertainty left me torn.

"Well, I'm going to go see the shrink," Halitov said, tugging at the collar of his new uniform.

"You're doing the right thing. And you know I'm here if you need me."

"Yeah," he said softly. "And you know, she's the only family I have left."

"Hey, man, you'll be all right. And maybe one day you'll get to see her."

He just glanced away and left.

The screen beckoned again, and I went back through the schematics, committing them to memory and whispering, "I'll get you out of there. I promise."

With my eyes growing sore, I decided to watch some war news, and there was my old friend, Ms. Elise Rainey, staring back at me from the screen and reporting from Kennedy-Centauri. Ten colonies had fallen to the alliances; with Icillica won back, nine of the seventeen were still under Alliance occupation. She went on with more local news about the riots, but my thoughts wandered back to the meeting we should have had and to the fact that she had contacted my father. I wanted to repay her, and I knew she wanted information, but I wasn't sure what I could give her without compromising my position. An incoming call from the bridge flashed on the screen's databar. I thumbed the remote.

"Major St. Andrew?" Callahan said from his command chair. "*Vanguard One* has just tawted in. I have Ms. Brooks for you."

I straightened in the chair and rubbed the haze from my eyes as our Colonial Security Chief appeared, seated at her desk. "Major," she said with a gasp, then took a moment to compose herself. "We received your message."

"Where's Paul now?"

"He's leading a joint operation of Wardens and West-

ern Alliance Marines. They're heading to Sol, to the
Exxo-Tally industrial ring station at Lagrange point
five. We're expecting an Eastern Alliance attack on the
station any day now."

"Whoa. Slow down. Wardens are working with Western Alliance Marines?"

"Remember when I told you how fourteen nations—
including the United States—split from the Western Alliance because of what happened at Columbia? Well, a
civil war among the Alliances has erupted, and we're
going to take full advantage of it. Paul's leading the very
first joint operation, and they just tawted out a few
hours ago."

"You let him go?"

"I had to. But Scott, can you prove beyond a shadow
of a doubt that he's a traitor?"

"Halitov and Jing are witnesses! He sold us out!
C'mon, you have to believe me. He's going to make sure
we lose the war. His mother's life depends on it."

"Scott, we're talking about Colonel Beauregard's son.
When I showed the colonel your message, he laughed.
Then he absolutely refused to believe it. Then he grilled
Paul. Afterward, he assured me that his son was *not* a
traitor."

"And that was enough for you? I don't believe this.
Why didn't you and the colonel find someone else to lead
the mission? Haven't I at least cast enough doubt?"

"As far as I'm concerned, you have. But the colonel
insisted. Between you and me, I believe he does have
some doubts of his own, and I think he's up to something, but I don't know what."

"Welcome to war. No one trusts anyone." I slapped a
palm on my forehead and rubbed my temples.

"Scott, I need you right now."

"And Jing needs me, too," I snapped. "She's being held at the Nereid Research and Testing Facility, thanks to the colonel's son. For all I know they could've brainwiped her already, or maybe she's dead. Paul really took care of us. The bastard!" I lost my breath, slammed a fist on the desk.

"I'm going to order a strike team to Nereid. We can't spare too many people, but we'll do our best to get Jing."

"And I'll lead that team."

"No, you're going to be my ace in the hole. Without the colonel's approval, I'm going to send you and Halitov to Sol. You'll board that station, arrest Paul, and take over the mission."

My heart told me to refuse and demand that I lead the team going after Jing. But being a good soldier meant making personal sacrifices. I knew what I had to do. "Ms. Brooks, do you promise you'll send that team for Jing?"

"You know I will."

"Very well. Rooslin and I will catch a shuttle back there. Have an ATC ready for us."

"It'll be standing by when you arrive. I'll meet you in the bay." Her expression tightened. "And Scott? I can't remind you enough of what's at stake here. If the United States and the other nations believe we're double-crossing them . . ."

"I know. Not only do we have to help them defend their territory, but we have to maintain good diplomatic relations as well. I'll do everything I can. I just can't believe you didn't stop Paul."

"Admittedly, my relationship with the colonel has grown more tenuous, and my time has been divided."

"We could lose the entire war because of the Beauregard family!"

"Scott, there are politics working here that you don't need to know about. Suffice it to say, that letting Paul go was a mistake. I knew that, but it happened too quickly, and at that time, I needed to do everything I could to make the colonel happy."

"Make him happy?"

"Yes. I'm sorry."

"I'm sorry, too. Because if Paul tips off the enemy, then a lot of good people are going to die for nothing—and with all due respect, ma'am, their blood will be on your hands."

She closed her eyes, and I broke the link, stood, paced the cabin, skinned up and called Halitov on our private channel. "Rooslin, we're leaving right now."

"I'm a little busy."

"That's right. You're tawting out to the Sol system to stop Paul Beauregard, who just happens to be leading a joint operation of Wardens and Western Alliance Marines on the ring station at Lagrange five."

"Now that's pretty funny."

"I'm serious, Rooslin. Remember he said there was a mission coming up?"

"Wait a minute. Yeah. He said it was the last thing he had to do for them."

"Well this is it. We've secured some allies in the Western Alliance, but he's going to ruin that."

"Goddamn. I'm on my way."

When our shuttle landed aboard *Vanguard One*, it wasn't Ms. Brooks waiting for us but Dr. Jim Vesbesky, who excitedly said that we would meet with the security chief following a brief treatment inside his newly modified Mnemosyne Reversion Stabilization Devices.

"We're working against the clock, here, Doctor," said

Halitov, double-timing at my side through the bay, with Vesbesky tagging behind.

"This will only take a few hours."

"I wish we had a few minutes," I said. "But if we don't get briefed and tawt out of here, growing old too fast won't bother us anymore. And to tell you the truth, we've been experimenting with a more, I don't know, thought-based approach to our problem."

"I'm intrigued. Tell me."

"Sorry, Doc," Halitov said as we crossed into a lift. He turned, lifted a hand, forcing Vesbesky out. "If we make it back, maybe, just maybe, we'll chase a little cheese for you."

Vesbesky smirked as the lift doors shut.

"The guy's only trying to help us," I said, working my tac to contact Ms. Brooks.

"Fine. You want to climb into one of his coffins while everything goes to hell?"

I shushed him. "Ms. Brooks. We're on our way up."

"Sorry I couldn't meet you there. Did you see Dr. Vesbesky?"

"Yeah. He needs a couple of hours. We'll have to catch up with him when we get back."

"A couple of hours? I thought he'd be brief. Well, I'm not comfortable sending you off in your condition, but I'd rather it be you than anyone else. See you in a minute. We have a lot to discuss."

PART 3

◀ ▶

The Blood of Patriots

18 February, 2322

13 ❯   **Ms. Brooks's face** haunted me during the entire trip to Sol. When she saw us off, there was something in her eyes, something I just couldn't place, a sadness perhaps, a longing for something, I wasn't sure, but it bothered me very much.

And now, many years later, I saw a similar expression on the face of President Holtzman as I entered his office. The big outdoorsman came forward and offered a firm handshake. "Colonel, it's a pleasure to finally meet you."

"Indeed," said President Wong, who rose from a plush leather chair positioned opposite Holtzman's desk. He offered his hand, which I took.

"To be honest gentlemen, I wasn't expecting a warm welcome, given the circumstances."

"We don't believe you understand the circumstances," said Holtzman. He gestured to the chair beside Wong's. "Have a seat."

I did so and politely rejected Wong's offer of water. "Can I assume we're being recorded?"

"We're not," Holtzman answered quickly. "As a matter of fact, I've had everything turned off, and the office has been swept for bugs. This is between the three of us."

"Sir, I don't understand."

Wong cleared his throat. "Colonel St. Andrew, we have some disturbing information for you."

"More disturbing than our present state of affairs?"

Holtzman approached, towering over me, his gaze narrowed and hard. "Colonel, your president is a traitor."

The absurdity of that remark left me grinning, but the smile dropped as I read their grave expressions. "Excuse me?"

"We have hard evidence indicating that she, along with a group of traitors in all three of our alliances, tampered with the congressional votes on Mars and Jupiter. The votes to secede will not stand once we release our evidence."

"If you're going to continue with these accusations, you'll need to show me your evidence," I said, my tone as unwavering as his.

Holtzman gazed back at his desk. "We're prepared to do that."

"Very good. Because I have a hard time believing that those colonies would endorse being abused by Inte-Micro and Exxo-Tally. The companies' grip on the tech market is as obvious as it is illegal."

"We agree," said Wong. "And we've been doing what we can to persuade them to lower their prices and work more openly with the colonies."

"Your attempts have obviously failed."

"They've failed because there are those in our alliances and those in yours—including your president—who want to start a war," said Holtzman with a grimace. "The Terran global economy has been taking a beating, and our losses have been felt by the seventeen. We're all getting our economic asses kicked, and a good old-fashioned war would bail us out."

Wong leaned toward me, and I thought I heard real emotion in his voice. "Your president and the traitors among us have taken advantage of our dispute with Jupiter and Mars. They're using it as a means to begin such a war. And they've done much more than violate the treaty."

"But what about your blockade over Rexi-Calhoon? That's not a violation? Come on . . ."

"We were hoping that an initial show of force would give your president pause," said Holtzman. "But she countered with her own 'parade' here."

They had yet to show me their evidence, but I had to admit that President Vinnery's behavior had been combative. "Instead of this show of force, why didn't you just go public with your evidence, indict those people involved, and call for another vote?"

Wong steepled his fingers. "At this moment our central intelligence officers, along with a special prosecutor, are working to identify and arrest the traitors among us. Going public would compromise that operation."

"Gentlemen, I'm floored. I came here armed with war stories and with a negotiations team of politicians, veterans, and citizens all meant to persuade you to allow the will of the people to stand."

"As it should," said Holtzman. "The people of Mars and Jupiter are pissed off, but they don't want to secede. The votes of their representatives were not counted properly because of the tampering of your president and this network of traitors. Colonel, the three of us want the same thing here: a peaceful solution. But first we have to deal with traitors, warmongers, and opportunists."

"So you want me to have my intelligence people investigate our president," I concluded, my jaw going slack even as I spoke the words.

"That's correct," said Wong. "And we hope your in-

vestigation will help uncover those who assisted her in
these acts. We can coordinate our efforts and put an end
to the dispute by arresting those involved."

"But you're talking about bringing down my president."

"Yes, we are," said Holtzman.

I suddenly remembered to breathe. My gaze lifted to
Holtzman, then to Wong. They wanted an answer. They
wouldn't get one until I was certain. "All right. Show
me your evidence."

Holtzman returned to his desk and activated a holographic projector. Numbers spilled across a flat display
glowing in the air above us. "First I'll take you through
the computer code to demonstrate how it was tampered
with, then I'm going to show you exactly how we traced
it back to Rexi-Calhoon and your president."

I folded my arms over my chest. "Go ahead."

For the next twenty minutes, Holtzman detailed how
Vinnery had carefully covered her electronic tracks—
but her thoroughness had been her undoing. Although
the Western Alliance President used a lot of computer
jargon, my cerebroed memory defined every word and
phrase so that I clearly understood the cunningness of
the acts. In the end, he illustrated that his experts had
identified Vinnery's tampering, and Western Alliance Intelligence had confirmed it. What was more, both he
and Wong were willing to submit to cerebral scans to
prove they were not lying to me and had not fabricated
the data. I watched as for another half hour they submitted to those scans, and, finally, I received proof posi-
tive that they offered nothing but the truth. The
shocking truth.

"So you see," began Wong. "This is, indeed, more
disturbing than our present state of affairs."

"I'll need to meet with my intelligence people and begin an investigation immediately," I said. "But it's going to take time. Months, probably. And we have these cruisers breathing down our necks."

"And now we can't withdraw ours with yours sitting up there," said Holtzman. "So it's a standoff until the truth comes out."

"Let's agree on this, then. No blockade. All ships are permitted through. We'll just continue to point cannons at each other."

Holtzman glanced to Wong, who nodded. "All right."

"I guess that's the best we can do for now," I said. "But someone's going to fire a shot."

"Which is why you need to move quickly," said Holtzman. "We'll provide you with whatever you need to coordinate with your people back on Rexi-Calhoon. And don't worry about getting an operative aboard Vinnery's command ship."

"Yes, we know you already have one there," I said, dousing his attempt to surprise me. "Will he be at my disposal?"

"I'll make sure of it."

I rose. "All right. I'll need an office to set up a command post. And now I suppose we'll have to address the media."

"I suggest we maintain an air of optimism," said Wong. "The negotiations are ongoing, insightful, and we're making progress."

"Those are the facts," said Holtzman. "But I'm having a hell of a time remaining optimistic." The Western Alliance president led me to the door. "You know, I read your dossier in preparation for this meeting. Ironic how history repeats itself."

"What do you mean?"

"I mean this isn't the first time you've had to deal with a traitor."

"No, sir, it isn't."

"Well, I hope the past has taught you something."

"Funny, Mr. President. I had a premonition before I walked in here that it would. Whispers from the stars, maybe. Who knows."

"We'll meet up with you in a moment."

"Very well."

Bren, Tat, Ysarm, and Jiggs sprang up from their chairs and met me in the waiting area as I hurried out. "How'd it go, sir?" Bren asked as we walked.

"Trust me, Bren. It was an eye-opener. We're going down to meet the press corps, then we're going to set up an office here."

"What about the negotiations team, sir?"

"Send them home."

The burly man's face creased in confusion. "Sir?"

"Just do it, Bren."

"Yes, sir."

The rest of my security officers made no attempt to hide their bewilderment, and I made no attempt to explain my actions. They, like everyone else, would learn soon enough. We took a lift down to the press corps auditorium and passed through the scanners before being escorted by one of Holtzman's spokespeople up to the dais. I gazed out across a crowd of journalists numbering in the hundreds, their cameras hovering like all-seeing metallic clouds. I reminded myself not to fall on my ass again, both figuratively and physically.

Presidents Holtzman and Wong arrived a moment later, and Holtzman whispered in my ear that I would go on first. Holtzman's spokesperson announced me, and the room fell remarkably silent. My hands trembled, and I clutched the ornate wooden podium bearing the seal of the Western Alliance. "Ladies and gentlemen, I'm happy to report that negotiations between the Eastern, Western, and Colonial Alliances have begun in earnest. It is our aim to reach a peaceful solution to this crisis. I can state with impunity that the negotiations are ongoing, insightful, and we're making progress."

Holtzman and Wong beamed at me. I added a few remarks regarding our schedule before taking questions from the press. A strikingly handsome woman with dark hair streaked gray, rose from the front row and lifted her hand. I grinned at my old friend Ms. Elise Rainey and called her name.

"Thank you, Colonel. Now, sir, how do you respond to accusations made today from the independent parties on Mars and Jupiter that the vote to secede is inaccurate? And I do have a follow-up."

"Of course you do."

That brought laughter from the crowd. Rainey's hard-hitting reputation was well known, but I knew she wouldn't corner me. "Ms. Rainey, with any controversial vote, there are often those who come forward and cry foul. I know that investigations regarding the process are currently under way, so I cannot respond definitively to any accusations until we know the facts."

"All right then. And my follow-up. Do you think anyone really believes Admiral Fitzower's claim that the colonial fleet here is merely engaging in an exercise or a *parade*, as they're calling it?"

"I'll confirm here and now that our ships in orbit are not here on an exercise. There is no parade. We're here in response to the fleet over Rexi-Calhoon. President Wong, President Holtzman, and I have agreed that ships will remain in place until this crisis is resolved. However, there will be no blockades. All vessels will be allowed past both fleets."

And that set off a fit of murmurs.

"Thank you," Rainey said, then mouthed the word "dinner" at me before taking a seat.

After a curt nod, I took the next question, already looking forward to a rendezvous with my old friend. Yes, there had always a been a spark between us, but we had been wise enough and strong enough not to allow that to interfere with our jobs or our personal lives. And while I couldn't divulge much information, I suspected that Ms. Rainey and her connections could help me gather a few facts. And therein might lie one answer from the past.

Five gravitationally stable Lagrange points relative to Earth and the moon provided engineers with the perfect coordinates for positioning ring stations, and the two located at L4 and L5 made slow, eighty-nine-day orbits in their regions. The Exxo-Tally station Halitov and I approached had a diameter of 6.4 kilometers, with an RPM of 0.53 to simulate Earth gravity. To the untrained eye, the station resembled a giant wagon wheel with a stable axis and a tire rotating around it. The tire actually housed the industrial city and protected it with a 1.6 meter-thick radiation shield. Behind that shield, the station's floor was set edge-on so that you felt the downward pull as the ring rotated. Massive mirrors angled within the wheel's spokes brought in light and solar energy. In truth, the station stood as a feat of engineering and research, but its aesthetic appeal had often been criticized. Some said it resembled a cheap prop from a campy science fiction film of century's past. At that moment, though, I scrutinized the station not because I agreed with that assessment, but because I was imagining exactly what Mr. Paul Beauregard was doing, deep within the city, at his command post.

Our ATC's pilot maneuvered into position, then let docking command take over for the link. We thumped against the portside module jutting from the ring's axis, and the ship locked in place. Wearing civilian tunics, we floated in zero-G toward the hatch. I keyed it open and pushed myself through the tube, into a narrow, pristine-white bay, where I was accosted by a security detail of three Western Alliance Marines wearing mag boots that kept them floor-bound. The sergeant, whose bloated face indicated that he had spent far too much time in zero-G, scanned my tac, then scanned Halitov's. He blinked hard at the tablet in his hand, then said, "Your orders indicate zero arrival and log-in, is that correct?"

"Yes, it is. Our orders come from the Security Chief and have already been acknowledged by Major Nicholls, Thirty-second Battalion, C-Corps."

"I understand that, but this is my watch, and I have a huge problem letting you two on board my station without any record of a log-in or verification of your IDs. You're the second party this week with similar orders."

"Look, buddy, your CO says you have to let us through. You want to have a crisis of conscience over it, do it on your own time," said Halitov.

The sergeant bore his teeth. "You fuckin' colonists coming in here. And a gennyboy to boot. Fuck you."

Shocked, I glanced to Halitov, his fuse already burned to the base, and shook my head fiercely before facing the sergeant. "I'm going to ask you once more for clearance."

The sergeant rolled his eyes and turned quickly to the

lance corporal at his side, who tapped a panel on his wrist. A hatch behind them slid open. "Jones?" called the sergeant. "Take them to decon."

"Sir, yes, sir." The lance corporal waved us over. "This way."

"Thanks for the hospitality," Halitov growled as he floated past the sergeant, then he added his poorly disguised threat: "I hope to see you again on the way out."

"Off my deck now!" the sergeant boomed.

"Nice," I said as we glided into the decontamination chamber. "Very nice. You'll make a fine ambassador some day."

Halitov flipped the sergeant the bird as the chamber door slid shut. "And these guys are our allies?" he asked.

"I'm sure that attitude prevails. You don't take former enemies and put them side-by-side without some of that."

"Or without some of this." Halitov beat a fist into his palm.

We stripped and went through the decontamination process, a formality since we had already been cleaned prior to boarding our ATC, but you didn't get on board without decon—especially after the smallpox plague of 2297. Following that, we took a lift down, passing the zero-G production facilities where purer metals and more perfect and larger crystal growth occurred. Signs posted along the catwalks indicated the days and times of free tours.

"You know, instead of stopping Paul and saving the colonies from Alliance tyranny, we could go sightseeing," Halitov suggested in a deadpan. "I've always wanted to watch crystals grow."

"I already have," I said, blank-faced. "My dad's a geologist, remember? It's fascinating."

"Do I laugh now?" he asked.

"No."

"Listen, Scott, I know you want to take him alive, but
if it comes down to it, you know what I'll do."

I took a deep breath and swore. *How the hell had it
ever come to this?*

We traveled directly toward one of the ring's hollow
spokes, where at a small hub we caught a maglev train
for the city proper. A computer voice piped in through
the overhead comm instructed us to strap into our seats
and anticipate a gravitational increase. Halitov withdrew one of the vomit bags from the seat ahead and
joked about it, just as gravity slapped its beefy paws on
our shoulders. Within a minute, Halitov turned green,
fumbled with the bag, and wound up puking on his
shoes. I wish I could say I didn't vomit. I wish I could
say I had time to open my own bag. Instead, I puked on
Halitov's shoes. It just wasn't his day.

At the next hub, feeling the full effects of Earth-
normal gravity, we sat on a bench for just a moment,
swallowing hard against our sunken cheeks. Halitov
rushed off to clean his shoes in a public rest room, then
we bought a couple of bottled waters from a street ven-
dor and hustled away from the hub, passing beneath a
broad quickcrete awning until we stood on a platform
overlooking the city. Although I had seen holos of the
station's interior, they did little justice. Ahead lay a me-
andering river paralleled by on both sides by mountain-
ous terrain upon which thousands of apartment
buildings, manufacturing plants, parks, shopping malls,
and sports complexes had been constructed. The land-

scape curved up and away from us, with more of it visible through a vault of literally millions of windows, obscured here and there by tendrils of clouds. I hadn't realized that there was actually weather inside the station, and for a moment, it was easy to forget that we were encased in billions of tons of steel.

"Where do we meet Nicholls again?" Halitov asked, then gulped down the last of his water.

"I'm glad you were paying attention during the briefing. What if I get shot and die? How will you finish this mission?"

Halitov squinted in thought. "We're going to his apartment. That's right. Just outside the base."

"And you should know the address. Let's get out of here."

As we double-timed down a staircase leading to the street, Halitov asked, "Help me understand why this guy is helping us."

"You heard Ms. Brooks. He's a valuable contact and we should trust him."

"I get the feeling that before the war, this guy was one of her lovers."

"I hope he was."

At the corner below the maglev platform, we caught a cab, and on the way to Nicholls's apartment, a squadron of EE60 Endo Troop Carriers, smaller versions of our own ATCs, jetted overhead, followed by a second squadron, then a third.

Halitov's gaze tracked the carriers. "Shit, something's going on."

"It's the big attack," said our cabdriver, an old man with a freckled pate and white teeth gone to bronze. "I knew it. Once we got in bed with the colonies, the Eastern Alliance would hit us. Fucking maniac politicians!

They're going to blow us all to hell!" The driver pulled to the side of the road, the engine still idling.

"What are you doing?" I asked him.

Ignoring me, he opened his door, hopped out, and just stood there in the middle of the road, shielding his eyes from the reflected sunlight and staring at yet another squadron of EE60s thundering overhead.

Halitov burst from his door, jogged around the hover, then knifed into the driver's seat, seized the half-wheel, and engaged the throttle.

"We're stealing his cab?" I cried.

"He needs a moment," Halitov said as we hissed off.

I glanced back at the driver, who still hadn't reacted to our departure. Nothing mattered anymore to him, and I understood his disbelief. The world that he knew—everything—was in jeopardy, more jeopardy than he could possibly know. I turned my attention to the tablet built into the rear of the driver's seat. I pulled up a local news feed. An Eastern Alliance fleet had tawted into the system, arriving just 10,000 kilometers away from the station. The Western Alliance's Second Fleet had set up an ambush, and while the two forces traded fire, Eastern Alliance troop carriers had penetrated the station's perimeter defense network and troops were gaining forcible entry through the docking modules. In the distance, over the hover's engine, I detected the report and echo of particle fire.

"It's already too late, isn't it," said Halitov. "Paul got them by the peridef so they can get their troops inside."

"Probably," I answered. "But we can still remove him from command before he does anymore damage."

"If he hasn't run."

"I don't think he can. I think he needs to ensure that the Eastern Alliance gains control of this station."

Halitov abruptly pulled into a small lot adjacent to a five-story apartment complex. "Okay, this it."

We hopped out, and a stout security drone was about to confront us when an explosion about a kilometer down-ring stole its attention. An alarm went off as we rushed past the drone's gate, then dashed frantically through a hallway, beyond the lift, and into the stair-well. We reached the fourth floor, found unit 491, and thumbed the hatchcomm. The door glided open.

"Hello?" I said.

"Come on in, gentlemen," came a man's voice.

A dimly lit living area lay before us, and on a small coffee table sat a tablet propped up on a stack of books. Colonel Nicholls, forty, with tiny eyes and gray temples, stared motionless at us from the screen. A databar be-low his image flashed the words MESSAGE AWAITING.

"He's not even here?" asked Halitov.

"Would you be?" I countered, tipping my head up, toward the booming outside. I touched the screen and Nicholls spoke evenly:

"Sorry I couldn't meet you in person, but by now I'm sure you know why. On the table you'll find a pair of particle rifles, along with two pistols loaded with six hiza darts each. The darts hold the antimnemo per your request. I've secured you some uniforms, temporary se-curity clearances, and this tablet to locate the target, though if he does run a personnel check, he'll pick you up, so you'll have to move quickly. Good luck."

"Three words, man," said Halitov, stripping out of his tunic. "It's all about three words: *element of surprise.*"

"Exactly," I said, undressing myself. "We'll only get one shot at him before he reaches into the bond and wills himself away."

"Man, I remember bullshitting with him back in the

mess at South Point," Halitov said, looking as wistful as I felt. "I just can't believe this."

"Hey, he asked me, so I'll ask you. What would you do if they had your mother and your father write her off?"

"Anything but this."

"That's easy to say, being on the outside."

"You defending him?"

"Just trying to understand. Trying . . ."

Dressed and fully armed, I accessed the tablet and learned that Paul, now a major, had established a command and communications post for his Twenty-first Battalion within an elevated maglev station in what we designated as Point Rattlesnake, one of thirty-one tactical defense positions lying opposite each maglev railway. Invading troops could enter the station only through the railways, lest they waste a whole lot of time trying to cut through the station itself. Thus, the bulk of our forces were concentrated in those potential breaches.

"All right, we have a choice," I said. "We see if that hover's still outside and drive the thirty minutes over there, or we pay the price and use our magic."

"Let's do one better," said Halitov. "Let's see if we can use an old miner's trick and bypass those bugs in our head. Call it our coupon for a free ride."

"This one's for you, Mr. Hardeson Poe," I whispered, then closed my eyes, reached into myself, found the point, saw the two images of myself, and lo and behold, Halitov and I stood beside a warehouse opposite the maglev platform.

"You all right?" he asked.

I gasped, looked around, grinned a little. "Son of a bitch." No drain. Nothing. Just force of will. I couldn't tell if I had any control over my aging, but I didn't feel any older.

We squatted near the wall, skinned up, and zoomed in to pick out Paul's snipers positioned along the roof, catwalks, and elevated walkways. I'd never seen soldiers looking more tense, all of them just waiting for those enemy troops who would come barreling through the tunnel in their airjeeps, particle cannons swiveling and blazing.

And somewhere nearby, inside that complex, Mr. Paul Beauregard waited to begin choreographing the demise of his own battalion.

"Ready?" Halitov asked.

I took in a long breath, held it, and we bolted across the barren street, into the shadows collecting beneath the maglev platform.

18 February, 2322

14>   **Had I been** in the same room with President Vinnery, she would have throttled me for not consulting her before I met with the press corps. As she had ripped into me for that convenient oversight, her cheeks had grown so flushed that I wondered if she were having a breakdown. "Ma'am, I apologize. I should have spoken with you first."

"You're damned right you should have. You're over there negotiating with them like you're the president, and you fail to notify me of your intention to divulge classified information to the press."

"Time was of the essence. And certainly my presence here represents our respect of their traditions. You know I'm hardly a replacement for you, and I thank you once again for allowing me to speak with them. I'm happy to say we're making excellent progress."

"Somehow I doubt that. Anyway, Colonel, by tomorrow you'll be relieved of your duties there."

"Ma'am?"

"The *Falls Morrow* is en route to Earth. We'll be tawting out in six hours."

"Coming here is too dangerous. Between the situation with the Aire-Wuian missionaries and the fleet, you're inviting another attempt on your life." I conveniently failed to add that her coming to Earth might make my investigation into her vote tampering a bit harder, since I had already hired investigators who were traveling to her ship, but they wouldn't reach the vessel before it tawted out.

"I've increased my security team. They assure me that I'll be perfectly safe. And I've already told Wong and Holtzman that I'll be having breakfast with them tomorrow."

"If you insist."

"I do. You're headed back home."

"I understand, ma'am. But if I stay, it'll be two on two. You won't be outnumbered."

"You're groveling, Colonel. And it's unbecoming."

"Yes, ma'am."

"You'll catch a shuttle out of there immediately."

"Understood."

She pursed her lips, gave a terse nod, ended the link.

I sat there alone in my makeshift and meager command post within the Western Alliance capitol, thinking hard about my next move. I called Holtzman, who told me that Vinnery's appearance might mean that she had been tipped off.

"But why come here? To destroy the evidence? She knows that'd be impossible. You've backed it up on satnet."

"I don't know why she's coming in person. Perhaps you've bruised her ego. I do know that you shouldn't leave. I don't care what she told you, Colonel. I believe your life depends upon you staying."

"Message read and understood, sir."

"And Colonel, we might need to go public with our evidence before we're able to round up all the traitors. President Wong and I have already discussed this, and it's something we are prepared to do. No matter what, Vinnery will go down, but we need to take as many with her as we can."

"Just stall as long as you can. When the *Falls Morrow* arrives, I'm going to contact your operative on board. We'll see what we can come up with. It's clear Vinnery had help, and I'm betting some of those people are on board that ship."

"We'll do what we can."

About two hours after my conversation with Holtzman, I sat at a small table in the president's private dining room, glancing over a candle and Caesar salad at Ms. Elise Rainey. Wong, Holtzman, and their guests had already finished their meals and had been leaving when we had arrived, so technically Ms. Rainey and I had the entire dining room to ourselves. I say technically because Bren, Tat, Ysarm, and Jiggs loomed warily in the corners, and I had warned them about ogling my dinner guest.

"Don't worry, sir," Bren had said. "We're all trained professionals."

"Professional wolves," I had said with a laugh.

Ms. Rainey sipped her wine, then asked. "Your daughter's just been commissioned."

"That's right."

"You must be very proud."

"Yes. And scared. We can't let this generation see the things we've seen."

"And oh, what we've seen . . ."

"Are you still having the nightmares?"

"It's weird. That was so long ago, but now and then they do come back. It usually takes something during the day to trigger them."

"Like a meeting with me. Sorry."

"No, it's all right. Even the slightest things will do it, like someone just casually mentioning Columbia

Colony. That night I'll go home, climb into bed, and
wake up in the middle of the night with bodies lying all
over my room. I've tried the drugs, seen the therapists. I
keep kidding myself that I'll heal in time. But we don't
heal, do we . . ."

"We manage."

She considered that, reached once more for her wine.
We ate quietly for a few minutes. When our entrees ar-
rived, she began cutting her vegetable pizza and asked,
"What's really going on here, Scott? Off the record."

"Off the record? It's big."

"C'mon, Scott. It's me."

"Not this time, Elise. But I'll tell you this: I've never
needed you more than I do now."

"You're scaring me."

I nodded slowly. "Talk to me about the *Falls Morrow*. You have a contact aboard, don't you?"

"Two actually. What do you need?"

The barest of hisses turned my gaze up, away from
my meal—

Even as Ms. Elise Rainey slumped forward onto the
table, a bloodstain swelling across the back of her
blouse. And there, standing behind her, was Bren, gripping his QQ60 pistol with attached silencer. "Fuckin' reporters," he muttered, then faced me, the pistol leveled
on my forehead. "Sorry, sir. But I'm afraid there's going
to be a war. And there's nothing we can do to stop it."

I reached across the table, and, with a trembling
hand, checked Rainey's neck for a pulse. I couldn't find
one. Then, I glanced up at him. *Don't trust anyone.*
"Bren? Why?"

"She's my president. And she knew you'd never go
along with this. You're all about duty, honor, and the
code."

I searched the room for Tat, Ysarm, and Jiggs. "You killed them, too?"

"The second hardest thing I've ever done." He thrust the pistol at me.

"You think you can get away with this?"

"Tomorrow's news will report that I was a mole planted by the Mars Militia. It's not the legacy I would've chosen, but you don't get too many choices when you've been hired to die."

The pistol went off as I reached into the bond, willing myself out of the projectile's path, but I wasn't fast enough, and the round grazed my head. I materialized next to Bren, who, before I could stop him, shoved the pistol into his mouth, jerked his finger, and showered me with blood and gray matter. He fell back, knocking me onto my rump, as pins and needles poked my cheek and wove into my ear. Blinking blood from my eyes, I caught a glimpse of Ms. Rainey before I passed out.

Skinned up and monitoring the Western Alliance tactical channel as well as Paul's channel, Halitov and I hit the maglev platform's stairwell and slipped up to the first level, pausing near a two-meter tall bank of lockers. A databar in my HUV indicated that Paul's tac was functioning and his position appeared on a 3-D map of his command post within a bookstore/café cordoned off by three particle cannon bunkers. Halitov and I would slip along the perimeter, dodging from bunker to bunker, until we got close enough to materialize in front of him, fire the darts, and pray the antimnemo took effect before he could escape. But as usual, our timing was shit, our plans torn from our fingers and express-mailed to Hell.

With a rush of air and a computer voice announcement, a maglev train rumbled around the corner ahead, its blue-and-silver nose slicing forward, the passenger compartments behind seemingly empty. I listened to the skipchatter over Paul's tactical channel:

"White Star Five, you secured that train, didn't you?"

"Affirmative, sir. Complete lockdown."

"Then why is it entering my perimeter?"

"Sir, I don't know, sir!"

"Aw, shit, they're getting set up," Halitov said over our private channel. "That train's loaded with troops. Here they come!"

At least the company commanders recognized the old Trojan Horse gambit and ordered their people to open fire. Cannon flashes erupted from all twenty-one bunkers lining the platform's perimeter, and the train's nose exploded under the barrage, tattered alloy tumbling across the tracks, crashing through windows, and hurtling into the lockers beside us.

As Paul's Wardens continued laying down a fierce barrage of suppressing fire, I realized exactly what the Eastern Alliance Marines were doing, but because I couldn't contact the Wardens without giving up my location and identity, all I could do was watch as enemy troops arrived in their airjeeps—not from the main entrance behind the train, but from outside. In fact, the train had not been a Trojan Horse but merely a diversion to misdirect the Wardens' fire while Marines penetrated the station via the nearest platform down rail. From there, they would advance on to finish Paul's battalion, the whole strike carefully coordinated by Paul himself.

With white-knuckled grips on our rifles, we sprang away from the lockers, hit the wall, then found the bond and sprinted sideways across a bank of windows that exploded behind us as Marines outside targeted our silhouettes.

"Maybe it's time we checked the classifieds for another job," Halitov groaned, hopping down from the wall and hustling to the first bunker, his skin coruscating with reflected rounds.

"Who are you guys?" asked a young, bug-eyed sergeant directing the two cannon operators.

"Don't mind us," Halitov answered the woman. "Just passing through."

"Sergeant, forget the train," I told her. "Direct your fire outside!" I pointed past the bunker, toward the shattered windows, as an airjeep raced by.

The sergeant eyed the train, the windows, saw two more airjeeps, then it dawned on her. "Palladino? Martin? Bring those cannons around!"

I flashed her a thumbs-up, then bolted on after Halitov, who was already halfway to the next bunker, some thirty yards ahead.

We kept tight to the storefronts, particle fire tossing up sparks and punching holes in everything, the incoming more fierce than anything I had ever experienced. Nearly every movement brought my skin into a round.

Above the storefronts, a quick salvo from a wild airjeep gunner shattered another bay of windows, sending the glass down on us as another three airjeeps, tight on the heels of that fire, penetrated the station. Two banked right, their single cannon operators leveling fire on the bunkers while the third pulled straight up, wheeled around, then strafed Paul's people from the rear. Two bunker cannons exploded, along with their operators and mobile fuel systems, and you couldn't tell what was metal and what was flesh anymore. But Halitov and I repressed the horrific images and kept streaking along the wall, drawing closer to Paul's command center. A red blip flashed in my HUV, indicating Paul was still there—and that blip drove me harder, faster.

A terrific thunderclap threw Halitov back toward me as a duty-free gift shop succumbed to a grenade blast, the fireball swallowing us before we dropped to our knees. My skin level plunged to forty-two percent as the ball passed, leaving a blinding black cloud in its wake. An infrared view via our tactical computers guided us forward, through the smoke, until we reached the next row of stores.

Opposite us, across the platform, ten, maybe a dozen airjeeps buzzed across the zone, their pilots deftly evading streams of cannon fire and small-arms fire from the scores of Wardens posted along the catwalks some ten meters above. I'd already seen a handful of those Wardens get maimed or shredded, what was left tumbling to thump on the deck. We were reliving the massacre at Columbia, and I couldn't stand it. Couldn't stand it at all.

"Jesus Christ!" Halitov cried as we threaded between bodies lying before a smoldering bunker. "Look at these guys! Where is Paul? Where is he?"

"Just go, man, go!" I shouted, then craned my head.

An airjeep some forty meters out swooped down, its gunner intent on locking his bead. I whirled, lifted my rifle, locked a bead of my own, wearing down his skin until he finally blew off the airjeep's back. The pilot switched gun operation to the computer, and the cannon swung back on me and Halitov. I turned and ran, rounds nipping my shoulders.

Back at South Point Academy, Major Yokito Yakata had shared with us an old saying: During combat, soldiers' brains turn to water and run out their ears. All they have to go on is instinct. And while I clung to my instincts, Halitov's brain turned not to water but in on itself, battling with the mnemosyne. He stumbled, fell.

I went to him. He looked at me, gaze vague, head shaking, words coming out, incomprehensible at first, then:

"Twenty-two-sixty-six. Mining of bauxite begins on fifth planet in Ross Two-fifty-eight solar system. Inte-Micro Corporation CEO Tamer Yatanaya names planet 'Allah-Trope' and declares it retreat for Muslims being persecuted by Eastern Alliance powers. Allah-Trope becomes first offworld colony with predominately one religion."

As Halitov went on, I stared at him and saw myself. The image scared the hell out of me. My friend convulsed a moment, then collapsed. His combat skin faded. I shouldered his weapon, dug my arms beneath his pits, lifted, and dragged him out there, as the particle fire sparked and ricocheted near his boots.

I reached the next smoldering bunker, hauled Halitov over the mangled bodies of fellow Wardens, then lay him behind the remaining blast plates that stood only a meter or so above the deck but should protect him from stray rounds. I shrugged off his rifle, lay it across his chest, then placed both of his hands on it, should he awaken and need to immediately fire. I checked his pulse: rapid but very much present. I didn't know what else to do for him, and I could already hear him swearing over his inability to help, but my own internal swearing was louder because I needed him. Badly. His prejudice was a lot stronger than mine. I understood too keenly what Paul was feeling, and I worried that my understanding might make me hesitate.

"I'll be back for you," I said, more a promise to myself than to Halitov.

Still hunched over, I pocketed his QQ60 pistol loaded with the hiza darts, left the bunker, and hightailed along

the last row of storefronts until, at the corner, I reached
a row of bunkers five abreast outside the café. The cannons there boomed, and an airjeep took a direct hit,
shedding smoke and metal as it flat-spun down to shat-
ter across the platform. Cringing from the explosion, I
slipped into the café, scuttling between bookshelves and
display racks. I abandoned my rifle and gripped both
QQ60 pistols. The moment I spotted Paul, I would
empty both magazines.

Two aisles later, I neared the back of the café, where,
according to my HUV, Paul had set up a bunker perimeter behind a serving counter. I peered around a shelf corner and lost my breath. I wasn't scared. I wasn't shocked.

I was astonished.

Paul crouched down beside the counter, aiming a pistol at his father's head.

Colonel J. D. Beauregard had come to stop his son?

"It's too late," Paul cried. "And it was all your fucking fault!"

"It's not too late!" the colonel hollered as automatic
weapons fire nearly drowned him out.

I thought back to the docking module, to something
the sergeant had said, something I had forgotten to ask
him about: *"I have a huge problem letting you two on
board my station without any record of a log-in or verification of your IDs. You're the second party this week
with similar orders."*

Colonel Beauregard must've been that other party,
and if he had planned to stop his son, his plan had gone
terribly awry.

And there I was, caught in the middle of a battle and
a domestic drama that could decide the war's outcome.

What the hell was I supposed to do? Make my move
and kill the colonel's son—right in front of him?

Could I even do that? As much as I hated Paul, could I really kill him?

I didn't know. I just didn't know.

Maybe if I had to, I would kill him.

Maybe I could just capture him before he hurt his father.

I weighed my options:

If I spring on him, he could still manage to fire that pistol and kill me or the colonel.

If I call his name, that would create a second-long standoff until he willed himself away.

If I will myself behind him, fire, then I might have a chance to get his weapon.

During my contemplation, Paul's XO, a Ms. Duma Knight, had slipped up behind me. She tapped the side of my head with the muzzle of her particle rifle. "Drop your weapons!"

I tightened my grip on the pistols, froze, considered taking her out before she could fire, but I couldn't waste time. I reached into the bond, and, without time to bypass the mnemosyne, used them to will myself behind Paul. I materialized there—even as Paul turned, saw me, opened his mouth.

There wasn't time to empty the magazines, but I got off four darts, all striking his chest and sticking before I chucked the guns and lunged at him.

19 February, 2322

Holtzman's security people had come just after the shots had been fired. I learned later that I had been rushed to the nearest trauma center, treated, and admitted overnight for observation. Ms. Rainey, Bren, Tat, Ysarm, and Jiggs had been pronounced dead at the scene.

From my hospital bed, I watched the midnight news reports as Vinnery's story spun across the airwaves. Bren was, indeed, linked to the Mars Militia, and while I had shared the truth with Holtzman and Wong, who'd come to visit me, they suggested I do nothing until Vinnery arrived, at which time we'd all confront her and go public with the evidence of her vote tampering and conspiring to have me murdered. But I couldn't bear the thought that those who had assisted her would vanish into the network, only to reappear at some future moment to once again undermine peace and stability between the alliances. I felt certain that something about my experience with Paul Beauregard would provide a clue in how to deal with Vinnery. I just couldn't put my finger on it. So I just lay there, grieving and reliving one of the most painful moments of my life, searching in vain for connections, sometimes seeing them then realizing that I saw only what I wanted to see.

Later, during the wee hours, as my wounded head throbbed and I drifted in and out of sleep, something emerged from my thoughts, something about the guilty conscience of a traitor.

15 ❯

Paul Beauregard had only wanted to save his mother, but he had been willing to risk far too much. He had not been willing to make the same sacrifice that his father had, and in his decision to betray the colonies, Paul had once and for all reminded us that in his heart he was not a soldier. Not a soldier at all.

As I threw myself at Paul, two shots rang out, one from the XO's rifle, the other from Paul's pistol. The first round knocked my combat skin to zero, the second caught me point-blank in the shoulder and blew off my left arm at the bicep. It all happened so fast that I didn't feel a thing and dropped onto Paul. I tried wresting the pistol from his grip as we both fell to the deck. Only then did I notice blood jetting from my stump. Paul shoved me back, and the drain from accessing the bond along with the sudden blood loss gripped me in dizziness and nausea. I rolled away, came up on my hand and knees, stared down the barrel of his pistol, my shoulder throbbing as I turned and glanced vaguely at my shattered limb. The shakes came on violently as I sat, tucked my stump into my chest.

"Let me shoot him, sir!" cried Duma Knight from behind us.

"Hold your fire!" Paul ordered.

I glanced past Paul to the colonel. "Sir, are you all right, sir?"

The colonel just sat there, sweating and leering at

Paul. "Letting my son come here was a test of his loyalty, Major. I couldn't believe he was a traitor. But he is. And he's convinced his XO that *I'm* the traitor."

"Maybe you both are," I said. "A lot of people died out there so you could test your son's loyalty. You suspected this might be a trap—and you betrayed their trust."

"The Eastern Alliance will not take this station, Major. And our relationship with our new allies in the Western Alliance will remain strong. I've made sure of that." The colonel regarded his son. "Now, Paul. Drop that fucking weapon."

Paul lolled his head back, swung the weapon drunkenly from me to his father. The hiza darts were taking affect. "You still think you can give me orders—after what you did to her? She's your wife! My mother! You didn't even try to save her!"

The colonel bore his teeth. "We do not negotiate with terrorists."

I glanced back to the XO. "What are you going to do? Let him shoot his father?"

The woman stood there, panting, shifting the rifle between me and Colonel Beauregard. "Captain," she called to Paul. "Is your father telling the truth?"

Instead of answering, Paul whipped around and fired, striking the XO in the face as she attempted to skin up. The single round blew most of her head off, and I winced as she crumpled.

Paul blinked hard at me, trying to focus. "You're the one who told them, didn't you. Somehow you got back and told them. But it doesn't matter, Scott. We're all fucked. And now I show you what duty and honor really get you." He thrust his pistol forward. "After everything you've done, you're going to die in this pathetic little train station. That's the military for you."

I closed my eyes, fought for the bond, but found only an amorphous feeling somewhere between numbness and sensation. I tensed, waiting for the report of his pistol, heard only a dull exhale, followed by the slight shuffle of boots.

When I looked up, a Ka-bar sprouted from Paul's back, a Ka-bar gripped by a horrified Colonel Beauregard, who slowly removed his hand, then suddenly wrenched the blade from Paul's back. The colonel rolled his son over, then took him into his lap. He cradled Paul's head, swore through his tears, and began rocking. "My only son . . . my only son . . ."

Several books dropped to the floor behind me, and there was Halitov, stumbling toward us, one-handing his rifle and rubbing his eyes. I couldn't read his expression as he gazed at the colonel and Paul, but when he glanced to me, saw my own tears, he just lowered his head and sighed. "I'm sorry."

We all were, but no one more than Colonel J.D. Beauregard, who, in the days to come, would enlist our new allies to help free his wife.

The attack on the Exxo-Tally ring station lasted no more than a few hours, thanks to the three battalions Colonel Beauregard had hidden aboard. We scored our first joint victory with our new allies, and rumor had it that the war would be over before year's end. I hoped so. My body couldn't stand much more abuse.

As the colonel's forces moped up from the battle, I was taken to a local hospital and received surgery on my stump, after which nurses wheeled me into a Spartan recovery room.

"I'm sick and tired of winding up here," I told Halitov, scowling at the machines and placards and canisters labeled biohazard.

He leaned back in the chair beside my gurney, folded his hands behind his head. "Hey, man. You're just living up to our mantra."

"I didn't know we had one."

"Shit, yeah." He winked. "Live dangerously, eat hospital food. And get this: their spaghetti and meatballs come from a can. From a can!"

I snorted, gingerly touched the nanotech regeneration tube screwed into my shoulder. The docs would try to grow me a new arm, but odds were I'd be fitted with a prosthetic within a year, just like my brother. I wondered if Jing would accept the fact that her fiancé had been maimed. Then again, I was assuming she was still alive and hadn't been brainwiped. I glanced once more to the tray near my gurney, where I had placed my tablet. I leaned over and drummed a knuckle on the screen.

"Relax. Brooks'll call," Halitov said.

"Maybe something went wrong, and she's thinking of a way to tell me."

"Maybe you should stop worrying about it until she calls."

"They either wiped her or killed her, I know it," I said. "Everybody dies."

"Except us. We get to watch."

"You call that a bedside manner?"

"I call it the truth."

The tablet beeped, and I ripped it from the tray. "Anything?" I asked Ms. Brooks.

"I'm sorry, Scott. I'm afraid the rescue team was shot down before they could land. Our allies tell me that the Eastern Alliance's flotilla is still there."

Halitov shouldered his way into camera view. "Ma'am, request permission to go after her."

"I'm sorry, Captain, but—"

"Don't make me go AWOL, ma'am. Nothing new there."

A smile nicked the corners of my mouth as I watched Halitov argue for leading his own rescue mission. Ms. Brooks gazed dubiously at him, unmoved.

"I'll be going, too," I told her when Halitov had finished. "I can still fire a weapon."

"If you think I'll let you lead a rescue mission now, you're not only insulting my intelligence, but you're betraying your lack thereof."

I winced, sat up. "We can't leave her there. Please . . ."

She fidgeted, finally met my gaze. "Let me talk to the colonel about this, and I'll get back to you."

The screen went blank.

Halitov grabbed my arm. "We're not waiting."

"We're going AWOL?"

"Does it matter anymore?"

"Rooslin, we can't."

"Oh yeah, we can."

"No, I mean how're we supposed to get there? Float around in the vacuum, stick out our thumbs, and try hitching a ride?"

"We'll just hijack an ATC," he said. "Remember how Eugene did it? All you need is a gun and an attitude. I got both."

"Oh, that sounds good. We'll go in with no team, no firepower, and a couple of pilots who don't want to be there in the first place. Then we somehow blast our way through the flotilla, get down to the moon, break into the facility, and rescue her."

"Exactly. And in that order."

"Forget it. We can't go without help."

"She's your wife, man."

"Fiancée. Now, wait a minute. Yeah, maybe that's it. If we can get a chip out to him, maybe—"

"A chip out to who?"

I sat up. "Let's get to a comm hub."

"What're you talking about?"

"What am I talking about? You're the one who gave me the idea."

"What?"

I sighed through a smile. That was Halitov. Fiercely loyal, incredibly dense.

Nine hours and forty-five minutes later, Mr. Eugene Val d'Or and eight guardsmen from Icillica docked with the station. They had come in a heavily armored ATC and had jammed the cargo bays with particle rifles and explosives confiscated from the garrison at Colyad.

"Didn't think I'd ever see you again," Val d'Or said, shaking my hand in the docking module and trying to ignore my missing arm. He regarded Halitov. "Didn't want to see you again."

Halitov wriggled his brows. "And I thought you'd miss me the most."

Val d'Or shot Halitov a crooked grin, then waved us through the docking tube and into his ship. "Too bad you couldn't get the colonel's blessing," he called back.

"The colonel claims he's sending a battle group to take out the flotilla there," I told him. "But Ms. Brooks says she's unsure when they'll arrive, meaning they might never arrive."

"You want a rescue operation done right? You have to do it yourself."

"Absolutely. So what lies did you tell to get here?"

"They were complex. They were many. But we three—as much as I hate to admit it in Halitov's case—we three are brothers. Like the old Earth Marines. Once a guardsman, always a guardsman, even if you now wear a Wardens uniform. One of us calls, we come. Now, then. If you'll deactivate your tacs, we'll get under way."

I knew the moment we did that, the colonel would be alerted, though he could no longer track our location via satnet. I didn't care anymore. I needed to know one way or the other about Jing, and I wouldn't wait for the colonel to get around to dispatching that battle group. Halitov was just as eager, and I had forgotten that he had his own agenda for going. But my memory was jarred when we reached Nereid and were hailed by two atmoattack fighters from the security frigate *Mao Triggor*. Somewhere behind all those cannons and alloy blast plates sat a midshipman at her station, a midshipman who just happened to be Rooslin Halitov's sister.

"Still hailing us," the pilot said.

Val d'Or stood behind the man, rubbing his jaw nervously. "We'll deal with them in a minute. The nuke is spun up. Stand by to take out the frigate."

"Belay that order," Halitov cried from his jumpseat. "Eugene, my sister's aboard that ship!"

"What?" he called back.

"My sister's aboard that ship! You can't take her out!"

"There's a piece of information you could've shared BEFORE WE TAWTED OUT!"

"Is there another way through?" I asked Val d'Or.

"No way. They've already pinpointed our position.

Two more frigates are en route. If we don't punch a hole and get down there now, this mission is over."

"Why don't you try an emergency tawt?" Halitov asked.

"You want to calculate the jump?" Val d'Or countered. "Because our computer sure as hell can't."

Halitov threw up his safety bars and stormed toward the cockpit. "Open a channel to the frigate."

Val d'Or placed himself between the cockpit and the hold, raised his index finger at Halitov. "Get back in your seat."

In one powerful motion, Halitov gripped Val d'Or by the shoulders and lifted him aside. Then he burst into the cockpit and grabbed the pilot's shoulder. "Just open that fucking channel!"

The pilot, a lean young man, knew better than to argue. "Channel's open."

"You're making a mistake," Val d'Or screamed.

"*Mao Triggor*, this is ATC Five-Niner-Seven. Request permission to speak with Midshipman Dobraska Halitov. This is a priority-one request."

"ATC Five-Niner-Seven, this is Captain Jung Park. We will not honor any requests until you broadcast your IDPO immediately."

Val d'Or yanked Halitov around, got in his face. "We tell them who we are and where we came from, they'll fire on us!"

"Send the IDPO," Halitov ordered the pilot.

"Belay that," cried Val d'Or, drawing a pistol from his waist and aiming it at Halitov. "You want my help? You do it my way."

Captain Park's voice boomed once more. "ATC Five-Niner-Seven. Broadcast your IDPO immediately. Otherwise, I'm going to blow you from my sky."

"Rooslin," I said firmly. "Eugene's right. We ID ourselves, he'll fire on us. But I have another idea. Let's go talk to the captain—personally."

"Oh, no way. No fuckin' way," said Val d'Or.

Halitov and I closed our eyes in unison, reached deep down, past the mnemosyne—

And opened our eyes on the *Mao Triggor*'s bridge. Two security officers were on us, even as I raised my good hand.

"Conditioned soldiers, and Wardens no less," said Captain Jung Park, a middle-aged Asian man with a crewcut and sinister-looking brows. He glanced to a monitor as a computer scanned our images and locked onto our identities. "Captain Rooslin Halitov and Major Scott St. Andrew, Colonial Wardens."

"That's right, Captain," I said. "Mr. Halitov has a sister aboard your ship."

"So I've just learned. She's on her way up." Park moved slowly to Halitov. "Tell me, Captain, did you come here for a family reunion, to surrender, or perhaps, to defect?"

"Rooslin!" shouted Dobraska Halitov, her blonde hair tied in a neat bun, her eyes bearing an uncanny resemblance to Rooslin's. She broke past the security officers behind us and nearly leapt on her brother. It had been a while since I had seen my friend cry, but he had good reason. On the day Halitov had shipped out to the academy, Dobraska had been there to see him off, and that was the last time they had seen each other before she had been conscripted into the Eastern Alliance Navy. As she pulled back, her finger went to the gray at his temples. "What happened?"

"We can't talk about it now."

"How did you find me?"

"Doesn't matter. I should've found you a long time ago."

"But now you're POWs. You shouldn't have come."

Halitov glanced to me.

I cleared my throat, not having a plan, only a premonition that if I could stall the captain long enough, an answer would come. "Sir, my friend and I are en route to the research facility on Nereid. My fiancée, Katya Jing, is a POW there. We're going in with a small commando team to rescue her."

Halitov's jaw nearly slipped from his face. "Scott?"

Park brought those sinister brows together, then abruptly smiled. "You expect me to believe that, Major?"

"Yes, sir. And we could use your help. All you need to do is let us pass through, and no shots will be fired."

"This is ridiculous, Major. I believe you've lost more than just your arm."

"Is my request any more ridiculous than this entire war? How many friends have you seen die for nothing?"

"They died defending the Alliances. They died honorably. But Major, we're not here to debate the validity of this war. You've willed yourselves into enemy territory, and unless you plan on using your conditioning to leave, you'll be placed under arrest, thrown in the brig, and probably be shipped down to the moon for study."

"Sir, the ATC has just tawted out," reported one of Park's tactical officers.

"So much for being brothers," Halitov muttered.

"Well now, it seems you've nowhere to go," said Parks. "Unless you can will yourselves down to Nereid. But from what I understand, bridging a distance like that is impossible."

"Scott," Halitov sang in a warning tone. "What the hell are we doing?"

"We're surrendering."

Parks gestured for his security officers to lead us out, and, surprisingly, he allowed Halitov's sister to accompany us.

Inside the lift, Halitov asked, "Did you do this for me? Because next time would you mind asking first?"

I glanced at him, then looked down, widening my gaze on my tac. He understood and discreetly reactivated his.

16 ❯ **I sat in** my cell, digging fingers between the regeneration tube and my arm, eyes tearing as I struggled for an itch I would never reach and fought against the phantom knives and ghostly flames. The docs had discussed some biofeedback treatment that would ease the phantom limb pain. I didn't know what that was, but at that moment I would have killed for it.

Halitov had been placed in the cell across from mine, and he'd been sitting there for hours, catching up with his sister. Again, I was surprised that she had been allowed to spend so much time with him. Despite those evil-looking brows, Captain Jung Park had a good heart. Siblings, once torn apart by the war, had finally been reunited, and Park considered that more important than blindly following protocols regarding prisoners of war. The man had earned my respect.

A battle stations alert sounded over the shipwide intercom, and Dobraska said a quick good-bye as a security officer opened a breach in the cell's force beams.

"What do you think?" Halitov asked.

"Well, if that's a Colonial battle group out there, then they should pick up our tac signals—hopefully before they engage this ship."

"You think we'll be that lucky? Linda Haspel is still out there. She's probably sticking pins in her little Rooslin Halitov doll right now."

We sat there for maybe another hour, ears pricked on

the bulkheads as we anticipated signs of incoming fire. I didn't know about Halitov, but my pulse raced. Every minute of not knowing drained the life from me as efficiently as my failed conditioning.

Finally, I shot to my feet as the brig's hatch opened, and Captain Jung Park strode quickly inside. Had he come to taunt us? Interrogate us? "Major, Captain, you'll be leaving now."

"Where are we going?" asked Halitov.

"You'll be heading down to the moon," he answered evenly.

My heart dropped. The colonel's battle group had not arrived, and we were being shipped down to the research facility so that Alliance military scientists could do everything short of lobotomizing us.

"Captain," I began somberly. "Thank you for letting my friend talk to his sister."

"I have a family myself, Major. And now I hope your people are as understanding."

I wasn't sure what he meant by that, but our situation became clear as we stepped onto a catwalk overlooking the main docking bay, where two ATCs bearing Colonial Warden insignia had docked. A full platoon of troops had fanned out, their rifles trained on Park's security detail.

"Sir?" I asked the captain.

"One of your battle groups is out there, Major. I'm sure that comes as no surprise. They've captured our entire flotilla and ordered your release, which is why I said you'll be heading down to the moon—to rescue your fiancée."

"Yes, sir," I said, then mounted the staircase.

"Scott, I need to talk to the admiral here," said Halitov. "There has to be something we can do about my sister. I won't let her be interned."

"I doubt we'll be in the admiral's or the colonel's good graces after this, but you can try."

"Sir," called the platoon commander, a young man of no more than twenty who marched toward us, his expression so intense that it bordered on comical. "First Lieutenant Tim Roth, sir! We're here to escort you back to the *Thomas Regal*, sir!"

"Negative, Lieutenant. We're heading down to the moon."

"Sir, those are not my orders, sir."

"No, Lieutenant. They're mine."

I left the confused boy in my wake and climbed aboard the ATC, accepting a tablet from the co-pilot. I immediately called Admiral Anne Forrick, the battle group's commander, who spent the better part of five minutes booming at Halitov and I for recklessly endangering our lives. When I told her that we hadn't finished "recklessly endangering our lives" and were requesting permission to head down to the moon, she flatly refused. But a bit more coaxing and the promise that we'd allow her troops to secure the facility before we entered finally made her give in.

A mere two hours later, Halitov and I were running frantically down a hallway within the facility's rotating ring that, like the Exxo-Tally station, produced near Earth-normal gravity. We found the personnel quarters, searched another hall for the hatch number given to us by a first sergeant, and burst into the room to find Jing lying on a gelrack, that same first sergeant standing nearby, skinned up and giving orders to his squad. "Sirs!" he said, snapping to attention.

I ignored him and dropped to my knees beside Jing's bed. I didn't know her status, because I had deliberately not asked when the sergeant had contacted me. I could not bear to have some noncom tell me over the tactical frequency that my fiancée had been brainwiped or was dead. I needed to learn for myself. Jing glanced vaguely at me, then at Halitov.

"Katya, it's me, Scott. Katya?"

She craned her head, squinted hard in thought, then suddenly widened her eyes. "Do you have any idea what I've been through?"

"Katya?"

"The drugs, the needles, the tests, day in and day out. All I can say is, you better have brought that wedding ring."

Halitov chuckled. "Yeah, she's all right."

I took her head in my hand, closed my eyes, and kissed her long and passionately.

"I get the next kiss," said Halitov.

Jing broke the embrace, smirked at him, then softened her gaze on me. "We'll have time later. Now," she added teasingly, "where's my ring?"

"I don't have the ring. All I have is me. Or at least most of me."

She touched my regeneration tube. "What happened?"

"Paul."

"Did you get him?"

"We tried. But it was the colonel. He did it."

"Oh my god."

"It's terrible, all right," said Halitov. "But the colonel did the right thing. He remembered Columbia."

On that grave note I stood. "Let's get out of here."

"I'm still drugged up," Jing said. "You'll have to carry me."

I lifted my stump and frowned.

Halitov lifted his brows. "I'll carry you."

"Sergeant?" I called, smirking at my sexually deprived friend. "Get two medics and a long backboard in here ASAP."

"Sir, yes, sir!"

A week after leaving Nereid, Halitov, Jing, and I sat in Ms. Brooks's office aboard *Vanguard One*, waiting for her to get out of a meeting. Halitov and I had just finished our most recent treatment with Dr. Vesbesky, and I couldn't say for certain whether it was his efforts or our own, but according to the good doctor's analysis, we were, at least for the moment, aging at a normal pace. Vesbesky said he and scientists on Exeter were developing a treatment to actually reverse the damage. We knew our aged bodies would revert to their prior condition if we spent an extended period of time inside the Minsalo Caves, but we also knew the effect would not last. The idea was to make it permanent. Halitov and I remained dubious of Vesbesky's efforts; still, we were two soldiers who actually did want to live forever.

Of course, that would never happen, winning the war was beginning to seem less improbable. Joint Colonial and Western Alliance forces had won back three more systems, and Ms. Elise Rainey's news reports took on an almost jovial tone. Inter-system communications were improving, given our new victories, and I sent off a chip to my father and brother. Amazingly, I received a reply just two days afterward. Jarrett was recovering slowly but steadily and getting used to the idea that he would become a cyborg. I had told him about my arm, said we would commiserate the next time we got together. He told me to stop feeling sorry for myself, then tilted the camera toward my father. Dad looked good and said he was working with one of Inte-Micro's subsidiaries. He said he liked the job and the people, but most of all he liked working under a real sky—even if you still couldn't breathe the air. As a geologist, he had resigned to living his life in a hole, but life on Kennedy-Centauri had freed him. He didn't miss our homeworld one bit and was getting ready to put a deposit on a small condominium located in one of Plymouth's suburbs. He did, however, miss me and told me no less than three times during the brief message.

A frazzled Ms. Brooks rushed into her office, apologized, told us to sit tight another moment, then called her assistant, saying, "Is she out there? Very good. I'll let you know." She pursed her lips and faced us. "Paul's mother, Mrs. Julia Beauregard, would like to speak with you."

"Why?" Halitov asked, already shifting in his seat.

"I'm not sure, and I'm not comfortable with asking. But this is up to you."

"Really? You don't call this an ambush?" Halitov glanced to the door. "Talk about pressure . . ."

"Actually, Mrs. Beauregard came by on her way out. She's going home, but she wanted to see you first."

"I think it's a bad idea," said Jing. "And I'm not sure I can deal with this right now."

Halitov's brows tightened. "She looking for closure or what?"

"I don't care what she's looking for," I said. "The colonel did something I doubt any of us could do. And now his wife wants to say something. We should listen. We owe it to the man."

Jing's gaze fell to her lap. She sighed in disgust, then said, "All right. Bring on the guilt and stress."

I cocked a brow at Rooslin, who groaned. "Bring her

in, but I can't promise I won't tell her what a rat fuck her son was."

"She doesn't need to hear that," I said sharply. "And you'll behave like an officer."

"Yes, you will," added Ms. Brooks.

Halitov threw up his hands. "Let's get this over with."

Ms. Brooks contacted her assistant, who escorted Mrs. Beauregard into the office. Regal-looking, with snow-white hair and sad, blue eyes, the colonel's wife managed to smile briefly as Ms. Brooks made introductions. Then came an awkward silence as Mrs. Beauregard took a seat and clutched her purse tightly to her breast. "This won't take long. I guess I'm here to say that I'm sorry for what my son did. Not many people know this, but everything that happened is my fault."

I glanced to Jing for her reaction, but she kept her head low and scratched nervously at her pant leg. Halitov set his jaw and nodded.

Mrs. Beauregard went on: "It was my fault that I got kidnapped in the first place. I was tired of having no privacy, tired of having rude and insensitive security people around me every hour of every day. So I slipped away. Went on a shopping spree. And an Alliance recon team snatched me." Her eyes brimmed with tears, and she began losing her breath.

"Mrs. Beauregard, if this is—"

The colonel's wife waved off Ms. Brooks. "I'm all right. It's just that if I hadn't gone fucking shopping, my son would still be alive."

"You don't know that," Jing said. "Anything could've happened. You didn't ask Paul to betray the colonies—did you?"

"Of course not. And I knew when they got me that

my husband would do the right thing. He and I understand that we don't live normal lives. There are respon-
sibilities much greater than the two of us. He would not
be blackmailed. He's a good soldier. He always has
been."

"And he expected the same from Paul, but that was
never what Paul wanted," I said. "What he wanted was
to tell his father the truth, but he never could."

She closed her eyes. "I've known that for years. And I
tried to tell my husband, but he wouldn't listen to me.
Only to Paul."

I took in a deep breath, then tried to exhale away the
uneasiness and the pain. "I'm sorry for what happened,
ma'am. And I guess you could go on blaming yourself,
but Paul bargained with the Alliances. That was his
choice. Not yours."

She pondered that, blotting her eyes with a tissue. "I
was a good mother. I tried to do everything I could for
him. And I don't care if you don't forgive me. Please try
to forgive him. Please . . ." Mrs. Beauregard stood, and
Ms. Brooks rushed forward. They exchanged a few
hushed words, then Ms. Brooks saw her to the door.

Halitov sat there, shaking his head.

Jing backhanded tears from her eyes, sniffled, then
reached for my hand. As I took hers, I leaned toward
Halitov and said, "Thanks."

"For what? Keeping my mouth shut? You know, she
came here to explain it to us. She couldn't leave it alone.
And you know what? I don't forgive her. And I don't
forgive her son. Think about it. Some rich bitch colonel's wife can't stand her bodyguards, goes shopping,
and fucks up the entire war effort." Halitov chuckled
darkly. "That's just great. Just great."

"What about you, Ms. Brooks?" Jing asked. "I've

never heard you offer an opinion on any of this."

Ms. Brooks dropped hard into her chair, leaned back, and shut her eyes. "People like the colonel and me, we've convinced ourselves that our duty is more important than relationships and families. But for me at least, being a martyr is getting old. Very old."

Jing edged forward on her chair. "So do you think the colonel did the right thing by refusing to bargain for his wife?"

"As horrible as it may sound, yes, I think he made the right call. But he could have never seen the consequences. And if I were him right now, I'd be thinking that the price of service is just way too high. First he had to come to terms with the loss of his wife. Then he was forced to kill his own son. I couldn't go on after that. I don't know how he does."

Halitov abruptly stood. "Ma'am? The captain requests permission to leave, go to the bar, and get seriously drunk."

Brooks smiled faintly. "I'm right behind you, Captain."

"Me, too," said Jing.

"I'll catch up," I said. "I'm not finished moving."

Ms. Brooks had secured larger and more comfortable quarters for us aboard *Vanguard One*, and I had transferred everything out of my old quarters, save for a few books, photographs, and that ridiculous tree Paul had given me as a get well present. He had said that I needed "a little greenery in my life." I had not watered the thing, and its limbs sagged a bit, its heart-shaped leaves and pink flowers brittle and turning brown along the edges. I stood there, staring at the tree, trying to decide what I should do with it. Paul's actions had already made an indelible mark. I didn't need a tree to remind me of him.

After asking around at the bar, Halitov's sister said she wanted the redbud, and later that evening I carried it down to her quarters. Thanks to Ms. Brooks, Dobraska had been "interned" aboard *Vanguard One* until such time that she would be transferred to a camp on Rexi-Calhoon. Ms. Brooks assured Halitov that that transfer would never happen. It never did.

The story of that tree does not end with Halitov's sister. About ten years afterward, during a trip to a nursery on Rexi-Calhoon to buy plants for a home I had bought there, I came across another redbud. An attached label explained that the redbud is also called the Judas Tree, from the belief that Judas Iscariot in the Christian Bible hanged himself from such a tree. Was it just a coincidence that Paul, a traitor to the colonies, had chosen to give me a tree named after one of the most famous traitors in history? Or had he been trying to tell me something?

19 February, 2322

I awoke with a start in my hospital bed and immediately accessed my tablet. I remembered that President Vinnery had, several weeks prior, sent me a list of intelligence officers she had wanted upgraded to level A7. Funny thing was, she had asked why I hadn't pried into the request. In truth, I hadn't given it a second thought until she had queried. The memo had seemed in order, and there was nothing suspicious about upgrading security clearances to people working in volatile zones. The list of names appeared on my screen, all fourteen of them.

"It can't be this easy," I muttered aloud.

The computer showed me log-in dates and times, then cross-referenced them with election postings from representatives of Mars and Jupiter colonies. Was it a coincidence that all fourteen officers had been logged into the system during the election postings? I checked their individual duty logs, which unfortunately looked in order. Then I reviewed the supervisor's log, and there was nothing suspicious there. A call came in from Holtzman's operative aboard the *Falls Morrow*, and while he believed the fourteen officers were working with Vinnery, had no other leads to implicate them and no hard evidence. We had nothing.

I called Holtzman with the news, then added, "I was thinking about a tree Paul Beauregard gave me a long time ago. Turned out to be a Judas Tree. I guess he couldn't keep all of that guilt inside, and deep down, he needed to tell somebody. The same goes for Bren, who, in his own way, tried to warn me. So I was hoping Vinnery might do something unconsciously to tip us off, but she didn't."

"I see. I guess we'll have to bring her down and let the rest get away."

"Maybe not."

"You have a plan?"

"I'm an old military man, sir. We always have a plan."

Holtzman thought a moment, nodded. "I think I know what you have in mind." He consulted his watch.

"Colonel, my breakfast meeting with Vinnery is in two hours. Will you be well enough to attend?"

"Mr. President, if this were my deathbed, I'd make them wheel it over there."

He smiled tightly. "See you in a couple of hours."

17 ▶ **President Holtzman had** loaned me four of his
security officers, and their leader, a dark-faced
lieutenant, raised an index finger before we left the hospital room. "Sir, just give us a moment to clear the
route." He barked a few more orders over his tactical
frequency. "All right. We're ready."

I gave myself the once over, smoothed a wrinkle from
my dark uniform and straightened one of my medals before heading briskly into the empty corridor with two
security officers in front, two behind. We reached the
lift, rode it down to the first floor, then caught a heavily
armored hover waiting for us outside a service entrance.
Holtzman's people were sneaking me out the back door,
but across the street, journalists and paparazzi had expected such a ploy and jockeyed for positions behind
force beam barriers. I glanced at those reporters and felt
a sharp, hollow pain in my gut. Elise Rainey was dead.
My entire security team was dead. And I was about to
confront the woman responsible. As I plopped into the
hover, I wished that I was just having a nightmare, that
in a moment I would wake up and realize that I should
have ordered something light for dinner.

Twenty minutes later, we reached the capitol, and my
borrowed team rushed me up to a small dining room adjacent to the presidential suite. Wong was already there,
and he took my hand in his own, covered it with the
other. All he said was, "Colonel." But he needn't say

more. He gestured toward an ornate table, where expensive silverware and fine china glistened atop a lace cloth. A waiter was already pouring me a cup of coffee as I sat.

"Good morning, Colonel," said Holtzman. He reached the table and gripped the back of his chair. "President Vinnery is on her way up now."

"She'll probably have six, maybe eight with her," I said. "Are your people ready?"

Holtzman glanced to the ceiling, then to the walls. "They're ready."

"Mr. President, this could get messy. Very messy. Still, I just got off the line with Fleet Command, and Admiral Corithius assures me that his ships will not move against Terran targets without proper authentication."

"So I assume your call with the vice president went well?"

"I wouldn't say it went well. He was shocked. But he is standing by."

"And our fleet is preparing to tawt away from Rexi-Calhoon," said Wong. "That may soften the blow, if only a little."

"Here she is now," said Holtzman.

I rose as President Vinnery crossed into the room, her blonde hair flawlessly styled, her dark green business attire revealing subtle but flattering curves. One look at her and you thought, strong woman. Professional. Words like cunning or corrupt didn't come to mind. She brightened a little as she caught sight of Holtzman and Wong, shook hands with them, then turned up the false congeniality as she regarded me. "Colonel St. Andrew. I didn't know you were joining us. My God, how are you? I just heard."

"I'm still alive, ma'am," I said, locking my gaze on her until she flinched and looked away.

"Gentlemen," she said, turning to the presidents. "I need a moment with the colonel."

I looked to Holtzman, who tightened his lips, shook his head.

"Madam President," began Wong. "We have urgent business to discuss, and it cannot wait."

"I know that," she said impatiently. "But Colonel St. Andrew won't be joining us. I've ordered him back home, and it's clear he needs some rest." She squinted at the synthskin repair job on my head.

"We want him to stay," said Holtzman, who shifted around the table and withdrew a chair for Vinnery. His gaze said get in the chair. Now.

She took a deep breath, glanced to her bodyguards who had taken up posts around the room, then tossed me a dirty look as she begrudgingly complied. "Before we begin, I'd like to remind you that my tac is linked directly to our admiral at Fleet Command. I am but one authentication away from ordering a strike on Terran targets."

"We know, Madam President," said Wong. "And our fleet is awaiting a similar order. But we're not here to discuss that. The people of Mars and Jupiter have not been properly heard. The votes of their representatives have been tampered with."

Vinnery laughed. "You actually believe those rumors?"

"Oh, there's no doubt that rumors equal ratings," said Holtzman.

Vinnery snorted. "Tell me something I don't know."

"But in this case, those journalists out there? They're dead-on."

"Dead-on? Really? If this is a joke, it's a bad one. Look at me. I'm not laughing anymore."

"There's nothing to laugh about," I said, just a few heartbeats away from throwing the table aside and strangling the woman myself.

But it was time to implement my plan, an old-fashioned bluff that might get her to admit the truth:

"Madam President, we have indisputable evidence indicating that you, along with fourteen colonial intelligence officers and nine more in the Eastern and Western Alliances, engaged in electronic vote tampering in the houses of the Jupiter and Mars colonies. We've already taken this evidence to a special prosecutor, who's in the process of drawing up a formal indictment. When those papers are complete, we're going to release everything we have to the press."

Vinnery, who had been adding cream to her coffee, didn't miss a beat as she stirred, then lifted the cup to her lips. "I know all about your evidence and your special prosecutor."

That took us all aback. "So you admit to working with those officers?" I asked.

She sipped her coffee, winced. "These Terran beans are always too strong."

"Madam President, would you like to see our evidence?" asked Holtzman, who traded an uneasy look with me.

She glanced innocently at him. "No."

I banged a fist on the table, rattling silverware and nerves. "Bren told me what you said, that I'd never go along with it, that I'm all about duty and honor. You ordered him to kill me, didn't you?"

"Scott, there are forces at work here, political forces, military forces, that you couldn't possibly understand. We both want what's best for the colonies."

"And what's best? Another war to boost the economy?" My voice came in a growl. "You don't know what that's like."

She widened her gaze. "Maybe not. But I will . . ." She tapped her tac, spoke rapidly. "Authentication five-niner-zero-tango-five, voice ID initiate. Orders batch nine."

"Now!" Holtzman cried, and even before he finished, a dozen conditioned security officers materialized in the room and confronted Vinnery's people. Particle fire thundered as I dove across the table, seized Vinnery's wrist, then dragged her to the carpet as rounds criss-crossed overhead.

"It's too late," Vinnery said, struggling to free her arm. "God help me, it's too late."

"That list of intell officers you sent me. Those are names, right?" I asked. "Those are the names."

"It doesn't matter anymore. I've ordered the strike. We're going to war. It's what we need."

A final round echoed, then someone cried, "Hold your fire! Hold your fire!"

My nose crinkled at a burning stench that nearly made me gag. Vinnery's security team lay crumpled, dead, along with three of Holtzman's people. Yet another security squad of ten rushed into the room, sweeping the perimeter.

"President Wong?" cried Holtzman.

"Over here," said Wong, sitting up against the wall and gripping his shoulder with a blood-stained hand. "It's not too bad."

"Get me a medic in here now!" shouted Holtzman to his security team leader.

I dragged Vinnery to her feet, glanced to Wong, then turned my blackest look on my president. "You're lucky. Very lucky. Now you'll come with us. We want to show you something. President Holtzman?"

We followed a breathless Holtzman out of the dining room and into his office. We remained standing as he activated the holo projector. A satnet image showed our Colonial fleet moving out of orbit, preparing to tawt. Vinnery's mouth slowly fell open. "How?"

"The order you just gave was not authenticated," I said. "But the one from the vice president was. He ordered the retreat, overriding your order based on vice-presidential protocol thirty-nine-A. Are you familiar with that protocol, ma'am?"

"That protocol details acts of treason, Colonel," she snapped.

"Yes, ma'am. It does."

"Madam President, we've ordered our fleet over Rexi-Calhoon to pull out. I'll have images of that within the hour. The standoff is over. There will be no war. There will, however, be a recount in both the houses of Mars and Jupiter."

"Then let me ask you this, Mr. President," Vinnery said. "What if the vote to secede stands? What then?"

"I'm confident that it will not."

"But what if it does? Are you prepared to lose those colonies?"

"I am. And so is President Wong. The will of the people must prevail—not the will of a select few. Now, two of my officers are waiting to take you into protective custody."

"We're not finished here!" Vinnery boomed.

"Madam President, I can't stand to look at you anymore. Get out of my office. NOW!"

Vinnery boiled for a second, then spun on her heels and marched off. She slammed the door after herself.

"Jesus Christ," muttered Holtzman. "What have we done?"

"I'm not sure, sir. But at least it feels right."

Holtzman came around his desk, dropped a hand on my shoulder. "Yes, Colonel, it does. So tell me, when all hell broke loose, you could have forced her into a round, got her killed. What held you back?"

"I don't know. Duty and honor, I guess. Sounds trite."

"You know, Colonel, those political and military forces she mentioned are still out there. We brought down a conspiracy, but we hardly whipped the special interests."

"No doubt. And now the colonial presidency will be tarnished for the first time ever. I'm glad I'm not the vice president."

"He's going to need all the help he can get. I'm glad he has you on his team."

"Thank you, sir."

During the week that followed, another election took place, and the vote to secede did not stand by a margin of sixty percent. With that nightmare over, I made a quick trip to Kennedy-Centauri. Elise Rainey had kept a small condo in Plymouth, and about a kilometer away, within a beautifully landscaped cemetery dome, she was set to rest. Her two sons, James and Michael, both in their early thirties, took me out to dinner after the funeral, and I shared with them the story of Columbia Colony and how their mother and I had helped each other over the years. While they were still bitter because their mother had put her career first, they understood that her contributions to the colonial community were great. They were proud of what she had achieved, yet a certain distance gripped their voices, a distance that prompted me to reflect on my own relationship with my daughter.

When I returned home to Rexi-Calhoon, I attended the funerals of Tat, Ysarm, and Jiggs, offering my condolences to each of their families. Bren was cremated, his ashes scattered in the vacuum by his brother, a police officer who had frequently appeared on the news channels and was hoping to get a book deal out of his brother's involvement in "The Sol Vote Conspiracy." I was still in shock over Bren's betrayal and might never come to terms with it. I had repeatedly placed my life in that man's hands, and he had been ready to kill me at a moment's notice. How could I have been so naïve? So foolish? I cursed him. But more so, I cursed myself and vowed never again to place as much trust in a security officer.

Still, there was a man, who, despite one unfortunate betrayal, had rekindled my trust and would be the best officer I would ever find.

"Hell no!" cried Rooslin Halitov, sitting behind his colossal desk, his sandaled feet kicked up onto his computer's touch screen as he stroked his sandy gray beard. I didn't notice the ponytail until he turned his head. "My sister and I are making money hand over fist. Do you know how many new accounts we racked up just last month?"

I kicked up my own expensive leather shoes onto his desk, threw my hands behind my head. "I don't care, Rooslin. Tell me you're happy, sitting here on Aire-Wu, running this little security business, and I'll leave you alone."

"I told you when I got discharged that this was the

plan." He set his feet on the floor, leaned forward, and motioned me closer. "That Hardeson Poe guy, all those years ago? He told me this. He told me my calling would be with her. We're very happy and successful here. She found a nice guy, started a family."

"And you're still chasing tail."

He winked. "College girls."

"Is that why you got the ring?"

He fingered the diamond chip glittering on his eyebrow. "They love it."

"You're a dirty old man."

"Only on weekends."

I grinned, took a deep breath. "Rooslin, they tried to kill me."

"Bastards. I saw it on the news."

"I need you, man. More than ever. The vice president is in a world of shit."

"So are you. In fact, it's blinded you."

"What do you mean?"

"I mean you can't see how shitty this invitation is, can you."

"Your sister can run this business."

"I know she can."

"Then pack your bags. We're shipping out tonight."

He came around the desk, leaned on it, folded his arms across his chest. "I have to pass."

"Rooslin, it's me."

"I'm sorry, man. I just can't do it."

I stood, began to choke up, realizing that he was really turning me down. I offered my hand. "Well, then. It was great seeing you. We should get together again some time. Maybe . . ."

He grabbed my hand, nearly squeezed it off. "You dumb fuck. Look at you, about to cry. Of course I'll help you. I'll lead your security team, and I'll get the moles for you, too. They'll never know what hit them—but I get to keep the hair and the brow ring."

I heaved a deep sigh. "You could've just said yes, you idiot."

"Too easy. Hey, you hungry? My sister cooks dinner for me every Friday."

"What's she making?"

He made a face. "You have to ask?"

21 November, 2326

Four years after I recruited Halitov to serve as my security team leader, we found ourselves standing in a large banquet room of the Exxo-Tally Astoria, one of the most posh hotels on Rexi-Calhoon. Along with a crowd of nearly two hundred, we watched a holo of all Seventeen Systems floating above us, planets revolving around their suns in real time. Beside each ghostly world hung databars reporting election results. In a few moments we would know who would be the next president of the Colonial Alliance.

Halitov gulped down the last of his Tau Ceti vodka. "Well, that's my first and last."

"Drinking on the job again? I should've fired you four years ago—the day after I hired you."

"I heard Joanna made captain."

"Don't change the subject."

He threw an arm over my shoulder. "Hey, man. We've got this entire area locked down. Don't worry about a thing."

"Easy for you to say."

Jarrett came hustling over, his artificial legs moving so naturally that you would never guess he had survived a nightmare made real. "Scott!"

"You made it," I said, taking his hand.

"We almost didn't. You know Dad. He has to stop and talk to everyone."

"Where is he?"

"He went off looking for the food. I'm sure he'll turn up. So how're you doing?"

"I'm dying over here."

Halitov nudged me. "Don't die yet—because here it comes."

Holo journalist Raverna Avery, perhaps the most familiar newscaster on Rexi-Calhoon, appeared at her desk, flanked by the shimmering star systems. "Ladies and gentlemen, the results have been tallied, and we can report with certainty that former Security Chief Scott St. Andrew has won his bid for president. I repeat, Scott St. Andrew will become the next president of the Colonial Alliance."

A deafening roar lifted in the banquet room as Halitov grabbed my shoulders and shook me. "Son of a bitch, you won, man! You won! Finally, after all the bullshit we've been through, we get to run the show!"

"What do you mean 'we'?" I shouted with mock seriousness, barely able to hear myself.

He glanced back as Katya came over, then made way as she hugged me so tightly that I lost my breath. "I am so proud of you, Scott. So proud."

"Daddy!" cried Joanna, rushing toward me in her black dress uniform, her captain's gon proudly displayed on her breast. You'd never know she was the daughter of two epineuropaths. Not a single birthmark marred her beaming face. "Daddy, I can't believe it. You won!"

"I guess I did," I said, accepting her into my arms. "And I know this'll be rough on you."

"I've lived in your shadow for this long. Trust me. I can take it." With that, she pulled back, winked, then willed herself across the room, to a knot of other Colonial Wardens, friends from her unit.

"I told you not to show off," I shouted, but she didn't hear me.

"Congratulations, Mr. President," said Jarrett, grabbing my chin. "My kid brother. Who would've thought . . ."

"Come on," said Katya St. Andrew, the Colonial Alliance's new first lady. "Acceptance speech. And it had better be longer than the one you gave when you became security chief."

"Longer, yes. Better? We'll find out . . ."

"I don't know why you didn't want my help . . ."

"I can handle this," I said, moving shakily toward the dais, people slapping me on the back during the entire walk. "Katya?"

"I'm right behind you."

"Stay close. Maybe I can't handle this. Maybe I'm going to pass out."

"Give the speech first," she ordered.

Finding strength in her tone, I reached the dais, gripped the podium with one hand, then hoisted a fist in the air as the microphone hovered into place. "To the person who said a kid from the mines of Gatewood-Callista, a gennyboy no less, would never grow up to become president, I say this: here I am. Here I AM!"

Chilled by yet another wave of thunderous applause,

I spotted Halitov near the northwest exit, whistling, clapping, as tears slipped down his cheeks. Then Katya broke down, even after she had promised she wouldn't. I'd forgive her for that. I'd forgive both of them for making me cry. After all, we were old soldiers, the three of us, standing there among the living, standing there in memory of our fallen comrades. I saw ghosts in the crowd: Joey Haltiwanger, Dina Forrest, Jane Clarion, Judiah Pope, Kristi Breckinridge, and even Paul Beauregard. Many more joined them. Hundreds more. Thousands more. We had all been brothers, rebels, and patriots fighting together for a just and lasting peace. Sure, some would forget us or take what we had done for granted.

But some would always remember.

**Astonishing tales of new worlds
and remarkable visions
edited by**

DAVID G. HARTWELL

YEAR'S BEST SF 8
0-06-106453-X/$7.99 US/$10.99 Can

YEAR'S BEST SF 7
0-06-106143-3/$7.99 US/$10.99 Can

YEAR'S BEST SF 6
0-06-102055-9/$7.99 US/$10.99 Can

YEAR'S BEST SF 5
0-06-102054-0/$7.99 US/$10.99 Can

YEAR'S BEST SF 4
0-06-105902-1/$7.99 US/$10.99 Can

YEAR'S BEST SF 3
0-06-105901-3/$6.50 US/$8.50 Can

YEAR'S BEST SF 2
0-06-105746-0/$6.50 US/$8.99 Can

YEAR'S BEST SF
0-06-105641-3/$7.99 US/$10.99 Can